THE BEST OF SOMMER MARSDEN

THE BEST OF SOMMER MARSDEN

A collection of erotic stories

SOMMER MARSDEN

Published by Xcite Books Ltd – 2011
ISBN 9781908086082

Printed and bound in the UK

Cover design by Madamadari

Contents

Sticky Notes 1

The Greed Jar 11

Take a Break 25

Discipline 38

Do You Trust Me? 48

Would You Like Fries with That? 59

My Good Boy 68

Grip 75

All the Boys 81

Spank Pants 87

Flexible 95

Black and White Photos 104

Just Like Your Father 113

Picket Fence 120

Worship 133

Rebound Guy 143

Stick Garden 151

Pants on Fire 157

One More Night 163

When We Were Two 173

Yes, Tim 178

Nothing but the Boots 188

Girl Crush   198

Tech Support   206

The Known   212

Vigil   218

Not All Love Stories are Great   229

Sticky Notes

I'd like to blame it on the wine but I'm not much of a liar. I will chalk it up to a really good sweaty romp and then a rather erotic thriller. The movie got me going all over again but by the time the good parts were over, it was time for Steven to go to bed.

'Good night, love.' He ruffled my short blonde hair and gave me a long lingering kiss. 'We need to do that again tomorrow but for now I'm off to bed. Early morning.'

And he was gone and I was horny. Again. I finished my wine, flipped through a magazine, and read a sex survey. That didn't help. Basically, I stewed in my own juices, so to speak.

I was just about to give up. Throw in the towel. When it hit me. Again, maybe the wine, maybe the thriller, maybe the fuck. I really don't know what did it. I didn't care. I grabbed the pad of sticky notes from the desk and began writing furiously. When I went to bed, it was stuck to the coffee pot. My little love note for Steven.

What do you want? Your wildest fantasy (or fantasies). Anything you want. Spill!
Love,
Loren

I had forgotten the note in the morning. It was Saturday so I lingered in bed. I was sad, I'll admit, that Steven had to go to work. His side of the bed, cold and unoccupied was enough to make me want to call him and tell him to come home. Come home and fuck your woman. In my mind's eye I could see myself dialling my cell. I could hear myself making this giggling but authoritative command. He had to work, though, and I was fine with that. I was just lonely.

I ran my hands over my soft negligee. Felt my nipples turn to hard pink pearls under my fingers. My pussy went soft and wet and I let out a sigh. Somehow, as horny as I was, the thought of rubbing one off alone in bed was disappointing. I would go downstairs and make some coffee and wait until Steve got home. Then I would attack him like a horny mountain lion.

I was still laughing at the thought of a hormone-induced attack on my studly guy when I wandered into the kitchen. There it was. Hot pink. Innocent to look at. A sticky note for me.

TO SEE YOU WITH ANOTHER WOMAN. NO TOUCHING FOR ME. JUST WATCHING.
LOVE
STEVE

Somehow the sight of his answer, boldly printed all in caps, did me in. I did it right there. Clutching at the pantry door, fingers working furiously and wetly under my nightie. It only took a few minutes. My fingers diving greedily into my humid wet cunt, my thumb rubbing roughly but expertly over my clit. I stared at the words as I came in one long, delicious spasm. Little animal sounds rushed out of my throat and I collapsed on the cold linoleum in a glowing, warm heap.

I needed to leave him notes more often.

My fingers still tacky and shaking, my knees still knocking, I claimed the hot pink square and stuck it firmly in my day planner. I made my coffee, enjoyed my afterglow and mentally calculated how many hours I had to wait for him to get home.

'I'm home!' Steven's face lit with a tired but happy grin. 'Thank God! Oooph–'

The last part was my fault. I launched myself at him like a lusty groupie and kissed him long and hard. I pushed my tongue past his soft lips and tangled it with his. I plundered that hot sensuous mouth and pushed my wet pussy against his belt buckle, my legs tightly clamped around his lean middle.

'Did you miss me?' he laughed as I slid my tongue down his neck, nuzzling him at the base where his cologne seems to settle. A nice warm, manly scent that hovers in the hollow of his throat.

His big hands palmed my ass and he groaned. Shifting me a little lower so my crotch was level with his, I could feel the growing bulge of his awakening cock.

'I liked your note,' I sighed and pushed myself against his hard-on. Shameless hussy. That's me.

'I can tell.'

'Come on, come on, come on,' I was practically barking as I set my feet on the cold floor and pulled him toward the sofa. 'Off with the jeans! Off with the shirt!' I directed, stripping my leggings and sweatshirt off.

'As long as you don't say, 'Off with his head!',' he chuckled. But he obeyed. He soon stood before me completely naked, his beautiful cock a blushing purple and standing straight up toward his flat belly.

'On the sofa!' I could hear my demanding tone but couldn't seem to control it. I was in a fog. A thick fog of lust and need. I always wanted Steven, but right now I needed him. My body thumped with a pulse of arousal and craving. I need him. Hard cock. Hot cunt. His. In mine. Now.

I straddled him, the soft green sofa cushions engulfing my knees. Without preamble I sank down onto his dick, sighing with what sounded like relief to my own ears. Within three desperate strokes, my thighs were soaked from my own juices.

'Correspondence is inspiring,' Steven muttered as his eyes rolled back in his head. He looked like he was in pain.

'Am I hurting you?' I grunted. It was all I could manage. I admit, though, I didn't slow my frenzied pace for even a moment.

'Fuck no!' He grabbed my hips as if for emphasis. Big fingers digging into my soft, flushed skin and propelling me faster with his strong hands. His hips pumped up as he drove into me.

'Best note ever...' I mumbled as my cunt seized up, gripped him greedily and then fluttered around him as my orgasm roared through all of me. Even the roots of my hair tingled and I swore I heard myself cry out, 'Evvvvvver ...!'

Steven yanked me against him and I felt him pump into me. Hot wet come. Filling me. For the first time ever I really felt it, the incredibly warm emptying of his body into mine.

I collapsed, exhausted and panting onto his chest; our breathing creating a nice little cha-cha number.

'Sorry about the ninja attack,' I giggled but my wet insides still fluttered and pulsed around his deflating cock. It would work for every last flicker of pleasure, it seemed.

'Loren, you can go ninja on my ass any day of the week.' And then he kissed me.

Steven went to bed early that night. I think I wore him out. I weighed the pros and cons and then my mind flashed to that first seductive moment of my body engulfing his and my mind was made up. Before I locked up for the night, I grabbed my faithful sticky notes and wrote another. I was humming merrily as I shut off the kitchen light. I could see its little square shadow as I left. I smiled, knowing what it said.

What else! I'm begging. Hands and knecs. Tell me.
Love,
Loren

I climbed into bed, snuggled up against a loudly snoring hunk of man and drifted off to sleep. Somehow I couldn't wipe the goofy grin off my face even as I slipped into dreamland.

Sunday morning didn't so much break in as creep in. Gray, murky light filled the bedroom. Another overcast February morning. I stretched and yawned loudly. My hands found the cool empty spot on the sheets where Steven should be. A momentary blip of sadness skittered across my internal radar screen and I sighed. Then I remembered the sticky note I had left and I tore down to the kitchen. I didn't even bother to put on slippers or a robe. I didn't care if I froze. I wanted to see

4

my note.

My bare feet slapped the cold linoleum as I ran to the coffee pot. There it was! I was so excited. My belly did a flip and my nipples grew hard.

I claimed my hot pink prize and read.

I WANT TO FUCK YOU IN PUBLIC. MAYBE THE DARK SMOKY CORNER OF THE CLUB. UP AGAINST THE WALL. HANDS UNDER YOUR DRESS. YOUR LEG WRAPPED AROUND MY WAIST...
LOVE,
STEVE

Oooooh. I caught my breath, sank into a kitchen chair and once again settled in for some self-abuse. My fingers made quick work of my swollen clit. Two fingers plunged into my flooded pussy as an accompanying finger played a rousing number of God-I-am-turned-on on my clit. I stared at the words, read the sentence over and over until my insides were so tight it was nearly painful. Then I focused on my favourite sentence: MY HANDS UNDER YOUR DRESS. These were his hands under my nightgown. Steven's hands. Under there. For all to see...

The orgasm left me bedraggled and flushed. A stupid smile on my face. I drank my coffee, puttered and counted the minutes. When he came through the door I was waiting for him. Only this time he was prepared.

I wasn't very creative, I'll admit. I once again did my animalistic pounce the moment he shut the front door. Only this time, he promptly dropped his briefcase and held his hands out. At least I wasn't afraid I'd hurt him this time.

'You're wearing a dress!' he exclaimed around my wandering, plundering tongue. He kissed me back and laughed against my lips.

'Yes, yes!' I hissed, 'Now put your hands under it.'

'Ah, our missives have done a number on you again.' His tone was teasing but his hands were big and warm as they slid under my short dress. Goosebumps and baby hairs along my

5

spine sprang to attention and my pussy did that persistent little thump, thump, thump! that signals impending orgasm. Dear Lord! He hadn't even touched me yet. Well, none of the naughty bits.

I didn't stop to ask what a missive was. I simply wrapped my legs around his waist and shoved my pelvis against his. I ground against the erection I found there, refraining from whooping in joy. Barely. 'Sofa, sofa, sofa!' I took up the chant as my brain seemed to short- circuit.

There it was again. An overwhelming need. Urge. Compulsion. I had to have him in me and it had to be now. Steven complied. Smart man. This time there was no upper hand for me. The moment we hit the sofa, Steven flipped me on my back and pinned my arms above my head. His other hand slid and groped and pushed its way greedily under my dress. His breath beat warmly against my throat as he practically panted.

'Good Lord, what has gotten into us?' he growled.

Steven didn't stop for an answer. My two thin wrists held tightly in his strong hand, he slid down my body and buried his face in my pussy. Like a crazy man he snuffled and licked and ate at me until I was making little *whoop, whoop* sounds. What the hell was that? Didn't know, didn't care. I let my thighs fall open and he burrowed deeper, shoving the rigid tip of his tongue into my tight, wet entrance. I clamped my knees around his head as his perfect lips worked their way back up to my clit. I came so hard, I feared I'd given him a head injury. But he was fine, forcing his way between my legs roughly. His cock was hard and already leaking a steady stream of pre-come. I licked my lips and he allowed me one good swallow and one good stroke of my tongue over his slit before he whipped it away. He got between my thighs.

'Fuck.' That was it. That's all he said as he slid into me. My cunt, still echoing from my orgasm, latched on and clenched him tightly. Little aftershocks of pleasure lit up my insides.

It felt so good. Unbearably good. I clamped down. I made my pussy as tight as I could until the friction of his thrusts nearly drove me insane.

'Fuck,' he said again.

A few more frantic pounds and his body went rigid in my arms. I felt his cock swell even larger for just a moment before he jerked against me and came with a long low moan. I joined him. Just watching his face and the power in his body as he came was enough to shove me right over the edge into another orgasm.

After a sweaty moment of tangled laughing, he stared up into my eyes. 'You're not drugging me, are you?'

I giggled until I thought I would cry. 'Nope. No drugs.'

Steven kissed me on the lips, the nose, the forehead. He climbed from me, steadied himself and ran a hand through his thick black hair. 'Beer? You want a beer? I need a beer. I'll get us some beers.'

I could only grin as he wandered into the kitchen buck naked and chuckling.

Now I was preoccupied. All I could think about was what might be going on in that handsome head of his. As usual, he went to bed long before me. I sipped a glass of Cabernet and watched a little TV and tried not to think of crisp square pieces of paper that could be stuck to virtually any smooth surface. I cracked. I knew I would.

Before bed, I wrote my now normal love note and affixed it in its usual place. My notes had become as intense as my sexual urges.

And!? What else? I need more!
Your slut,
Loren

Monday morning dawned just as bleak. It was even more depressing because my alarm went off at 6:30. A work day. Yippee! I turned it off and stretched, taking a moment to sniff at Steven's pillow. The warm, familiar scent of him clung to the pillowcase and I felt a stirring of my now ever-present arousal. Then I remembered my note.

I barely noticed that it was snowing outside my kitchen

window as I yanked my pink prize from the coffee pot.

I WANT TO SHOVE YOU UNDER A VERY ELEGANT
TABLE IN A VERY ELEGANT RESTAURANT. PUT MY
COCK BETWEEN THOSE PERFECT PINK LIPS AND
HAVE YOU BLOW ME UNTIL I BREAK MY WATER
GLASS.
YOUR SEX MONKEY,
STEVE

Ah! Just the thought. The wonderful taboo thought of doing
that in one of the very nice, very posh restaurants we
frequented was enough to bring a warm sluice of fluids
between my thighs. This was too much. This was not a
masturbate in the kitchen note. This called for the big guns. I
eyed the clock, calculated my allotted time to get to work. I
nearly broke my neck getting up the steps to the bedroom. I
opened my middle dresser drawer and rummaged until I
found it. Ahhhh. My vibrator.

All pretty and pink and smooth and jelly filled and
vibrating; at my mercy and very talented. I clutched the note,
flipped the ON button and dove onto the bed. No lube needed,
I was soaked, I worked it inside myself and let out a blissful
sigh as it danced inside of me. I closed my eyes and saw
myself in my most elegant black dress, strappy black heels,
under the table. Dark and warm. Steven's naked cock. His
hand on the back of my head. Pushing me. Urging me. Not
always gentle. Fucking my mouth. Me under there. In the
dark. Warm and cosy and cave-like. Licking up his shaft. His
spasm in my mouth. Drinking in his warm milky come.

I gave the vibrator a run for its money as I came with a
bellow and a long lusty laugh. My heart was beating so hard
my eardrums vibrated. I climbed from bed, my body like
taffy. Warm and happy. Completely loose. I've never been so
happy to get ready for work.

The day at work was a treat. I was so content I just didn't
care. I didn't care that they screwed up my pay-check. I didn't
care that the voice recognition system had made a grievous

error in a legal report. It should have read: 'The client was injured at work while dragging a trash can'. What the system entered was: 'The client was injured at work by a dragon with a tin can'. This should have been enough to send me into a tailspin. Oddly enough, I found it extremely humorous. The sigh of relief from my assistant was audible.

Even rush hour traffic didn't bother me. Sitting and inching my way home didn't set me off like it normally would. Every time I had to sit and wait, I pulled Steven's sticky note out of my day planner and read it. And got hotter. Hornier. Crazed.

This time he was waiting for me. He grabbed me the moment I shut the door, took my bag and pushed me to my knees. Then, never taking his eyes from mine, he unzipped his khakis, freed his cock and pushed the already engorged head against my lips.

I opened for him compliantly and played my tongue over the weeping slit. Then I fell on him as if I were starved. And I was. The taste of his salty warm skin on my tongue was heaven. The hot hard length of his erection, like suede covered marble. So hard and yet so pliant. He tasted like sex and love and man.

I licked my palm several times, plunged his cock back in my mouth and moved my slick fist in tandem. Steven buried his hands in my hair and rocked against me. Moving back on his heels, head tilted back, eyes closed. All harsh breath and rumbling growls deep in his throat. The urgency in his sounds sent a thrilling shiver down my spine and I sucked harder and deeper than ever before. I couldn't settle for anything less than making him lose control.

I loosened my throat and burrowed my nose against his pubic bone. Let him slide all the way home in my throat and I palmed his balls and let my middle finger skim his perineum. That did it.

Steven roared, 'Loren!' as he came and just the sound of my name tearing out of him like that soaked my panties.

Steven scooped me up and collapsed in the overstuffed arm chair with me on his lap. He kissed me, opening my mouth with his tongue. He kissed me deeply until we both tasted like him and warm wet kisses.

'Think we'll ever do any of them?' I asked, squirming just a little in my wet panties.

Steven shifted under me. My squirming had done wonders. I could feel him getting hard already. He acknowledged my observation by pushing his cock against my ass. 'Well, I'd say just talking about them is keeping us busy at the moment,' he said with a grin. He pumped his hips up again and I noticed that hardening had turned to hard.

'I'd like to try them all some day,' I laughed, squirming just to be evil. 'But you're right. Just talking about it is making me a sex addict.'

'Well, if you're curious,' he said, sliding his hand up under my skirt and hooking a finger in my panties, 'I have a few more.' Then he plunged two blunt fingers into my cunt and I shuddered around him. 'For instance–'

I shoved my palm against his lips and pushed my pussy against his hand. Forcing him to probe and push deep inside of me. 'Don't tell me! Don't tell me!' I sighed, squirming some more. 'Leave me a note.'

The Greed Jar

Long ago, the jar was put under a spell. Some say by a genie and some say genie can't use spells. People will always argue about these mystical things. The bottom line is that the jar was cast under a spell. And there are only two reasons to put a spell on something: to keep it away from others and for yourself, or to keep it away from people for their own damn good. Either way, most magic is all about keeping people away from something.

The jar looked very much like a jar of golden honey. A huge jar of deep amber syrup with a decadently ornate lid, but there you have it. It sat in a hole in the desert forever and a day. But jars like this don't stay hidden for ever; they crave to be found ...

'And you call yourself a UIC?' Jim was teasing but Alice had to resist the urge to smack him just the same.

'That thing is God knows how old. How many items are supposedly cast upon by genie, Jim?'

Her partner shrugged. 'I've never heard of any. There are some who would argue that genie cannot work magic beyond wishes. Curses and spells are for witches and warlocks and demons.'

'Why not? They are certainly mystical, magical beings. Why shouldn't one be able to curse?' Alice took a final swig of her espresso and sighed. 'I am a failure as an Unnatural Items Collector if we don't find that jar. It was a friggin' miracle that the woman who sold it to me was willing to part with it.'

'She inherited it?' Jim looked vaguely bored as they sat in

11

the office at the airport waiting to file a lost claim on the Lucite cube that contained The Greed Jar.

'It was passed down from her dad who won it in a poker game. Jesus. What if someone opens it?'

'Wouldn't be surprised,' Jim sing-songed, staring at a burly porter and then, in the next breath, a buxom blonde by the counter. Jim was an equal opportunity ogler. Handsome man, beautiful woman, he'd hit on either. Sometimes both.

'Well, that's reassuring.'

'Al, it looks like a damn jar of honey.'

'But the cube.'

'OK, a very expensive imported jar of honey,' Jim amended. A tall, strapping man with silver hair and a matching moustache called her name. Jim said, 'Oh, man. Why don't I come with you?'

Alice could only laugh as she fought her way to the counter. 'Slut,' she said under her breath and then she was lost in trying to explain how she had misplaced a rare 'collectible' of archaeological interest. Hard to do while your assistant flirts like a shameless hussy with the airport representative.

They had to explain it twice because the guy – Ted – kept staring at Jim. Alice was ready for a big, big drink and said so on the way to the car park.

There had been sexual tension and flirting between Alice and Jim since they started working together, but both tried to ignore it. She felt jealous of his other attentions sometimes and attracted to him at all other times. But Alice still wasn't sure if it was a good idea. Guys like Ted the airport man or flirtatious young things who automatically assumed that Alice and Jim weren't together really ticked her off. What if Alice and Jim *were* a couple? But no one ever seemed to think they were. Which really made her seethe.

'What kind of drink are we talking about? A Long Island Iced Tea? Wine, beer? Maybe a nice Sex on the Beach.'

'An Italian Surfer,' Alice sighed, trying to locate her old Chevy in long term parking.

'Oh, I'd like one of those, too,' Jim sighed.

'A drink! Not an actual surfer.'

Jim shrugged, 'Either, or.'

Alice rounded a Ford Escape and just as she approached a Hummer the size of Texas a bright yellow-orange glow lit up around them. It hung low to the ground like a neon fog and then flashed, huge and gaudy. Nuclear attack, mushroom clouds, radiation. All of this flashed through her mind before her brain kicked into gear and supplied the answer. 'The jar!' she said to Jim and they both turned to the walkway between the two vehicles.

There stood a tall, lanky man who made Alice immediately think *rock star*. He was leanly muscled and dressed in jeans and a black T-shirt. High top, black Chuck Taylor's and a leather wrist band. A chain hung loosely on his lean hips and it tethered him to a wallet that rested somewhere in his faded jeans. He looked like a rock god, but she bet he was a thief. 'Hey, that's ours!' she shouted and she expected him to take off. Instead, he turned to them with a dazed, slightly drunken gaze and gave a loopy grin.

'Shit,' said Jim, eyeing up the stranger.

'I think we know at least one thing the jar does,' Alice said. Then to the man, 'Hi, there. I think you have my jar.'

'Oh?' he said. He sounded confused, like he'd been sucking on a bong for the better part of the day. Then he pointed to it, 'Mine.'

'Yeah. Look, I won't say anything to anyone if you just give it back. I had to travel a long way for it – and it cost a lot. I'm sure it simply fell off that caddy's cart.'

'Yeah. Yeah ... it did.' He smiled a beatific grin and moved toward Jim. 'Hi.'

'Um ... hi,' Jim said. 'So is this the effect of the Greed Jar? Oh, those wily genie. Turn the opener into a stoner. Big whoop. That's not very greedy, it's more like fucking stupid.'

Alice barely registered the man moving, but he reached one long, pale arm out and yanked Jim in like a bear yanking a fish from a river. Then he planted his thin pink lips to Jim's and pulled him in close. Thrusting his hips eagerly against her

13

assistant, the man groped Jim's ass.

Jim twisted her way but the newcomer just kept kissing. His pink lips latched onto Jim's neck. His collar bone. 'Um, Alice?'

'Yeah, Jim?' Her eyes searched the ground for the jar. It had rolled half under the Escape and it glowed with a sherbet-coloured light. The lid to the Greed Jar had rolled under the Hummer. Alice was calculating how fast she could get them and get the lid back on the jar, when the stranger started shoving his hands down Jim's pants.

'Alice!'

'What?' she shouted. Panicky and frazzled.

'I think I know what the jar does!'

'Makes you horny?' She lunged for the jar but, before she could get it, the man's arm snaked out and tugged her in. Alice slammed up against him and felt the long, hard ridge of his cock against her pelvis. And then there was Jim, right up in her space, his hard-on pressed to her leg. The stranger leaned in and kissed her. Entirely too long and wet and hard. Her body warmed and she shivered. It was all of those things but it was also intoxicating.

'More,' the stranger said and pushed their faces all together and his tongue flicked out to try and kiss them both at once.

'I'm thinking this is decidedly greedy behaviour, yeah?' Jim asked.

Before she could answer the man had pushed his tongue into her mouth again. His fingers on her breasts, his cock rubbing eagerly against her pelvis. God help her, she was getting turned on.

'We need to get him to the office!' she gasped to Jim.

'Hell, yeah,' Jim said, his head rocked back, eyes closed because the stranger's hands were still busy in his jeans.

'To fix him!'

Jim sighed, but said, 'Yes, of course. To fix him.'

It damn near took an act of God to get the man in the Chevy, and his lips never did break from Jim's. When Jim did manage to ask his name, the stranger muttered, 'Mal.'

'Like malicious,' Alice grumbled, trying to strap him in the back of her car.

He caught her tit in his hand and squeezed. The other hand shot out lightning fast to her jeans and he grabbed her by the crotch before she could block him. The arousal she felt from his sexual frenzy was not easy to ignore but she did hear when he corrected her, 'Like Malcolm.'

'OK, then, Malcolm. We're going to take you home.'

'To fuck?' He pawed at Jim who didn't seem too concerned and then at her. Finally, Alice managed to get in the driver's seat.

'No, to fix. We're going to try and right you.'

'I'm hungry,' Mal said. It was sort of like talking to a hyperactive toddler, he switched topics so fast and so randomly.

Alice drove them through the insane loop of airport parking and he said it again. 'I'm hungry. Really hungry.'

Jim had a tent in his pants, her panties were wet and, if the rear-view mirror was correct, Mal, the new addition to their motley crew, was rubbing his cock through his jeans. 'OK, we'll get you something.'

The moving was slow and grid-locked and she literally heard Mal's stomach rumble. The Greed Jar was back in its Lucite cube it the trunk and Alice was still waiting to see if from putting the pieces back together she would be affected. 'I'm starving,' Mal said.

'We know!' Jim barked. He got grumpy when he was horny and unfulfilled.

The first fast-food restaurant she spotted, Alice hit the drive through. 'What do you want?' she asked Mal. She turned and he was furiously stroking his hard-on through his pants. By the way his hips shot up and the look on his face, she guessed he was close. 'Jesus Christ,' she said.

'Go on, get it,' Jim laughed. 'I want a Number Two meal,' he said to her.

'I guess we'll all eat.' Alice ordered a Number Two for Jim, a chicken sandwich and a diet coke for herself and then it was Mal's turn.

'A Number Three meal and extra pickles.'

Alice repeated and asked for the total.

'And a Number Six meal with extra hots,' he said.

Alice amended and started to ask for the total when Mal said, 'And a side of onion rings, a chocolate shake, an apple pie, chef salad, two boxes of cookies and a diet limeade.'

Jim turned to stare. 'Holy shit, man. You running a marathon?'

'I'm hungry,' Mal said and then leaned in and kissed Jim again.

'And we're off!' Alice said, but happily took a break in Mal's ordering frenzy to drive to the window and pay. 'I guess I'll have to use my credit card,' she told the cashier. 'I wasn't expecting *that* big a bill.'

She took the huge order, loaded the food around Jim who was still being (joyously) groped and then tossed a meal to Mal the way a zookeeper tosses a carcass to the lion cage. 'Mine! All mine!' Mal said in a giddy, drunken voice.

Jim brushed his kiss bruised lips with a napkin and cleared his throat. 'So ... how do you propose we fix him?'

'I have no fucking clue, but we have to get him home and I have to look it up. You deal with him, I'll check the records. I think there was something about the jar in that book I got at the Simon's auction.' They travelled to auctions held by any families who dealt in occult memorabilia. You never knew just what tidbit of information or lead you might find about an unnatural object in one of the many tomes to be found.

'That'll be hard.'

'What?' She ate her sandwich and stole one of his fries. Alice turned left on Summit and parked in front of her house. In the back, Mal had eaten two meals and his onion rings. His face was coated in chocolate shake and his dick was still hard. What a mess.

'Being alone with loverboy.'

Mal turned his love-struck eyes on Jim when he spoke. Alice rolled her eyes and snorted. 'You are a terrible liar, Jim.'

16

Jim laughed.

Alice found it in a book from an estate auction for the Grayson mansion. The man who'd owned it had been reported to be a necromancer and a fellow collector. In the book, bound in what was possibly human skin with a clasp made of bone, it gave a very brief description of the jar and below it said: *If the soul affected by the overwhelming urgency of greed is to offer something of his or her own heart, naturally, and without instruction, the spell will be broken and the effects will wane over the days. Twenty-one sunrises and sunsets will find the afflicted well and returned to normalcy.*

She rushed to tell Jim but, as she approached the old summer kitchen where Jim had taken Mal, she heard them first. Alice tiptoed, avoiding the squeaky boards. The wet sounds went straight to her lower belly, heating her pelvis with arousal. She knew that sound. She had made those sounds with lovers over the years. Alice peeked around the doorjamb and her insides turned molten. Her heart fluttered and her pussy throbbed.

Mal, his brown hair hanging over his closed eyes, was on his knees on the dark red linoleum. His mouth stuffed full of Jim's cock. Jim was oblivious to anything but the sucking going on as he thrust in harsh, eager strokes. His fingertips only rested on Mal's shoulders but, from the looks of the new man, he could very well have been yanking him forward roughly. Mal looked ecstatic. High. Completely blissed-out. His eyes opened, bottle green in the slants of sun from the blinds. He saw her and her breath stalled in her throat. But Mal didn't react, his eyelids drifted shut and he raised his hand and cupped Jim's balls. Squeezing, kneading, stroking. His fingers danced over Jim's thighs, cupped his ass, moved over the other man's skin. Alice leaned in and let the doorjamb press her clit. She wanted so badly to be in the middle of that. Just seeing them reminded her how long it had been. How much she missed affection, touch, sex.

Jim opened his eyes, his mouth working but no words coming out. He saw Alice and grinned. 'Hi, Al.'

'Jim.'

Mal raised his head and held out his hand. 'You, come. You too,' he said around a mouthful of cock.

'Come on, Al,' Jim said and he held out his hand too.

'I can't,' she said, but Alice had already taken a step into the room. Her body humming like a live wire with electricity and excitement. It was just the worst idea in the world but she did it. She put the book on a sideboard and reached out her hands. The moment their skin touched hers, her mind was full of white and her heartbeat thudded in her ears, her throat, her cunt.

'Lose the jeans and tee, Al,' Jim said and let his eyes fall closed again as his hips continued to rock gently forward and his cock disappeared inch by wet inch into Mal's sucking mouth. Alice didn't really remember taking off the clothes. They were on her and then they were off. She stepped up to the two men.

It was wrong. So very, very wrong. Mal was basically ill. His greed was a direct result of the jar's spell. What if he had no interest deep down in his original self to be with Jim or her? But his fingers, thick and strong wrapped around her wrist and tugged her forward. His mouth, ruby-plump from friction, broke from Jim's cock and pushed to her pussy. His tongue diving right in, finding her clit and pressing her there. Sucking, licking, biting just enough to make her stomach bottom out and her nipples go hard. Jim reached to her and stroked first one breast, then the other. 'I've always wondered about you buck naked,' he said.

Her breath ripped in and out and her hips arched up as Mal licked her, inches closer to coming. 'And?' She almost feared his answer.

'And you're pretty hot, boss.' He pinched her and Alice moaned. Jim moved behind her, angling her just a touch so that his slippery cock accessed the sopping opening of her pussy. He rubbed the head there, back and forth, his rhythm opposite to Mal's licking. Alice couldn't figure up from down and right from left. Her body was pulled between the soft, probing strokes of Mal's tongue and the velvety, hard tip of

Jim's cock. 'Here's your time to back out,' he said right up against her ear.

She was there between them. One hand pulling at Mal to get his face closer, his tongue harder and deeper. Damn near bending the poor man in half at the angle he had to manage. But he did it. He suckled her and she shook her head, the pleasure curling up from her clit to her belly button to breast to throat – where it tickled ever so slightly. Her other hand fell back, finding Jim's flank. She pulled at him just a touch and he took the signal, sliding into her with an effortless stab of his cock.

'Oh, Jesus.' She wanted to watch but couldn't quite manage. Her eyes fell closed and she was lost to the sensation. It was bigger and brighter and warmer in the dark behind her lids. Her pussy began its perfect fluid contraction as her orgasm sidled up to her like a long lost lover. 'I'm going to come,' Alice told no one in particular and Jim laughed softly in her ear.

'Mine,' Mal said, working his mouth on her harder. He reached around and grasped Jim's flank as Jim fucked Alice from behind. 'Mine,' he said again and the low rumble of his voice travelled through her and her pussy went taut. The sweet constriction made her cry out as she came and Jim groaned. She knew by that sound he didn't want to come yet. When he gripped her hips hard and pumped into her faster so that she nearly tipped forward onto Mal, she came again.

Alice sank to the floor, sitting on her ass hard, heart pounding. The moment she moved, Mal shuffled forward on his knees, saying 'Mmm-ine' again and taking Jim's wet, red cock deep into his mouth and throat. Mal's hand pumped, a white blur of motion on his own now-exposed erection. Alice noticed in a detached, stunned kind of way that he was uncut. That turned her on for some reason. She had never been with a man who remained uncircumcised.

'Mine, mine, mine,' Mal was saying it in a monotonous, eerie cadence now. His hand moving in time on his dick, his mouth sliding with slick sucking sounds along Jim's cock.

'Redundant but pleasant,' Jim said, tipping her a wink. He

then tilted his head back and grabbed Mal's face, fucking his mouth as roughly as he had just fucked her. He came with a hiss and a growl, the muscles in his neck and biceps jumping wildly as he emptied.

Pearly white come arched from Mal, sliding over his fist, hitting her red linoleum in pretty patterns of white.

'What now?' Alice gasped. Now that sanity was returning.

'I'm hungry,' Mal said in his dazed robot voice. His hand moving automatically worked the last bits of pleasure from his cock.

'Shocking,' Jim said, but helped him up. 'Come on. We'll get you some food.'

Mal didn't answer, instead he leaned in and kissed Jim on the mouth. A long, lingering kiss that made Alice horny all over again.

Halfway through his submarine sandwich and a pint of cherry ice cream, Mal sat in Jim's lap. He wriggled and moved and bounced until Jim was gritting his teeth. Alice felt the whole day to be surreal. Maybe they were all under the influence of the jar. Or maybe that's just what she needed to tell herself. But a thrill of excitement pulsed in her chest and she said softly, 'Go on. You know you want to.'

Mal ate the last spoonful of ice cream and dropped his jeans. He sat on the table swinging his legs like a coquettish girl. 'Please, if I'm a good, good boy?' he asked. His dark hair in his eyes, his surreal green eyes flashing in the late afternoon sun. Then he lay back and waited, his cock standing straight up in the kitchen as hard and true as a wooden spoon.

'Jesus. What am I supposed to do now?' Jim asked, but Alice could see him touching his new hard-on through his khakis.

'Fuck him,' she said. The eagerness in her voice was audible.

'You want me to fuck him?'

'Do it for me,' she said, giving him the out he needed.

'Why?'

'I want to see.' Then she shucked her own damp-in-the-crotch jeans and spread her legs, bearing her cunt to both men. Flushed and swollen, she could feel her pulse between her legs. She touched herself softly and Jim's eyes grew wide. 'Please. Do him for me. I want to see.' And she was telling the truth despite how surprised she was at her bravado.

'But what are we going to do about him?'

Alice shrugged. Her eyes were pinned to where his eyes were. Jim was watching her fingers and Mal was watching Jim. Alice said, 'There's not much we can do until we break the spell.' She slipped one finger, then another, into her wet cunt. Working herself with slow slips of her fingers so he could see. Jim's chest rose and fell rapidly and he licked his lips.

Mal made a soft sound, arched his hips, and stroked his cock in his slack fist. 'Jesus. Fine. I'll do it.'

'You're such a martyr.' But she laughed and pressed her G-spot firmly so that the first ticklings of orgasm could be felt.

With only spit and nimble fingers, Jim parted Mal's ass cheeks and opened him up. Slowly and surely, and gently like a good lover should, he had the man arching and tossing on her table, his dick steel hard and his fingers groping his own erection, palming his own balls. Then, Jim ducked and sucked Mal into his mouth. Going down low and letting his eyes drift shut. Mal gasped and jerked up to meet Jim's mouth.

Jim pushed himself to Mal's ass and thrust. One agonizingly slow and perfect stroke had him in and Alice thought she would come right there on the spot. Instead, she took a deep breath and stilled her hand for a moment as she watched Jim fuck the man.

Mal's fingers gripped the edge of the table, his legs up high and wide, his cock bobbing with each jerk of the wooden table. 'I want to come. I want to come. I do. I want my orgasm. I want my orgasm.'

Jim grinned at Alice, his jaw set harshly from holding out his own pleasure. His eyes found her stroking, working fingertips again and the flushed red flower of her pussy lips. 'I see why it's called the Greed Jar. *I want, I want, I need, mine.*

He's like a broken record.'

'Yes, yes, yes.' Mal was barking it out and he moved in jerky little bobs to meet Jim's hard cock. 'Give me mine. Give me mine.'

Alice would have laughed if the sight of Jim fucking Mal so spectacularly didn't have her hovering right on the precipice of coming like a freight train. 'Give him his,' she joked. But there was no humour in her voice, only soft arousal.

'I thought that was what I was doing.' Jim smiled and he grasped Mal in his hand, jerking his cock with sure pumps of his fist. Mal bowed up like he was being murdered but in the best possible way.

He stopped saying words and lost his voice to nothing but sounds. Alice watched the contrast of Jim's tan hand on Mal's pale dick and she was done. Her orgasm blindsided her and she cried out, her hand coated in her own juices just as Mal came, coating Jim's hand with white cream.

'Fuck. You two did me in,' Jim said, thrusting a few more times before roaring at the ceiling as he came. 'I had another five minutes in me without all the noise and orgasms and stuff,' he said.

Alice laughed and he laughed with her.

Mal leaned up on his elbows, his pupils as big as saucers. 'I'm–'

'Hungry!' Alice and Jim said in unison and Mal looked confused but nodded.

He'd decided he was thirsty too. And for wine. Mal was currently on his third bottle of wine. Talk about being a thief. First, he stole her jar and now he was drinking some of her most expensive vino! But, still, there was a blooming affection for the man. He seemed sweet, even if he was sneaky enough to lift the jar at the airport.

Alice and Jim watched him through the doorway into the kitchen as he ate and drank like a Viking. Every once in a while, Mal would pause with his mouth stuffed full and utter one word. 'Mine.' He said it to no one at all, but it seemed important.

'What do we do?'

'Somehow he has to offer something on his own. Not a good shot at that considering everything is 'mine' to him. God.'

'It's worth a shot.' Jim watched the other man. He touched her chin without looking at her. 'We'll be OK?'

'Sure we will. I wanted it just as much as anyone.' Alice blushed when she said it, but it was the truth, so fuck it.

'And we have him for how long if we get him to be giving?'

'It translates to roughly three weeks. It will wear off over time. Then I guess it's up to him. I don't think he'd be with us if he didn't want it to begin with. It makes him greedy for more. It doesn't give him the urge to start with.' She liked the feel of Jim's fingers on her skin. She closed her eyes remembering the feel of Mal's mouth on her pussy. Relived Jim fucking her, his fingers anchoring her by just a touch.

'Did he look like he was having ... uh ... fun?'

Alice laughed so loud that Mal paused at the kitchen table and looked around. 'Yeah. I think that's safe to say.'

'Come on.'

Alice had stashed the jar way up in the closet with other boxed unnatural items she had collected. A witch's recipe book from the 18th century, instructions on building a golem, a shaman's medicine bag, a petrified tulpa and a claw reputed to be from Bigfoot. There was a haunted sword, a cursed buck knife and an enchanted walking stick. The Greed Jar was locked in its cube on the third shelf behind several doors with padlocks. Now they just had to deal with Mal.

He looked up when they came in. 'Mine,' he said, indicating the food.

'We know.' Jim got a new bottle of wine and opened it. He poured two glasses and handed one to Alice. 'I think we've earned it.'

She toasted him and took a hearty swig. 'Amen.'

'Whatcha eating, Mal?'

'My food,' Mal said.

23

Jim leaned in and stared at Mal's food. Mal cringed. Jim licked his lips and Mal flinched. 'Mmm,' said Jim and then he leaned in and said something in Mal's ear.

War showed on Mal's face for a moment. Hope, fear, greed, excitement. Then he pushed the plate toward Jim and indicated a chip. 'Want one?'

There was a brief flash of light, like a magician's flare and then Jim took a chip.

'What did you say?' Alice asked, relief with just a hint of loss flooding her.

'I told him I sure was hungry and if I weren't so hungry I might have the energy to bend him over the table in the living room this time.'

Alice laughed and clapped. 'His greed for sex overcame his greed for food! And you didn't ask, so it was given freely.'

'I really am clever. I should get a raise.'

She would think about it. For now, Alice ran in and kissed him hard and fast. But then he yanked her back and kissed her slowly. His tongue trailing over hers. His hands tight at her waist. Then Mal stood and said his mantra and leaned in and managed to give them a sloppy kiss simultaneously.

'What now?'

'Now we eat up and I take care of that business.'

'What business.'

'Me and him in the living room.'

'Oh.'

'And you and him, of course, boss. I saw you checking out his package. It wouldn't really be a celebration without you.'

She smiled. 'I wouldn't miss it for the world. The celebrating or the package. I can't seem to get enough of you and him. Even without the jar.' They'd have a few weeks to figure out if Mal would stick around after all was back to normal or if they just needed to cherish the magic.

Take a Breath

She was perfect. He couldn't help but notice; a long lean body, a perfect hour-glass, wide, slender shoulders; a subtle feminine flare at her hips. Her eyes were the colour of whisky and she had a fashionably messy tangle of tawny hair. There was a steely determination about her but Jon saw through that. Underneath it all was a shadow of exhaustion; the look of someone just waiting for another person to take control. Take over. Allow her to take a breath.

'It's a lovely reception,' he murmured so as not to scare her. He handed her a glass of Merlot. He had noticed her choice much earlier in the night and had approved. No fruity white wine for her. Something full-bodied and bold.

Her eyes found his and again he caught a flicker of fatigue, a sense of drowning in her eyes. She accepted the drink and gave him her full-wattage, well practiced smile. 'Thank you, Mr…? I'm sorry, we haven't been officially introduced. I'm Elise Prevost.'

He shook and ran his finger along the gentle curve of her palm. Made a slow circle with the pad of his thumb and stared directly into those captivating eyes. Jon planned on showing her the real him from the get-go. It would either fly or he'd be wearing a glass of Merlot for the rest of the evening. 'Jon Leavey.'

'Mr Leavey, you are…?'

Her mouth was lush and full and Jon stared at it openly. He watched her slender throat contract as she swallowed hard. His guess was the lovely Elise wasn't used to men eyeing her as if they could eat her whole. No, his guess was most men were much more subtle about their dirty desires when it came to Elise. They took the wolf in sheep's clothing route. Jon showed her the wolf and waited for her reaction.

'Enchanted,' he said, bearing his teeth in a grin. It wasn't the answer she wanted. She wanted to know if he was affiliated with Aero-King or Alton Airlines. She wanted to know on what side of the merger he represented. He wasn't interested in business.

'No. I meant –'

'I know what you meant,' he said, again taking that slender hand and working his fingers over the mysterious grooves and dips and valleys. 'But this isn't about the merger. Or even your party. Spectacular as it is, by the way. This is about you. Me and you.'

'Me and you?' she echoed. Another forced swallow. Colour high in her cheeks, eyes sparkling with a delicious mixture of fear, uncertainty and yes, excitement.

'Exactly. But only if you're on board. I'm not the kind of guy to chase and chase and beat my head against the proverbial wall. I'm more of a take charge kind of guy. I think you're spectacular. Sexy. Stunning. I want to fuck you,' he said it low but looked her in the eye when he said it.

A high shattered titter escaped her throat and her colour went higher. Her cheeks a blazing shade of raspberry. But her eyes – Jon took note – her eyes shone, deepening from whisky to cognac. He did a full scan of her, reading her body the way he would read a menu. Puckered nipples shoving against the creamy black cashmere of her dress; thighs clenched so her hour-glass figure became nearly cartoonish with its perfect proportions. Her pulse jumped high and wicked at the base of her throat. And her hands…they came together instantly, twisting and pulling against one another like writhing animals. Jon smiled again. He had her.

'Mr Leavey. I…well, I am flattered. But –,' She stopped cold. Those perfect pink lips opening and closing on words, arguments and terribly logical reasoning that wouldn't come.

'I'm waiting.'

She looked stunned though something else twisted just

below the surface. Excitement. The excitement was the fuel behind the jumping pulse. Jon felt his cock grow even harder. He'd had a hard-on from the moment she sauntered in on those classy but clearly 'fuck me' heels. It had only made matters worse as she worked the room, hips swaying, smile flashing. Now, at the deer-in-headlights look on her face he thought if she didn't talk soon and distract him, it might just snap off. This made him laugh and a flicker of confusion stained her face.

'I'm not laughing at you,' he assured her. 'Just imagining my dick shattering in my pants. You've got me hard, Elise, and, see, this is the part where you come into the equation. You either give me ten great reasons why I should go fuck myself and stomp off in a huff. Or...'

Her eyes grew wider and a pale hand fluttered to her throat as if to stop the words from coming. 'Or?' It came out on a breathless whisper that was like silk on his skin.

Ah! He had her.

'Or you give me the green light and we have a very special night. Together. With me in control.'

He watched for her reaction. He had to make sure she understood that part. None of this sharing the reins. Not with this one. With this one he wanted no holds barred. No confusion of power. He wanted her but only if he could have all of her. Mind, body and soul. Total control. He would not tamp down his nature. Not with Elise. With Elise, he wanted the wolf in him to have its night to howl.

Nothing. She was barely breathing. Jon was pleased, though. She hadn't slapped him. She wasn't lecturing him on decorum and manners while showing off that body in those deceptively modest clothes. She was just standing there. Staring. He stared right back.

Jon surveyed the room. They were positioned behind a potted palm that shielded them from the view of everyone else. He grabbed her free hand, gave it a squeeze and placed it over the tented fly of his tux pants. 'See, Elise. I told you. Ready to snap off. All because of you and those whisky eyes.'

He waited. She didn't jerk away, didn't start wailing like a siren; she didn't do anything. She left her hand there and eventually her eyes found his. Wide and scared and slightly unfocused but she met his gaze. 'What do I have to do?'

He took the chance and pushed her hand against him harder; felt himself jump in response. A low keening issued from her throat and he thought he might bend her over the potted palm right there. It was the sound of an animal in heat. Desperate. Hungry. Ready. He couldn't contain his smile. 'Just whatever I say. Think you can handle that?'

A nod. Then, surprisingly, a gentle squeeze of her delicate hand. He felt himself swell and stifled a groan that would have matched hers. Damn. He hadn't counted on that. 'Don't do that again,' he growled. 'I didn't tell you to, so don't do it. If and when I tell you to pleasure me, that will be the time to comply. Clear?' Even to his own ears his voice sounded like sand and broken glass. Slightly ugly. All control.

Another nod that caused that sexy mess of hair to shift and sway. The light from the chandeliers accenting the colours of honey and wheat in the strands.

'Now who's that?' He pointed across the room and in the same moment removed her hand from his crotch. She reached for him blindly for a moment before hearing the low growl in his throat and controlling herself. Now that he had her, she was eager to go. Pleasing, but she had to learn his ways first.

'Him?' She indicated a short, thin weasely man with a nod of her head.

'That's right. Who is he?'

'Jackson Beckner. He's a small-time guy who thinks he runs the show.' She said this in a soft slow voice. He wondered if her brain had caught up with her mouth yet. Did she realize what she had just signed on for?

'He seems to have a fascination with your ass,' Jon laughed.

Another sweeping blush stained her cheeks and she nodded. 'That he does. Not necessarily me in particular. Any female behind will do.'

Jon shook his head. 'You're wrong about that, sweetheart. I'm sure he'll reach for any piece of ass if he thinks he can get away with it. But you, Elise, are special to him. He's definitely hot for you.'

She shrugged and he watched her ample breasts shake beneath the tight sheath of her dress. Nipples still hard, pulse still jumping. Jon had to take a deep breath. Slow himself down. What good would it do to slam her against the wall and fuck her senseless? It would satisfy his physical needs, sure. Not the other needs, though. Not the need to have her bend to his will and do as he pleased: no matter what.

'Come here,' he sighed into her ear and pulled her into the alcove that held yet another gigantic potted palm. Without preamble or apology, he slid his hands beneath her skirt and hooked his fingers in the silly little side straps of her panties. And she opened to him, just like that. She opened her thighs and moved her cunt forward to him with a sigh.

'That's not it, sweetheart,' he whispered in her ear and heard her half cry, half mewl in the ambient light. 'These are what I'm after.' He pulled the panties down her generous thighs, down past her calves and urged her to lift her heels one at a time as he peeled them off. 'Now go over there and shake that ass in front of that slimy little fuck.'

This time the arguments found their way past her lips. 'But...why. I thought you...I thought we –'

'Oh, we will,' he assured her. 'Only after you do as I say, though. Trust me or forget it.' He touched her chin gently but firmly as it started to tremble. Just enough that you would notice if you were paying attention. 'Go.'

God help him, she did.

She went over and feigned looking over the offerings on the buffet. Jon watched Beckner's eyes on her. The predatory gleam. The oily aura the man gave off. He grabbed his cock through his trousers, giving it one good, strong stroke before letting it go. No time for that. He'd get to the good stuff soon enough.

She bent forward, amazingly enough, reaching for the crudités platter. Ample ass high and rounded, presented right before the wolfish gaze of Jackson Beckner. As he watched, the man cast a glance around the party, and judging it safe, reached out to palm her ass as she scoped the food. Across the room, Elise's gaze found his, *what now?*

He nodded and smiled, moving forward. Feeling the urge to run across the room and throttle the man or break his face with several well thrown punches. His girlish bone structure would be no match for Jon's large, heavy hands and the strength that lay within them. He took a deep breath and sauntered up to the buffet, making sure that the three of them were the only ones there, the only ones paying attention.

'I think these are yours,' he said to Elise as her face went from raspberry to plum. She stayed straight and tall, though. No shrinking violet routine. No nervous laughter or hysterical fleeing of the scene. She regarded him coolly, ignoring the flood of colour and heat in her pale face.

'They are,' she whispered as the other man blinked owlishly.

'Now how can we be sure about that?' he asked, pinning her with his gaze. He allowed his eyes to roam and tack on to the other man who now looked like he wasn't sure whether he should run or fight. He *had* managed to cop a feel, after all. She hadn't slapped him or shouted or even threatened him. Should he fight this man for the tiny morsel he had won?

'You could put them on me to make sure they fit,' she suggested. It was so low that no one else would have even been sure she had spoken. But Beckner knew. He swallowed hard, his Adam's apple bobbing. Then, wisely, he turned on the heels of his cheap dress shoes and fled.

'Let's do that,' he said taking her arm, tucking the panties into his jacket pocket. He took a moment to trace the deep swell of her cleavage even as it rose and fell with her hurried breathing. 'Let's find the coat room, Elise. Point the way. You rule this roost.'

'Here?' she nearly squealed, then steadied herself. 'I thought you meant…off site. Maybe a hotel room. Your house. My house. But here?'

'Take it or leave it,' he said, reminding her of his rules. Of her agreement.

'Take this left,' she promptly replied. He took her arm and

pulled her closer to his side. And she stayed, snuggled in actually, a relaxed and somewhat relieved sigh coming from behind those perfect lips. He could nearly read her thoughts. Wasn't this nice to not have to be in control? Responsible? His hand found her ass and he gave a possessive squeeze. His. For tonight. Maybe longer. But his.

Everyone was at the party. The coat room wasn't occupied and Jon pushed her forward into the near dark with just enough force to rush the blood through his veins, heightening the anticipation of taking her and making her his.

'On your knees, Elise. Right here is fine.'

Without hesitation, she dropped to those perfectly white, dimpled knees and folded her arms behind her back without being told. Wow. She was good. Had she done this before? he wondered. Not likely but you never can tell. Just submissive by nature perhaps, but oh so very good at hiding it from the world.

He lowered his zipper slowly, making sure she could hear the metallic growl in the near perfect silence of the deserted room. 'Open that pretty mouth, Elise. I want you to suck my cock and I don't want you to do *anything* unless I tell you to. That includes breathe. I'll tell you how deep, when to touch me, when to breathe. All of it.'

No words. She simply parted her lips after licking them slowly, unconsciously. He felt another growl swell through this throat and without thinking thrust between those petal pink lips. Sank in hard and deep without giving her time to adjust or relax. But she took every inch without flinching. Without a sound.

He fucked her mouth, working her harder, keeping a steely grip on both his desire and resolve. He would not come. They had too many other things to do.

He waited until her knuckles were white, her hands clenched into little fists. 'Breath, Elise.' And she did. Sucking in a great amount of air but never releasing him, never pulling back. She simply inhaled deeply, like a swimmer breaking the water's surface, and then played her gently pink tongue along his length.

31

Jon sank his hands into that hair. It made him crazy. The messy, tawny pile of silk that swayed with every move she made. Forcing himself against her mouth, raking his flesh along her teeth, he took her hard. Curious and amazed by how well she was handling this. 'Touch me now,' he commanded and she did, cradling his balls, playing them over her fingers. He had to focus or this could be the end. 'Breathe.' Anther gulp of air and she was back for more. He felt himself go rigid and grunted against the will of his very eager member, 'Stop.'

She froze. Delicate fingers still on his sac, mouth wrapped around his dick in a way that just looking at it made him skate that razor's edge of release. He pulled out of her mouth and she didn't move. She didn't close her lips or sit back or say a word. She waited.

'Stand up, Elise.' He extended a hand which she accepted. She moved gracefully from her place on the floor as if she were being presented to royalty instead of being interrupted in the middle of blowing a virtual stranger. 'Back behind the coats.'

He pushed her hands against the wall, pinning her hips flush against it, too. He knelt behind her, taking a none too gentle bite on one firm ass cheek. She whimpered but otherwise remained silent. He slid his hands down the backs of her thighs, ran his thumbs along the sensitive skin behind her knees and circled her tiny ankles with his fingers. 'Don't move,' he said quietly. His voice was nearly threatening and he knew it. In response she gave an involuntary shiver but stayed still. 'At all,' he finished. Just so she knew. Understood the rules.

As slowly as he could manage, he ran his hands back up her legs, dragging the soft cashmere in their wake. He bared her. Her panties were still in his jacket pocket, so, bare of the black fabric, she was completely bare and spread before him. He watched her skin pebble with goose bumps under his breath. He ran his tongue along the sweet crack of her ass, stroking the spot where her butt met her thighs. She sighed but managed to stay still. Her stance denoted someone struggling to control their movements – their instincts. Taking his hands, he pushed her knees further apart so she was spread wide, her legs planted firmly atop her ridiculously high heels. 'You're gorgeous, Elise,' he breathed, running his fingers along the wet seam of her cunt. He let two fingers take the plunge into her velvety heat and she bucked. Just the tiniest bit but she did. He could tell she had fought it and lost. Ah well, a lesson to be learned though.

'You moved, Elise. That's a no-no.' He removed his fingers and she made a sound that was nearly a sob. 'Now you have to wait.' He grabbed her hips and spun her to face him. The colour was high on her cheeks and the slightest sheen of perspiration dotted her forehead. Eyes wild, hair wilder, she begged him with her eyes but said not a word. 'You want me in you, right?'

She nodded.

'Any part of me will do right now. My cock,' he grabbed himself and ran the head along her crux of her thigh. Her eyes rolled back for just a moment and he saw the war beneath her skin. She wanted to respond to his touch but didn't dare. 'Or my fingers,' he cooed, enjoying playing with her now. 'Or even my tongue, I suspect.' He traced her lips with the tip of his tongue while his fingers found the tangle of curls at the vee of her thighs. 'Say you're sorry,' he said, twisting the curls around his fingers, yanking just enough to make her gasp.

'I'm sorry,' she moaned. 'I'm so sorry.'

'I bet you are,' he laughed. To reward her for her sorrow, he flicked her clit with a fingertip, tracing a circle along the high hardened nub. 'But not for long. You're new, Elise, so I'll take pity.'

'Thank you.'

'My pleasure. And yours, soon enough.' He captured her nipple between his teeth. Still sheathed in cashmere, he nipped her hard enough so that her eyes flew open and she squeaked.

'Good girl. Again, no complaint. You play well, Elise.'

She nodded, staring only briefly into his eyes. She bowed her head and he saw tears shimmering just along her lower lashes. Taking her wrists in his hand he pinned her hands behind her back and bit her again. She stayed steady, not flinching from him, not rushing forward to meet him. He hummed his approval and felt her heart jumping just below her breasts.

As a reward he plunged his fingers back in, sinking deep, curling them gently to find her G spot and stroking her there. She groaned against his neck but held her movements in check. She was learning. He sank to his knees, keeping his fingers busy and employed his tongue to her clit. Not gently but fiercely. He could feel her, pressing her back against the wall to keep from jerking against his mouth and tongue. Again he hummed his approval and the sensation must have pleased her because she shuddered against him, her channel jerking around his fingers and clenching him tight.

'Hello?' came a voice and he froze. Elise stayed pinned to the wall, breathing in deep stuttering breaths, eyes wide and haunted. Someone was at the door of the coat room. 'Don't move,' he warned, fingers still lost in her depths. 'Not a muscle.'

'Anyone back here?' It was a man. He heard the man talk to someone else and a female answered. The half door squeaked on its hinges as the man entered. Jon rose, fingers still inside Elise and stood in front of her, his chest crushing her breasts, his head shielding her face from view.

The coats were moved along the rack, hangers jangling on the metal rod.

'What coat did you wear, mother?' A mumbled answer. 'Ah, here it is. The fox. Very good. Now where's my brown wool overcoat?'

The hangers continued their jingly song as the coats danced along the rack getting closer and closer to Jon and Elise. Unfortunately, they parted and Jon stared into a startled, elderly face he didn't know.

'Sorry. Just some business,' Jon said, with a charming smile. The bulk of his body shielded Elise's face from view. 'The brown wool is down that way, I believe,' he said with a jerk of his head toward the opposite end. 'Help yourself.'

34

Then he pulled the line of coats closed again as he heard the older man scurry to claim his coat and leave.

Elise stayed still, her head bowed. His fingers were still embedded in her slick entrance. Again it looked as if tears would threaten but she held it together. Her breathing was slower, more controlled.

'I'm impressed,' he murmured, lowering a kiss to her lips finally. She tasted like woman and mystery and him. 'You deserve a reward, Elise,' he said.

She shuddered in response. Not sure if she should speak, she remained silent. He didn't miss it, though, when her pulse started to jerk and jump at the base of her throat.

'Turn around again and spread your legs. Wide.'

She complied and when he pinned her hands at the small of her back with his own she sighed. 'That's a good girl. Push your ass out for me. As far as you can. There you go,' he grunted, running the head of his cock along her slick entrance, playing with her just a little. Truth be told, he was all out of play. He just wanted to sink into that perfect cunt and watch her jerk and tremble around him. Listen to her come. She'd scream. The quiet ones were always the screamers.

He didn't hesitate once he was slick with her moisture. He simply pushed into her. One long, hard stroke that took him home in an instant. Her fingers curled within his grasp and for the first time she growled long and low. He felt his pulse jump at the primitive sound of her relishing his penetration. She didn't push against him, though, kudos for that. She simply took what he offered and he made sure to offer it all. He thrust into her, each stroke high and hard as she made little desperate sounds. Taking one hand from hers, he stroked her clit, plucking it hard and then soothing with circles and swirls that made her gasp like she was drowning. 'That's it. You're a good student, Elise,' he said, keeping tabs on his own impending orgasm. Not long now. She was so wet and tight. So eager and good. She had done better than most first timers. It made him want to know what else she could do. What else she could learn.

'I think I need a new Senior Administrative Assistant,' he

said, forcing into her, bucking against the willing flesh of her ass. She cried out softly as he tweaked her clit between his forefinger and thumb. 'I think I've found her. You'll be in charge of me, of course. Basically run my life. Unless of course, I tell you that I have a task for you. If I have a task for you, will you know what I mean?'

Thrust, push, pound. He drove into her, working her with now slick fingers, biting briskly where her fragile throat met her slender shoulder. She bowed against him as her cunt tightened along his cock, feeling as if it could blissfully tear him in two. 'That you're in charge?' It whooshed out of her as she tipped over the edge into another orgasm. A cry tore from her throat that made him waver along the border of his own release. Not yet.

'That's it, good girl. I. Am. In. Charge.' Each word was punctuated with a near brutal thrust as she continued to constrict and flicker and squeeze around him. Grabbing her hips, he released her hands. 'Clear?' *Not now. Not yet.* He had to hear her say it.

'Clear,' she barked, bowing her head, bracing her body for his with palms flattened against the pale blue wall.

His orgasm tore out of him along with a sound that sounded nearly evil with its primal nature.

Jon fell against her, his head on her shoulder. His arms clutched, possessively, around her waist. He let himself fall free of her, smoothed her skirt, spun her to face him.

'Jon Leavey, the new CEO,' he said, offering his huge hand to her small one. 'Just came on board. Pleasure to meet you.'

She eyed his hand. Not warily, he noted, but hungrily. 'Elise Prevost, new Senior Administrative Assistant to the CEO. The pleasure is all mine.' She shook as if he hadn't just fucked her nearly unconscious. She was coming back to herself. Her normal take-charge attitude shining through. Even with her dress still hiked up around her naked hips and the smell of her all over his fingers, his face.

'We'd better go, Elise,' he sighed, holding out her panties as she stepped into them. He smoothed her skirt and gave her a brief but wet kiss. 'They'll be announcing me soon enough. Then I will be announcing you. Think you can handle that?'

She nodded, briefly, smoothing her sheath, fixing her hair.

'I thought so,' he said, parting the coats. 'When I first saw you, I had the feeling you could handle just about anything. You're just what I need. Do you think I'm right?'

A ghost of a smile lit her face and she tucked her hand into his. 'I think I can handle you,' she said.

'And when I take you to task? Any time I want. Any way I want. What then?'

'I can handle that too,' she said, and led him back to the party.

Discipline

I remember saying it to him. I remember it clearly. My first book was out, my second in the works. I had a looming deadline and absolutely no fire under my ass to make any sort of progress.

I would panic, calm down, and bitch. But I could not throw myself into my work. I was on the verge of tossing my laptop into the bathtub and turning on the faucet when Austin walked in.

'Babe? What's wrong? You've got the crazy hair from running your fingers through it.'

Normally Austin's warm, deep voice and easy smile were enough to take me off edge. It didn't work.

'I need discipline!' I blurted out. 'I am the most undisciplined person I know. I have exactly ten and a half days to wrap up this manuscript and turn it in.' I gave my hair one more raking for good measure and let my head thunk on the desk. I would wallow in self pity. It wouldn't help, but I would do it anyway.

Austin rubbed my back and neck and gave a little chuckle. 'Then finish it, Lizzie. Just finish it.'

That put my hackles up. 'I can't! It's right there. I mean, it is right there in my head, all ready but...'

'But?'

'No fire. No fire to write. I'm content to let it sit there all ready and waiting until the deadline is screaming in my ear. Then the fire will be there and as usual, I will be flying by the seat of my pants. It sucks.'

'Change it.'

'I can't.'

'Ah, you won't, is what you mean.'

I hated when he called me on something. It was even worse when the something was a character flaw that I truly loathed.

'Fine,' I grumped, 'I won't.'

'We'll have to do something about that,' he said on his way out of my office.

'What?'

He just smiled.

Six days left until my deadline. I clicked my email icon. I checked my website. I checked my favourite blogs. All the while, I mentally calculated. I had thirty thousand words left to meet my length requirement. I had six days. That was an average of five thousand words or more each day. Panic swelled in my chest, making my head swim and my ears ring. Yet, I didn't open the document containing my novel. Instead I went to my favourite used-books website and looked around.

Austin popped his head in. 'Super busy or you up for some grocery shopping?' His dark brown eyes found the website and he grinned and shook his head. 'I guess super busy is out.'

I sighed. 'Sure. Let's go. Maybe realising that we'll no longer be able to buy food if I don't finish this fucking book will give me the kick in the ass I need.'

'I don't think you need a kick in the ass,' he said, reaching for my hand. 'You need something, but not to be kicked.'

'What do I need?'

'I have an idea, but it's a secret. Let's go. Errands! It'll be fun.'

'Fun,' I muttered and let him hug me. I put my hand in the back pocket of his faded jeans and gave his ass a squeeze. 'Maybe a good romp in the sack will get me fired up.'

'We might have to give it a try,' he said, walking me to the front door. He handed me my jacket and then pulled me in for a hug. 'You trust me, right?'

'Of course.' Had I been that down? That snippy? For him to think that I no longer trusted him? 'I love you and I trust you. You know that, right?'

'Yep,' he said, winking. 'Just needed to hear you say it. Now let's get our errands done and see if we can help Lizzie with her self-imposed writer's block.'

'I'm not blocked, just lazy,' I sighed, climbing into the car.

'Not lazy,' he corrected, 'you were right. You just need a little discipline.'

For some reason when he said it, a little tingle swept up my spine followed by a satisfying shiver. And a tiny touch of arousal. Confusing but true. I let it go. Time to focus on groceries and then on my issues with working like a normal person.

I shuffled through our errands and tried to mentally digest knocking out five thousand words. And then doing it again. And again. I was getting more distressed with each stop we made. Finally, after dropping off overdue books at the library, Austin turned to me and patted my leg.

'Ready to go home and have a fire lit under your ass?'

Zing! There was that arousal again. What was wrong with me? On top of being a top-notch procrastinator, I was getting turned on by his completely innocent comments. I gulped and shook my head a little to clear it. 'Sure. You have a plan?'

'Yes, Lizzie, I do,' he said and then quickly tweaked my nipple through my thin hoodie. 'I have several plans.' The normally warm look in Austin's eyes now bordered on dangerous. His gaze darker and more intense than I had ever seen it.

'OK,' I managed, though to my own ears my voice was unstable at best.

'Let's go.'

I pondered his comment all the way home. What did he mean? Surely, he wouldn't... hurt me. Never. Austin would never hurt me. Ever. I knew that for a fact. However, denying the look I had seen on his face was stupid. I had seen it. After seven years, I knew his facial expressions. I could honestly say that I had never seen that particular look before. And it excited me. A lot. The nipple he had pinched was still hard and sensitive. The other one was simply hard for moral support.

'You go up and get undressed. I'll be there once I unload the car,' Austin said it as if he were asking me to shut the car door for him.

'What? I'll help. We can both unload the car and–'

Austin turned to me slowly and let his eyes roam my body for a second. Then he levelled his gaze and stared me right in the eyes. 'I said, go up and get undressed. Wait for me. Take everything off. I will be up as soon as I've unloaded the car.'

He said it quietly and slowly and each new word he threw out into the air sent another jolt of excitement from deep in my belly to the now wet place between my thighs.

'O-Okay.'

'Good girl. Go on. Hurry up.' And then he turned his back to me.

I felt dazed. Confused. I made my way upstairs and tried not to turn it over too much in my head. I trusted him. I had always trusted him. I would trust him now. Plus, I would be a liar if I said that my whole body was not radiating a pleasant, tingling anticipation. My cunt was already wet. Nipples hard. The smooth skin of my belly fluttered just from the friction of my denim waistband as I moved. I shivered when I pulled the ocean blue hoodie over my head and dropped it to the floor. Next my pink bra. Jeans. Lacy white thong. Socks. Shoes.

Then I sat on the edge of the bed and waited. I held my knees together, my spine straight, ankles crossed. Austin hadn't told me how to sit and I felt uncertain. Realising what a completely bizarre thought that was, I giggled. Austin would never tell me how I was supposed to sit. Or how to do anything else for that matter.

But he just ordered you upstairs and stripped naked and waiting... and you listened.

Another shiver, another pulse of excitement, another streak of liquid between my thighs. All true. I waited. I was cold. I sat. I didn't know what to do, so I sat patiently and waited.

He made me wait forever. Austin is quick but surefooted. He moves fast, talks fast, works fast and thinks fast. The only time he is languid and slow is in the bedroom. There he sees fit to take his time. Relish our acts and our time together. I adore that side of him. This time, as I waited I could hear him moving methodically downstairs. He seemed to be deliberately pacing himself. To make me wait. To draw out the excitement. It worked.

By the time he finally appeared in the doorway, it was a struggle to keep my spine straight. My knees kept banging together no matter how hard I tried to keep them still. My heart beat so rapidly I felt almost sick and my ears felt stuffed full of cotton. Worst of all, I was positive that I had created a nice sized wet stain beneath me. My pussy was so slick and impatient it just kept generating more and more lubricant for the cock it so desperately awaited.

'I like that,' Austin said almost nonchalantly. He nodded at my posture and gave me a very small, smile. 'Nice. You look like you'll catch on quickly to this discipline thing.' As he spoke he pulled down the blinds on all three windows. Then he pulled the armchair from the corner of the bedroom and nodded. 'I want you here.'

I rose slowly, fighting a sudden and overwhelming light-headedness. I walked to the chair and sat, hoping not to stain the butter-coloured brocade with my fluids. Austin shook his head and twirled his finger in the air.

'The other way. Knees on the cushions. Arms on the back of the chair. Forehead on your arms. Legs spread wide so your knees touch the inside of the arms. Your weight will be spread evenly. You won't lose your balance.'

'Lose my balance? Austin what–'

'Time to listen and not speak, Lizzie. I will not tell you again.'

There it was again, I realised as I changed position. That surge of fear tinged with pleasure. I was out of my comfort zone but in hands that I trusted. The fear and the arousal were a heady mix. I swayed a little as I turned. Austin's big, warm hands pushed the insides of my knees until the outsides of my thighs bumped the padded arms of the chair. He pulled my forearms back a little so they were evenly on the headrest and crossed them. Then he pushed my head down a little further.

This forced my ass out. Out in the air. Vulnerable. Then his finger pushed into me and I gasped out loud.

'I see that you have had plenty of time to anticipate. And think. And work yourself up.'

His laughter was soft and dark. Nearly sinister. And yet, I trusted. He would never hurt me. Not really.

'Choose a word,' he said. I could hear him removing his socks and his shirt. The soft whisper of fabric being folded and discarded.

'What?'

'A word. I would like you to choose a word. To keep you safe. A word that you will say if you truly want me to stop. At any time. What's the word?'

I didn't even thing. It popped right out of my mouth. 'Procrastinator.'

'Good choice, Lizzie. Because that word, related to you, is about to become a thing of the past.'

My skin rippled with goose bumps and I bucked involuntarily as if he had touched me again between my legs.

'Do you hear me, Lizzie?'

'Yes. I hear you.'

'Good girl.'

I heard the clank of his belt buckle, then the long sinuous sound of the wide leather being withdrawn from the denim loops. 'See, when I was a little boy, before my dad left us, I got whippings.'

My nipples seized up and I couldn't seem to swallow or speak. I was ready to blurt out the word right then and there but all that came from between my lips was an airless, hollow sound.

'When I did not do the things expected of me. Things I was *paid* good allowance money to do, he didn't take my allowance. He took the pay out of my hide. That's what he called it. Taking payment.'

I was paid to write. Paid fairly well, too.

He spoke directly in my ear on my left side. He hadn't touched me yet. I didn't raise my head or my eyes. From my position all I could see of him was his bare flat stomach, the

43

belt in his hands, his denim clad legs and his bare feet. My heart jittered in my chest and I struggled for air.

'And I hated it. I hated him for doing it. It was humiliating and shameful and it pissed me off. I got better with my chores. I did things the way I was supposed to. I became faster and more efficient and more responsible. There was one thing I always noticed, though. I never admitted it to anyone. In fact, I've never spoken it out loud. Would you like to know what it is, Lizzie?' His fingers stroked my hair so softly that I couldn't believe he was talking about whipping me with his leather belt. The thought seemed ridiculous. But that was exactly what he was doing.

'Yes,' I said so softly I doubted he heard me.

'I noticed that when all was said and done. When he had left the room after collecting his payment, that I was hard. Every single time. Hard as a rock. And the moment I could get into the bathroom and lock that door, I jacked off. They were the best orgasms. Those pleasurable releases stained with pain.'

I felt a little sob well up in my throat. Now it wasn't because he was talking about whipping me. About intentionally striking me. It was because I realised I *wanted* him to. Very much.

I nodded but didn't speak.

'Are you willing to let me teach you some discipline? Make you a better writer? More efficient and conscientious?'

Another nod. Another shiver. Another trickle of fluid down my inner thighs.

'Good. Remember your word and count them off for me. I won't hurt you too much, Lizzie. He did it to hurt me. I'm doing it to help and to give you something you've never had before. That release. You trust me?'

This time I spoke aloud. 'With my life.'

'For this first time, we'll start with ten.'

He touched my hair one more time. Very softly. Reverently. Then he positioned himself behind me and I felt myself tense. I had never tensed up around Austin. I had never felt the need. With this new experience looming over me, I tensed. Thrust into a new sexual arena I felt a clawing terror in my chest mixed with curiosity and desire. I wanted this. To feel what it was like. To put myself in his hands.

What you see in the movies is real. That whistle through the air. The shift of oxygen molecules. I felt the stinging bite of leather on my skin before my ears picked up the sound. The overwhelmingly loud *crack!* of it biting into my skin. The sound of my pain tore out of my throat as my body bucked in the chair. Breasts banging the back of the chair, legs twitching involuntarily.

'One,' I sobbed and then wondered how I would weather nine more.

The second one connected in a different place with a different sound. Higher on my buttocks, overlapping to some degree flesh that had already been traumatized.

'Two.' I gritted my teeth when I said it but there was a hint of scream in my voice. I wanted to scream. I wanted to cry. I wanted to beg. And I wanted him to go on.

By the time we hit five, my face was doused with salty tears. They ran off my forearms in little rivers. My ass was on fire. Throbbing agony that made way into softer flickers of pain. This wasn't to hurt me, I reminded myself. Austin's father had meant to hurt him. What must *that* have felt like?

The next blow was so much lighter than the others. A kiss of the leather across my pulsing bottom. 'Six,' I said. It was almost a sigh. So pleasurable now. It had… had… what? Felt good. The pulse of my abused skin had reached my cunt and I felt it constricting with anticipation.

Each one got a little lighter then as my counting grew to moans of pleasure. 'Seven…eight…nine…' I had relaxed into the chair. My weight rested on my head and my ass was raised almost whorishly.

I heard the belt whistle but I was too late. That had been a tease. The final one was for real but my body wasn't ready. It ripped across my flesh with a vengeance, igniting every nerve in my body. Burning them up with fierce, toothy pain.

'Ten!' I shrieked and collapsed, sobbing against the chair.

The belt thudded to the floor and his hands were on me.

He smoothed them over my bottom, so softly it felt like an air current. His mouth found my ear and dropped a wet kiss there. Then on to behind my ears. My neck.

'I am so very proud of you,' he whispered. Even though I was still wracked with sobs, I couldn't help the smile or the swell of pride.

His fingers pushed into me. One finger, two fingers, three. I gasped and pushed back against him. Felt my body clench hungrily around his digits. Felt the beautiful light of pleasure swirl up my insides and settle somewhere around my ribcage.

'Lizzie?'

'Hmmm?' I pushed back against his hand, forcing his fingers deeper. He knew my body so well. He hooked his fingers and stroked my G-spot.

'Do you feel the difference?' As he spoke, he probed with his fingers and smoothed his other hand over the still-throbbing flesh of my bottom.

'Yes. Yes, I do.'

'Good.' Now he was gentle, pushing the blunt head of his swollen cock between my slick folds, finding my entrance. He slid into me slowly. Just the head first. Then a little more. My body stretched then pulled. Pulsing around him. Beckoning him deeper. Right at the end he thrust hard and high. All the way into me. I cried out as the first orgasm shot through me. Just like that. One hard thrust and it rocketed up through me until I felt as if my ears were burning and my head was swimming. He pushed in gently and pulled out slowly and let me ride the long, slippery waves of pleasure that didn't seem as if they would end.

Very gently he smacked my bruised skin and thrust hard again. Smaller, but just as intense, a second orgasm pulsed through my body. I hadn't even recovered from the first.

'So beautiful,' he said, finding a rhythm now as I pushed back to meet him. I wanted to soak him up. Take him all the way into me. The beautiful feel of his body in mine was like a drug. 'You were gorgeous. Counting them off, taking the blows. Your back bowed and shaking. Your ass striped and welted and angry red. But you did it,' he growled, his motions growing faster. 'So much more brave than I ever was. A fucking warrior. One who should never be afraid of her own talent. Never try to hide from it,' he grunted.

As soon as he said it I came. The truth. It was the truth. I felt overwhelmed at times, so I ran away. Hid from what I wanted to do with my life and my words. Austin came with me, yanking my hips so hard I screamed as my bruised ass banged his hipbones.

Little dots of white light danced in my vision. I put my head down and took a deep breath, not wanting to break contact. Austin's body was still linked with mine, his diminished but still firm cock in my cunt. I wanted to stay here for just a minute more.

Finally, he placed kisses along my spine and across my upper back. Then he pulled free and started to dress. I turned and sat in the chair then promptly jumped up with a screech.

'Five thousand words, Lizzie. Right now. I'll make dinner,' he said, handing me my clothes.

I put them on slowly and watched his face. He smiled his normal smile at me. I felt something loosen in my chest.

'I'm going to do it right now,' I assured him.

He handed me a throw pillow from the bed. 'You'll need this.'

I couldn't help it, I laughed. 'Think I'll ever need a refresher course?' I asked, secretly hoping I would.

'We all need refresher courses from time to time. I'm sure you'll be needing one in the future.'

I didn't say it but I thought it. *Good.*

'Do You Trust Me?'

'May I use that for a minute?'

I turned to hand over the corkscrew. Warm hazel eyes met my gaze. Dark hair, just a little too long. It fell boyishly over his forehead. I tracked the edge of his jaw with my eyes, took in the perfectly shaped mouth. Red lips. Not too red, just red enough to make me wonder what it would be like to kiss them.

'May I?' he asked again with a smile.

I realised I was still holding the corkscrew out. Offering it up but not letting it go. I shrugged, tried to cover with a laugh. I released the tool into his broad palm and wondered for a split second if that palm was soft or calloused. What it would feel like sliding under my skirt and along my stockings. 'Sure, sorry. Maybe I shouldn't have this glass after all.'

'Oh, I don't know about that. I think you just became a little absorbed for a moment. It happens to the best of us.' He flashed that smile again and I felt a warmth start low in my belly. I liked his smile very much.

'I was. Just a little.' I shrugged. No reason to lie, I had been obvious enough from the get-go.

'Well, my ego would prefer it if you said a lot, but I will take a little and be happy with it.' He began to uncork the bottle of Chablis he was holding. 'Not for me,' he explained. 'I prefer red. I was told someone with muscles needed to open a fresh bottle. Not that I'm riddled with them, mind you. A respectable amount, though.'

I took this as an invitation to scope out his muscles, so I did just that. He didn't have the over-inflated look of a gym rat, but a respectable amount was not an understatement.

Broad shoulders that hinted at strength. His arms, cut just enough that the contours showed through the cotton Henley he was wearing. It looked soft, too, that shirt. I repressed the urge to run my hands along the swells and dips cloaked in frequently washed cotton.

'Still a little absorbed?' he laughed as the cork broke free with a jubilant *pop!*

'No.' I took a sip of my wine and smiled. 'A lot.'

He let out a laugh and the hair on the back of my neck stirred with appreciation of the sound. He grabbed his chest and sighed. 'It does an ego good to hear it. I'm Eric.'

He took my hand before I could offer it. He didn't shake. He just squeezed it gently. Another stirring of baby fine hair, this time up my arms.

'Ashling. Ash to most.' He hadn't let my hand go and I didn't try to remove it. I liked the feel of his warm skin surrounding mine.

Eric leaned in close and whispered. 'I like your dress. Very deceptive.'

I glanced down as if I had never seen the dress. It was my favourite. Snug without being too tight. The front cut so that it fell just below my collar bones. Very modest. But the back. Well, there was no back. From behind my neck where the dress buttoned to the small of my back, I was bare. 'Thank you. I like it, too.'

Eric didn't back up. He stayed close to my face, his breath on my cheek. His mouth nearly touching my ear. I suppressed a shiver. 'Turn around for me so I can see. Up close.'

I turned slowly. I didn't even question why I was humouring him. He asked, I felt compelled to oblige. He still held my hand gently but firmly so I let my arm stretch out behind me as I turned. With my back to him, I waited. I held my breath. My skin felt as if it was on fire. When he touched me I heard a gasp tear out of me. A single fingertip. He traced the edges of the cut-out back, the gentlest touch I had ever felt and yet my head was swimming. He finally released my hand.

I stayed, frozen, back to him. Not moving. Unsure of what to do but determined not to break the spell that had settled over us. I heard the wine bottle bang on the table as he sat it down. His hands slid around my waist. He pulled me back so my ass was flush with a prominent erection. Another sound escaped me, this time a sigh. My dress whispered as he spread his hands across my waist and anchored me. He bent in low again, another kiss of hot breath against my throat. 'Would it scare you terribly if I asked you to come upstairs with me?'

I shook my head. My voice could not be trusted. Words would not come to me. I just shook my head. No. It would not scare me. Not at all.

I allowed myself to be led through the crowd. The smoke was thick, laughter loud, music blaring. No one noticed us. No one cared. Up the steps, I walked, hand back in his. My heart beating erratically and a pulse throughout my body. Captivated. Spell. I had no idea and I did not care. I wanted him. It was that simple.

My dress made secretive sounds against my stockings as I ascended. I did take a moment to thank the lingerie gods or whoever it was who put it in my head to wear the sexy unmentionables tonight. No standard pantyhose hiked up to my waist. No. My very best thong, the garter belt, the seamed hose, the whole nine yards. I smiled in the fading light. I was very thankful to whoever had guided my hand.

The party noises faded as we made our way down the darkened hallway. My hand still nestled in his, I felt a slight moisture seep from me, staining the crotch of my panties with a wet warmth. I managed to draw a breath and fight off the light headed feeling.

'Won't Derek mind us being up here?' I whispered. 'I only know him from work. I'd hate–'

'I've known him since I was nine. He won't mind,' he whispered right against my lips and kissed me.

I sank into the kiss. Into him. Wantonly. Like I never had before. I pressed along the full length of him, feeling his body meld against mine. I opened my mouth, accepted his tongue and met it thrust for thrust. He tasted sweet. Like wine and candy. Like sinful things.

'In here.' He propelled me through a door, his mouth

never leaving mine, the kiss never letting up.

I shoved my hands into his dark hair, grabbed handfuls as if I could kiss him more deeply if I held on for dear life. My back slammed against the wall and I used the resistance to arch my pelvis against him. Positioned myself to feel the delicious slide of his hard cock along the seam of my sex. I hummed my appreciation and continued the kiss. Let myself get lost in the slick humid moisture that was his mouth.

He broke away first and I found myself instinctively chasing after his mouth with my own, intent on reconnecting with him. He dropped to his knees and ran his hand up the inside of my calf and rested his forehead against my belly. 'What's on under this deceptive dress, Ash? It's been driving me insane since I saw you come through the front door. Proper pantyhose? Thigh highs with elastic, which is cheating by the way. Thong? Bikinis? Nothing? I've been dying to find out.'

His large hand moved up to my knee and just a touch beyond. I was panting in the dark. I could hear myself. There wasn't enough air and only a tiny bit of light. An antique table lamp that gave off no more light than a nightlight. His hand stilled there, so warm and big that I thought my skin might ignite. 'May I?' he whispered, lips pressed flush against my abdomen. His words vibrated up my body sparking a blissful shiver.

'You may.'

I whispered it. I barely heard myself. He heard me, though. His hands started a slow northward ascent. The room so quiet I could hear the sensuous sound of his hands moving up my thighs. The sound so amplified by silence and the adrenaline in my body, it sounded unbelievably loud. His hands reached the tops of my thighs. The sweet spot where the stockings were secured by the snaps of my garter. I hitched in a breath as he murmured appreciatively and dipped a finger below the gauzy material.

'This is what I was thinking,' he sighed and kissed the vee of my thighs through my dress. One chaste kiss and I was soaked. I felt it rush from me and my nipples hardened. 'I was hoping… praying, actually, that I would find something like this if I managed to get you alone. I saw the seams on the back of the stockings. I had to know,' he laughed quietly and the sound was like being stroked, 'if they were the real deal or a cheap imitation. I would have been very disappointed to find thigh highs with elastic. A woman like you should wear the classics.'

A woman like me. A woman who, at the moment, couldn't form a coherent sentence if her life depended on it.

Eric lifted my dress almost demurely. A slight tug of the fabric, a nearly dainty motion, like drawing up a curtain. Without thinking, I took the hem and gathered it to my waist. Holding it out of his way and offering myself up for display.

'And this thong… perfect,' he breathed and this time his breath feathered across my belly. I felt the fine hair stir and lift in its wake. I pulled the fabric tighter against myself just to do something, to take my mind from the fact that I felt unstable. Consumed. Just by his gaze.

First his eyes and then his fingers, warm and blunt, outlined the satin triangle of my thong. Heat blossomed in my cheeks and my chest, spreading like liquid fire down to my cunt. I made a small noise in my throat.

'Do you trust me?' he murmured, kissing the soft skin that bordered my panties. My entire body weight pressed against the wall. I nodded, though I had no reason to trust him. Not a reason in the world. But I did. Instinctively, I trusted him.

His lips never left my body but his voice got a little louder, 'I need you to tell me. Out loud. Do you trust me?'

'Yes,' I whispered.

As soon as my answer fell from my lips, he began. He released my stocking from their clips. The now empty straps brushed against my bare thighs. Eric peeled the stockings slowly, rolling one down with exaggerated care and patience. When he lifted my foot free, he put the rolled stocking carefully aside. The other leg received the same care. By the time both stockings were laid neatly on the floor, I was barely breathing. Taking in just enough oxygen to stay alive. His fingers hooked in the side straps of my thong and he tugged gently then stopped. He kissed the stripe of naked flesh above the waistband and then slowly dragged the scrap of material from me.

I could hear it whispering in the near dark. The fabric sounded almost as joyous and aroused as I felt. When the thong pooled around my ankles, he lifted first one foot then the other to set my legs free. Then he stood. Stockings in one hand, thong in the other.

'Now, Ash, I want you to turn around for me. Face the wall.'

The words startled me but the tone soothed. Demanding but gentle. Meant to be obeyed but also meant to set me at ease. He lowered his head, sucked my nipple into his mouth and sucked until a stripe of fire shot from my breast to my sex. 'Go on, now. Turn around.'

I did it without hesitation.

Eric's trailed his knuckles down the base of my spine, I could feel the satin and nylon he held rasping against my skin. I shivered when he leaned in, his breath hot on my neck. He bit me just hard enough to make me whimper and make my nipples pucker. The pleasure from the pain slid over my skin as I tried to figure out his plans. He bent down and I felt that hot breath on the base of my spine.

'Spread your legs for me,' he said calmly. I felt anything but calm. Scared, excited, bad. I felt all of those things but not calm. He pushed his palms against my bare calves, forcing my stance wider. I felt the slippery nylon loop around my ankle and then he moved to my left. The hosiery snickered in the near darkness as I watched him tie it to a dresser leg. 'Now the other,' he murmured as if he were talking to himself. My right ankle was encompassed and then he moved to tie it to the foot of the antique bed.

Eric stood and slid his hands along my sides, dragging my dress up with him. He lifted it over my head as I held my arms up like a child. 'The bra can stay,' he whispered and kissed me for a few moments. His tongue warm and sweet with wine. The gentleness of the kiss helped the fear beating away in my chest calm a little.

I stood with my legs bound wide, feeling like a prisoner ready for frisking. Instead of feeling embarrassed, I felt incredibly powerful. I could feel his eyes on me. Feel him studying me and soaking in the site of me splay legged and nearly naked just for him. 'Arms above your head, Ash. Normally, I'd like to bind them behind your waist but you seem just a little nervous. It's not as scary if they're bound above your head.'

I almost told him to go for it. Tie them behind my back. I didn't. His judgment was probably better than mine in this situation. I was a virgin at being trussed up. He obviously, had done this before. I slid my hands up the plaster wall and clasped my hands together.

'Do you have any idea how spectacular your back looks like that? A work of art. Those long lean muscles taut and tense. You are a vision.' His voice snaked into my ear and my nipples grew harder, little pebbles pushing eagerly against the black lace of my bra.

He looped my own thong around my wrists, tying it tighter than I had expected. His tongue dragged the length of my neck from nape to base and then another bite was administered. The insides of my thighs felt hot and slick. My body pulsed. All I wanted was for him to fuck me. My world had narrowed down to the stranger standing behind me. To the nylon that circled my ankles and the satin that bound my hands. And my vulnerability. I was helpless and the thought of being helpless for him brought a flicker in my cunt that was damn near close to an orgasm. A little burst of hot pleasure that demanded more pleasure in turn.

I heard his zipper, the rustle of fabric. The almost inaudible sound of clothes being tossed to the floor. I waited.

He smoothed his hands over my back, his words ringing in my mind as he slid his warm palms over each muscle in my back. I shivered. Then his hands gripped my hips and yanked me back. I nearly lost my balance but Eric kept me steady. I balanced as best I could, legs set wide, ass thrust backwards, hands above my head. Beyond doing my best I had to trust him.

Two fingers dipped into me, sliding into my warm waiting body. I sighed.

'You are very ready, aren't you? Positively dripping. Do you want me to fuck you, Ash? I need you to answer. No nodding that pretty little head. I need you to say it.'

Though my face grew so hot I felt feverish, I took a deep breath and said it. 'I want you to fuck me, Eric. Please,' I added for good measure and without thinking I stuck my ass out further. Beckoning. Pleading with my body.

The growl rumbled from low in his chest, his hands bit into my hips and he shoved into me so fast my breath stuck in my throat. Then I sighed, sinking thankfully back onto his cock as he fucked me.

I wasn't much good on trust. Not under the best of circumstances. Nearly dark, tied up, with a stranger wouldn't be considered the best of circumstances. Many men had taught me that trusting a male of the species was an earmark of stupidity. For whatever reason, I trusted him, though. I trusted him to have me bound, keep me nearly blind, and fuck me. It was freeing, this blind trust and I let the thought slip from my mind as he pushed a little higher. The head of his cock was smacking my G spot repeatedly. I tried to fight the orgasm, the clench that was beyond my control as my body gripped his. I lost. A spectacular loss that was trumpeted with wave after wave of pressure and release. All I could do was rest my forehead against the cool plaster as I sobbed out my pleasure.

'Good, good, girl,' he whispered against my ear. His hands roamed the taut muscles of my ass as my cunt continued to flicker and jump around his cock. 'Don't move. Stay just as I have you.'

He pulled from my body and I felt empty. Cold. I wanted him back.

'Be patient,' he whispered as if he could read my thoughts. 'I'm not done with you. Not in any sense of the word.' He untied the stockings, readjusted them so that my legs were even farther apart. My body even more vulnerable. Once the knots were retied, he slid along the wall so that he was in front of me. My bound hands over his head, my breasts smashed to his chest. I realised I would give anything if he'd take off my bra and suck my nipples, but I didn't ask.

'Now, I want to see what you taste like after you come,' he said. He kissed me. A fleeting kiss than left me wanting more. And though he didn't remove my bra, he yanked the cups down and nibbled slowly on one nipple and then the other. By the time his tongue left a hot trail of spit over my belly button and towards my waiting pussy, I was light-headed.

His mouth found me. Lips and tongue and teeth doing a spectacular dance across my pussy lips, suckling my clit. The rigid tip of his tongue swooped into me and he murmured against me, most likely at the taste of my come. I tried to stay steady flattening my upper body against the wall and prayed I wouldn't fall over. His hands gripping my waist tightly were the only things that kept me from sinking to the floor. Of that I was certain.

Only when I came again, a second crushing orgasm that wet his face and lips, did he release me. When he came up and kissed me he tasted like wine and my moisture. I could have kissed him all night. Even as he kissed me, his fingers stayed busy, playing and kneading. Stroking my clit, sliding into my cunt, keeping me perpetually on the edge of another orgasm.

'Are you OK? Not uncomfortable?' he asked.

His teeth went back to work on my nipple and the sensation shot straight to my cunt. I moaned but managed a weak. 'No. fine.'

'Good.' Then he was gone. Behind me again. His presence fiercely palpable.

I felt his cock rub against my slit again as my body jumped eagerly. Back in me. That's what I wanted. Him back in me, moving, slamming, pounding. While I remained helpless and at his mercy. Just the thought made me push back against him, trying desperately to speed up his re-entry.

'Behave. Don't move.' I felt his erection break contact with my body. Punishment, I assumed. I breathed. One breath, two breaths, three breaths…

Without warning he slid into me. One forceful stroke that filled me completely and left me gasping. His hands covered my hands as he leaned his full weight against me, pressing me to the wall, smashing me. His cock slammed high and fast as he grunted in my ear and I kissed the cool plaster beneath my lips. Teeth bit down in the soft flesh of my shoulder and I came again. My keening wail complimented the guttural sound of him spilling into me. He jerked against me forcefully as our combined orgasm took over.

We rode out the silence and the aftershocks. His large fingers encircling my bound wrists. I could feel his heart beat slamming against my shoulder blade. The bite on my shoulder sang with the sweetest pain. Like being branded, marked. I felt owned. And oddly, safe.

'Don't move.' Eric untied my wrists and I felt pins and needles settle instantly in my flesh. I kept my hands together, arms raised, afraid to break the spell.

I heard him bend down. Heard the whispers of nylon as he untied my hose. Felt the slack in my thighs as the tension disappeared and the burn of my trembling muscles. I stayed in that position too. Legs spread wide. I wouldn't move until I was told I could.

'Turn around.'

I did. I faced him. He smiled. The most handsome smile I had ever seen. A secret smile just for me. I had been at his mercy and now I felt oddly protected by him. I didn't question it, I just smiled back.

'I want you to leave this alone,' he said, helping me step back into my thong. 'Don't wipe me away. Leave it. Let my come dry. I want it in you, on you and on these lovely delicates. OK?'

I nodded as he slipped the sidebands onto my hips. I could feel it pooling in the cotton crotch. Hot and thick. In my head I could picture its milky opaque texture. I could smell it, too. The room was thick with the smell of pussy and come and sex. I smiled again.

He slid my stockings up my thighs and it felt beyond

sensual. To be dressed, to be tended to. I was sore and happy and a little confused. He adjusted the clasps and murmured to himself, 'looks as if they only stretched a touch.' I didn't care.

Next came the dress. He slid it over my head, adjusted the seams, smoothed the wrinkles. He fluffed my hair and helped me back into my shoes. Then he held my head in his big strong hands and kissed me. The same kind of kiss that had started it all. I fell into it. Let myself go. Nothing mattered but his hot mouth, his velvety tongue and the feel of him cradling my head.

'Do you trust me?' he asked again.

'Yes.' This time I knew to say it out loud. I meant it. Now I had reason to trust him.

'Good. You're coming home with me.' It wasn't a question.

'Of course.'

Would You Like Fries with That?

Feel free to laugh if you must. I have a friend Charlene who will go on and on when drunk enough about how she loves a man in uniform. Charlene, being a friendly, fun-loving slut, means a Navy uniform, fatigues, police officer, fireman, EMT and the like. I will drink shoulder to shoulder with her, nod and agree. But what I mean by a man in uniform is entirely different.

It isn't much of an issue but for certain days when lunch break takes me out into the bustle and crunch of the city. *Then* it's an issue. I both look forward to and dread these days. I anticipate them wetly and warmly because I know I'm going to get off. I dread them because I know I'll probably end up gaining about a pound from the food.

Today it's McWilliams's. I slip into the warm, neon-lit clatter of the fast-food joint and suck in a breath full of grease and salt and fat. Heaven.

The lines are long. It's lunch time, after all. There are five raggedy lines and a crush of people. The staff look frazzled and overworked but one stands out. He's tall and lanky and barely legal. Definitely graduated because it's a school day and he's here, but not by much. This is probably his college money job and that makes me smile.

His shoulders are broad but still thin from youth, his face is peppered with light stubble and a shock of unruly dark hair pops out from under his regulation cap. I check him head to toe. McWilliams's striped uniform shirt – a white shirt with a navy blue pinstripe. Yellow tie with a tie tack shaped like a burger. A navy cap with the big McWilliams's logo. Dark navy pants, yellow belt and a smile.

I love a man in uniform.

I can't help but fidget with the hem of my dress as I wait in line. Each satisfied customer that passes, I get closer to my server. I can just imagine the starchy feel of his nifty shirt under my fingers as I get him naked. The tinkling jingle of his bright yellow belt complete with logo as I undo it. I shiver, rubbing my thighs together, listening to the subtly sultry whisper of my cable knit tights.

My boots clack over the bright red, not so clean restaurant floor and it's my turn.

'Welcome to McWilliams's,' he says. 'My name is Todd. May I take your order?'

Todd. His name is Todd and he is fabulous. White teeth and red lips. Blue eyes and smooth skin. He must not work the fryer. There isn't a single blemish on his beautiful face. 'Yes, I would like ...' Well hell. What would I like? I have no idea. 'An ... um, chicken sandwich, no condiments. A diet cola and ...' His lips are distracting me and I swallow hard. I can feel the annoyance radiating off the person behind me.

'Ma'am,' he says, exhausted already despite his young age. 'Would you like fries with that?'

'Um ... are they good?'

'For crying out loud!' The woman behind me barks and I turn to her, narrow my eyes.

'Oh, I'm sorry,' I say. 'I was under the impression that it was *my turn*.'

She is frazzled, obese and has three kids in tow. I turn around quickly because I get the feeling she might want to do me bodily harm.

Todd leans in and my pussy twitches at that. Already under my pretty crème-coloured tights, my satin panties are wet in the crotch. My nerves are all jaunty and my skin is buzzing with anxiety and excitement. 'Miss, you really have to order. People tend to get a bit aggressive during the lunch rush,' he says.

'Oh, of course. I would. I would like fries with that.'

Todd nods and smiles. The smile goes straight to my cunt and then swiftly burns a trail from pelvis to nipples. I smile back. When I pay Todd, I slip him the note I brought with me. It's simple, really.

MEET ME IN THE PLAY COURT AT FIVE. I WANT YOU. WEAR YOUR UNIFORM. XOXO J

No phone number. Not even my whole name – Jamie – just orders to meet me if he wants to fuck. It's as simple as burgers, fries and shakes. I walk to the condiment counter and watch him open it. His eyes look up, he searches, finds me. Nod. He smiles again and it is all I can do to eat my chicken sandwich and hurry back to work. I lock myself in the small blue powder room, plant my boot on the toilet lid and push my hand into my panties.

It's Todd the counter boy in his stiff ugly uniform that I see when I rub slippery circles over my clit with my fingertips. I am kissing him, the bill of his McWilliams's hat brushing my forehead as I slide my other hand into my panties and push my fingers into my sopping cunt. I'm grabbing his tie while he fucks me as I get myself off two times, my pussy bunching eagerly around my juicy fingers as I thrust deep into my own body and I come.

I wash my hands, fix my face, and smooth my hair. The rest of the day is all business. My phone rings at three, it's Charlene. 'Meet me for a drink!' she commands. Her voice high and eager and bossy. She makes me laugh.

'I can later. I have to be somewhere at five, but I'm free after that.'

'Ooooh, fancy busy woman. That's fine! Where do you have to be?'

'I have a meeting,' I say and say my goodbyes. Maybe I'll tell her, maybe I won't. I kind of like having this little secret. This odd little thing that drives me sexually. That makes me fantasize and dream and wonder about what a man has under his ugly fast-food uniform. So far I have been with men from the fish and chips fast-food place, the taco place, the Greek place. Sometimes I like to think of it as an around the world with counter boys. No need to travel. I have a trophy from every stop.

'You look pleased,' Pat says from the doorway.

I start and then laugh. 'Oh, I am. Just having a good, good day,' I say and beam at him.

Pat has hit on me. I don't want him. Not now, anyway. He wears a grey tie and a black suit and wingtips every day. He also frowns a bit, worries and is rushed. I like my men a bit more young. And a bit more colourful in attire. And I like them to offer me a free refill or a baked pie when I order.

I snort, Pat frowns and I give him a finger wave. 'Sorry, back to work.' I shift in my office chair and feel the quiet moist thrill of a woman who has just gotten off and is anticipating doing it again. 'Come on five o'clock,' I breathe and try not to think about what his mouth will taste like.

It tastes like cherry soda and salty fries; his lips are sweet. He pushes me up against the deserted and defaced sliding board and slips his hands into my long blond hair. Such a gentleman, grabbing hunks of hair instead of handfuls of ass. 'Here or in my van?' he asks.

I rear back, pleasantly more excited than I already was. 'You have a van?'

He nods, looking so pleased with himself I almost laugh out loud.

'Here?' I squeak.

'Yes, I do, J – what does J stand for?'

'Oh right, *I* do *not* have a nametag on, do I?' I ask, flicking his shiny gold badge with my finger. 'My name is Jamie. Nice to meet you,' I say.

He shakes the hand I offer but uses it to pull me in for another kiss. I run my hand up the gorgeously tented blue slacks he has on. I rub the head of his cock through too much fabric with my thumb and he stops kissing me for an instant, his lips still on mine, he just can't manage feeling all that and kissing at the same time. I smile against his soft mouth. 'I like that,' Todd says.

'My name or when I rub your cock like that?' I ask, doing it again.

'Yes,' Todd says and I laugh. He tugs me and my coat gapes open in the sudden wind like I might float away from him. A fairytale princess lifted from earth by gusts of silvery magical air. I squeal playfully and he tugs me harder. Then together we run and slip through the late winter slush to a horribly rusted green van with a small rear window shaped like a spade.

'Smooth,' I tease and he has the good humour to blush and laugh it off.

He opens the rear door and pulls me into the small square cocoon of not quite warmth. It's still chilly as hell but we're out of the wind. His hands are back in my hair, his lips are back on my lips, my fingers are plucking again at the gorgeous hard-on he's sporting.

I pull at his buckle and stop kissing him so I can hear the merry tinkle of the cheap gold fittings on his belt. His dick is long and smooth and so, so warm in my hand. When I squeeze him, he sighs in my ear like a long-time lover. 'Nice?'

'Nice,' Todd says. I can still taste salt on my lips from his kisses, so I dip my head to take the head of his cock into my mouth. His skin's salty taste rivals the fried treat he's eaten today. I suck and he bucks against my mouth gently. Still a gentleman. Still so sweet and nice. A nice young man in a nice shiny uniform with a nice big cock. This time *I* sigh and he pulls me up to kiss me, wrestling with the mess of my tights and my panties. My dress is shoved up, my underthings shoved down and Todd says, 'I wasn't expecting this today.'

'Does it happen other days?' I ask, but I lie back when he pushes me gently. I land in a bundle of blankets and jackets and some more uniforms if I'm not mistaken. My cunt clutches up at that. I wonder if I can beg, borrow or steal a whole shirt and not just some small token when all is said and done. But the thought flies right out of my head when he pushes his lips to my pussy.

'No. Not most days,' he chuckles and then seems to make it his life's mission to lick my clit until I beg. I fist my hands in a blanket and arch my hips up to meet him. He pushes me down with his big hands, he latches to my clitoris and sucks until bright yellow spots fire off behind my closed eyelids.

'You taste like sweet tea,' he laughs. 'Anyone ever told you that?'

I shake my head. No one's ever told me what I taste like period. 'Is that good?'

'Good? Jamie, girl, I could stay here all day.' I come in a long liquid shudder and he just keeps eating me, lapping at me with a tongue that possesses such a talent it has chased all the chill from the hollow, cavernous van.

'Oh, I don't know about all day.'

'All day,' he assures me, drinking me slowly now. Letting my body readjust and calm down and flicker its last bits of release through my pelvis. When my breathing stabilises, he pushes his blunt fingers into my cunt. One, two ... three. I gasp under him as if no one has ever, ever put their fingers in my pussy before. It's almost laughable but it is a new sensation. The intensity that he brings to what he is doing is staggering. And nice, if you really must know.

'I ...'

Todd looks up, tongue still gliding over my pussy lips, my clit, fingers still buried deep inside of me. My mind goes blank. I shrug. I have no idea what I was going to say. He's wiped all logical thought from my head. 'Will you come for me again, Jamie? You really have the sweetest juices,' he says and he grins. His grin is a mix of mischievous boy and the devil. I come for him. I come hard watching him eat me with his long eyelashes brushing his pale cheeks. His face is stunning – a work of art. When he shucks his pants and boxers, I realise that his cock is too.

'Wait,' I say, because he's coming at me and I know, I can tell by his face, that all he wants to do in the world is bury himself in me and fuck. And I want that too, but first ...' Come up here, please.' I whisper.

Out in the parking lot, people are laughing and yelling and dusk is falling because out of his tiny porthole window is the purple air of evening.

He comes up to me, putting his thighs on either side of my arms like I ask. He's basically pinning me that way on my back, arms soldier straight at my sides. His cock slips between

64

my breasts and Todd pushes them firmly together, forming tight cleavage to fuck. Every time he slides high between my tits I lick my tongue out and slide it along the weeping slit at the head of his cock.

He's lost somewhere, I can tell. His face almost shadowed, mesmerized as he watches his own cock slide up between the seam of my breasts and then takes in the sight of my red tongue darting out to meet him. His eyes are blue and wide when he looks at me and says bluntly, 'I'm going to come like a bottle rocket if we keep this up. It's too much.'

I laugh at his honesty. 'OK.'

I tug the shiny pearlescent snaps of his shirt and stroke them like good luck charms. My fingers tickle along the logo stitched on his pocket and I say, 'Ask me something fast foodie.'

Todd pauses but doesn't seem shocked or turned off. You'd be surprised at how often they get flustered and pissed. Instead, he spreads my legs wide and nudges my dripping slit with his cock. 'Um ... let's see, would you like fries with that, Miss?' He thrusts in before I can respond and all of my words fly off when he fills me. His cock has stretched me wide and my pussy is thumping with my pulse. I don't see myself making it long before I come again.

Where has Todd been all my life?

'I would. I would like fries with that.'

He's playing along and I adore him for it. He turns his cap around so that the back logo shows and I tug his tie though only his top button is done. He comes down with a crushing kiss and then nips my ear with his even white teeth. 'Do you need ketchup packets with your fries?' Todd flings my legs high on his shoulder, angles me, fucks me deeper so that I have to struggle to pull a single shuddering breath.

'Oh God, I do. I do need ketchup packets with my fries.'

Todd nods, his face set with concentration as he watches his dick slip into me and then tug free. Slip ... tug ... slip ... tug. 'Do you want relish?'

'I ... I hate relish,' I gasp. My cunt is growing tighter with each thrust. His fingers are so harsh on my skin I want to beg and scream and tell him to hold me tighter.

Instinctively he does. He grips my ankle in one hand, turns his head and nips my ankle with his teeth. 'Would you like a pie for dessert?'

The pain sings up my calf and I shake all over as the orgasm rips through me. He's thrusting hard and fast and his muscles are trembling like it's everything he has not to just come right that instant. 'I would. I would love a pie. I love pie. I loooooooove piiiiiie!' I sing as every flicker and spasm dances through my pussy and I am grabbing his tie and possibly choking him to death.

Todd does not die. Todd pulls free, grabs my ass with both hands and turns me. The secretive sound of fabric being manoeuvred fills the van and then his golden tie drapes around my neck and I am ready to come all over again. 'My name is Todd and I'll be training you, trainee. First order is you must always be in uniform.'

He's rubbing the head of his cock to my pussy from behind and I'm holding my breath. When his hand snakes around and grabs the tail of the tie and slides it around so he can hold it behind my head like a rein, I moan.

Todd pushes into me slowly and then he tugs the tie like a leash. I feel my body grow tight and hot. I hang my head and inhale the smells of him. Young man, aftershave, fryer grease. He's fucking me and tugging that tie until his movements become fast and frenzied. 'You will always be in uniform or there will be a reprimand,' he says.

He tries to sound authoritative. But he sounds like a young man about to shoot his load, but I am on the verge of coming again so I give him a hearty, breathy, 'Yes, sir. I understand, sir.' My fingers are pinching my slippery clit desperately.

'Good,' he says and gives my ass one firm smack. The smack does it for us both. No one is any more good. Todd comes with a roar. I sigh, my fingertips rubbing over my clit until I bear my weight on my forehead alone and come with him. Mine is much more quiet and exhausted.

We sit there in the dark van, breathing hard. Then Todd leans in and kisses me. It is a surprisingly tender, sweet kiss for a hook-up. 'I have something for you,' he says.

I hold my breath, hoping against hope and yes, he hands me a striped McWilliams's shirt. My very own. Not a badge or a hat or a tie or a key-ring. A *shirt*. That I can wear any time I want to remember this. 'Thank you,' I breathe. I kiss him again. I rather like kissing him.

'I don't expect to see you back, but you know where to find me if you want ...' he seems to consider his words. 'A refill,' he says, finally and grins.

I have never wanted a refill before. But I just might want one this time. Todd is not your average counter boy. I kiss him one more time, push my starched prize in my tote and run off into the cold darkness, my body still thumping and quivering like a cooling engine.

'Seriously, you are all glowy. What have you been doing, girl?' Charlene demands, downing her fizzy pink drink.

'Just taking care of myself,' I say quite sincerely. I sip my Merlot and relish the fruity dark flavour on my tongue. I almost imagine I can taste salty fries with it.

A group walks in and Charlene singles out a guy in sailor whites. His crisp white shirt is jaunty with colourful decorations and medals. 'Colonel? Sergeant? Corporal?' she asks me, practically salivating.

I shrug. 'I haven't a clue. They don't make any sense to me.' Now talk to me about burger joint versus taco hut and we're talking my language.

'Whatever,' she says, staring. 'I do love a man in uniform.'

I brush my fingers over the stiff cheap shirt in my purse and smile. 'Me too,' I tell her.

My Good Boy

The first time I saw Joshua he was stumbling down the Avenue at twelve in the afternoon. Snookered, drunk, high as a kite. He was wearing a three-piece suit that any fool could tell cost a pretty penny. I'm not one for suits but even I wanted to run my hand over that dark grey fabric. I just knew it would feel like liquid silk. His shaved head radiated a lobster-like glow from the alcohol and he was smoking a cigarette in *that* way. The way an extremely plastered person smokes. Not just smoking it, but drawing on the filter so hard I half expected him to suck the entire smouldering cylinder into his mouth.

I was drawn to him. I admit it. He positively radiated submissive. This was a man who felt out of control and he needed some help. Some tender loving care. Or a good whipping. It was a toss-up.

My feet carried me to him before I could reconsider. I was hoping I had struck gold. A man who carried the weight of the world on his shoulders but craved a woman who would push him. And push him around. I get off on power. I get off on men who can be broken. For whatever reason, I wanted to get off with this man.

'What's wrong with you?' I said down to him. He was sitting on a concrete planter that held a sickly-looking palm tree. 'Why are you fucked up at noon?'

I figured it best to let him see exactly who I was right off the bat. If he was going to be mine, then he had to see the real me from the get-go.

He squinted up at me and took another severe drag on his cigarette. 'I am not drunk,' he said very carefully. The caution

68

and slow speech obviously earmarked him as a completely bombed individual.

'You most certainly are,' I sighed and planted one of my black stiletto heels on the planter. His eyes were level with my crotch and my short skirt rode up with the movement. No doubt he had a perfectly wonderful view of my crotch. That was good.

'OK, so I am,' he said directly to my pussy.

'Good. At least you're being honest. Now tell me why,' I barked. Oh, if only I had a whip. Hell, I'd settle for a ruler.

'I am...' he slurred, '...having a bad day. I have too much stress. I feel like I might...' he trailed off and took a final drag of his cigarette, practically licking the fucking thing. I snatched it out of his fingers and flicked it into the street.

'Explode? Cry? Jump off a large building?'

'Yesh,' he sighed. 'All of the above.'

'Come on,' I said and grabbed his hand. I hauled him to his feet and stood there waiting for him to fall over or fall on me. He did neither.

'Where're we going?'

'You're coming home with me and we are going to get you straightened out.' I marched him toward my waiting Jeep.

'You don't even know me!'

I stopped turned and said, 'Diane. And you are?'

'Joshua Davies.'

'Good. Now I know you. Get in the fucking car,' I said and pointed to the door. He nearly broke his neck getting in but he managed.

I could not wait to get him home.

He slept the twenty-minute drive to my house. He was snoring to the point of annoyance and I knew the first thing I'd make him do was brush his teeth. Stale beer breath is not a turn-on.

I pulled into the driveway and unbuckled. Went around and opened the passenger side door. 'Joshua!' I barked.

He came awake in a series of grunt and snorts. He blinked at me and wiped his mouth. 'We here?'

'Yes. Get out. Let's go.' I helped him out, though. The last thing I needed was for him to take a header in the driveway and knock himself unconscious.

Inside, I set about making a pot of coffee in case he'd need it. 'There are towels in the linen closet. The bathroom is the last room down the hall. Get a towel, take a shower and brush your teeth. Use my toothbrush, I'll get a new one.'

Now I waited. Was he what I thought he was? Most men would tell me to fuck off. Or complain or try to hump me in the kitchen. He dropped his head and nodded. 'OK.'

I smiled. I could smell them a mile away. 'Well? Why are you just standing there? Get moving.'

By the time he came out of the shower, his skin pink like a baby, I was in my corset and boots. My big red boots. They make me feel like a superhero. I love boots. In a sexy pair of boots I feel like I can beat the devil.

He gaped at me. His eyes skittering over the boots, the corset, the stocking, the thong. They settled on the thong, widened, shot back to the boots, widened further.

'Better be careful or they'll pop right out of your head,' I said softly and then brought the whip from behind my back and gave it a crack. I made it snap and sing to show him what he was in for.

He grew pale but his cock bobbed to life in an instant. I managed not to laugh but I did smile. 'Ready?'

'Yes,' he said and swallowed hard.

'Yes, what?'

'Yes, ma'am.'

Ah. A boy who had been raised with manners.

'Rules,' I said and cracked the whip again. 'You give me a word that you will use if you want me to stop. My rule is, if I stop, then we are done. Not just for the day. For good. However, I will stop at any time if you give me the word. What's your word?'

He blinked and cleared his throat. 'Pressure,' he croaked.

'Good. Now let's go. Leave your towel on the floor and follow me.'

In the living room, I pointed to my grand-mamma's ottoman. Covered in faded brocade with a lovely sea green

70

fringe, it was so very proper, and the perfect height for whipping a man's ass a lovely cherry red. I pointed but didn't speak and Joshua complied without direction. Had he done this before? I wondered. Either way, I would know in a moment.

He draped his broad chest and flat stomach over the top of the ottoman so that the edge was flush with his hip bones. Instinctively, he gripped two of the legs on the ottoman. He thrust his ass high for me, knees together, feet flexed, head down. Nice.

'Count them off. Be polite.' Let's see what he did with those directions.

I went slow with the first one even though the crotch of my panties was already wet. Just the anticipation of hearing the whip slice and whistle through the air was enough to make me hot. It was the most sensual sound I could think of. With the toe of my boot, I forced his ass a little higher and took the time to run the soft leather low enough to stimulate his sac. He moaned and it made me want to moan.

I reared back with my hand, gulped a deep breath and let it unroll through the air with a nice sibilant swish. The sound of the leather biting his skin beaded my nipples instantly.

His head flew back and he grunted. Like magic the stripes appeared on the pale flesh of his ass. 'One, ma'am.' He sounded almost calm, number two was harder.

'Two, ma'am!' he barked and a flood of fire burned under my skin. I felt the flush of power creep across my breast and chest bone. I felt it snake around my throat and heat the back of my neck.

I let the whip fly with its own ferocity. It knew what it was doing. The tendrils danced across his skin. The marks crosshatched white, red, pink. Little dots of purple in the mix. A shiver worked through me and my pulse beat between my legs. I rubbed my thighs together and felt the wet fluttering in my cunt.

'Three, ma'am!' Joshua threw his head back, teeth gritted, tears seeping from the corners of his eyes. Beautiful, big green eyes. He looked tortured and serene. Ethereal and demonic. All those at once and then some.

The breath tore in and out of him as the whip and I rained blows down upon him.

Four…six…eight…

I paused briefly, toeing his thighs apart some so I could see his balls. I pushed them hard with my foot and he arched back against my boot shamelessly. I nudged his perineum just enough to make him jitter a little. The sound that escaped him was that of a desperate animal.

'How hard is your cock, Joshua?' I demanded, stepping back and regaining my stance. We were about to finish up.

'Very hard.'

'Very hard, what?' I growled and gave him the hardest lash yet. His body did a dance that looked like a seizure.

'Very hard, ma'am! Nine,' he sobbed, his forehead pressed deep into the cushion.

'Don't forget your manners, boy.'

I delivered the final lash. So hard and fast my wrist ached from the force.

'Ten…' he said in a whoosh of air. His body bucked and he sobbed openly as I stared at the vibrant marks on his bone white ass.

Power and need sizzled through me. And I fingered myself as I watched him. Broken and weak but humping my grandmother's ottoman for all he was worth. Mindless at this point. Lost somewhere in that grey area that lives between extreme pain and extreme pleasure.

I pulled Grand-mamma's chair up to the ottoman. The old fabric threadbare in some spots. As far as design, the chair was perfect. I took off the thong but that was it. After all, this was our first time. I sat, threw a leg over each cushioned arm and bared myself, opened wide.

'Slide that up here, Joshua, and eat me. And this better be good.'

He scooted forward eagerly, pushing the ottoman across the hardwood floor. His face was pale and drawn but his eyes were burning fiercely in his face. He pushed into me without preamble. Tongue seeking my clit blindly, suckling, swirling.

Slow licks, fast licks, broad tongued and pointed. His mouth was a blur of hot, wet movement over my clit and lips. I let my head fall back and in my mind I heard the sinister whisper of the whip during descent. The echo of remembered sound mixed with his exuberant, noisy, ministrations. I grabbed his smooth, shiny head and fucked his mouth until I came. The muscles of my legs jumping from the force and intensity of what that tongue could do.

'Who's my good boy?' I said softly. My eyes finding his and holding his gaze.

He looked away, blushing the same lobster-red shade he had been when I met him. 'I am, ma'am.'

'Joshua is,' I corrected.

'Joshua is your good boy,' he amended.

'He is. And my good boys get rewarded.'

I moved around behind him and covered his body with mine. His cock was hard and long in my hand. He had as much girth as length and my mouth watered at the thought of sucking him. My cunt thumped at the thought of riding him. My ass ached to feel that much filling me. But I don't do things that way. Not the first time. All of those would come. Most likely before I dropped him off at his car later. But the first time, they never get what they want.

I wet my hand with my own juices, and, with my palm slick from my orgasm, I started slow and easy. Stroking him, jacking him off. I squeezed and released. Alternated fast and slow. Kept him just on the edge as I ground my naked pelvis against his sore ass.

Joshua tensed under me and I said softly, 'Not yet. I haven't told you that you could yet.'

He stayed tense, his breathing harsh. He moaned off and on as if he were in pain. Maybe he was.

I rolled my thumb over the sensitive crown, gathered the drop of pre-come from his weeping slit. When I couldn't stand it any more, I started a fast steady pace and when his body signalled to me I shouted, 'Come now, Joshua.'

So well-behaved. He covered my hand with thick, hot ropes of his come. The bleach-like scent of semen filled the air. I raised my hand to his face and I didn't have to say a word. He licked it clean. His tongue warm velvet on my skin as he tongued my hand clean. I shivered when he sucked my fingers into his mouth and moaned.

Now that he was sober, we had the rest of the day ahead of us. 'My good boy,' I cooed, 'we're just getting started.'

Grip

'Jesus, Annalee, what have you done?'

Jacob stared at my hair and I tried not to shift. It was my hair. I could cut it any way I wanted. I would not feel bad. The only reason he was pissed was a small reason. Ninety-five percent of the time he didn't give a shit about my hair. Not the colour, not the style, not any of it. It was that five percent of the time that my hair was cherished.

'I like it,' I sighed. 'Look, don't get pissy. I needed something new and I went ahead and did it. You'll get used to it.' I set about making dinner, intent on ending the turmoil right then and there.

'But you know how much I love your hair. Loved,' he corrected himself. There was venom in both the statement and the tone.

'You love it when you fuck me,' I sniped. 'More specifically, you love it when you fuck me from behind. You like to twist it up around your fist and yank me back with it. Yes, Jacob, I love that, too. However,' I banged the stock pot down and cringed at the loud noise, 'during the times when you are not playing caveman and using my hair as a reign, it's a pain in the ass!'

We stood there, eyeing each other in the kitchen, both of us angry, both of us thinking we were right. He could think he was right. That was fine. But it was my damn hair and I was sick of the work and the struggle of keeping a waist length mane clean, detangled and neat. I liked the new hair; just below chin level, layered to be shaggy but not messy. I threw my shoulders back. No guilt.

'I'm sorry if you don't like it but you'd better adjust. I am not growing it back out and I will not apologise for doing it.' Then I turned my back on him and started the water to boil.

Jacob barely spoke to me for three days. Every time I said or did the slightest thing he didn't approve of he would pause for several beats and stare at my hair. As if to say; look what you have done.

While he was busy frowning upon my new 'do, I was falling more and more in love with it. No more long mornings steaming myself in front of the mirror with a blazing hot hair dryer. No more combing out knots so big and stubborn I ended up in tears holding a fist full of my own hair. No more torture, muss, fuss and annoyance. It was freedom, this wonderful short flirty hair. I loved it enough for both of us.

Needless to say, it was a while before I got laid. Without my crowning glory of long chocolate coloured hair, I seemed to have lost my appeal. Or so it seemed.

The first time Jacob stooped to touching my new hair was the night of his boss's dinner party. Stewart J. Beckett was a prick and a blow hard and he loved my husband. We were expected to attend dinner. We were expected to be amusing and classy. We were expected to dress the part.

I straightened my taupe and black wrap dress. I fidgeted with the black satin collar for the millionth time. I flipped the cuffs up to show the black satin. I flipped them down to create bell sleeves. Designers who make dresses that can be worn several different ways should be shot. Do they not realise that the woman wearing their dress will most likely be a nervous wreck, which will result in her having absolutely no decision making skills? Black cuffs, bell sleeves, black cuffs…

Jacob took pity on me. 'Leave them flipped up. Let the cuffs match the collar.' Then he put his arms around my waist, temporarily it seemed forgetting my traitorous behaviour. 'You look stunning, by the way. It'll be fine. We'll eat, we'll be fake, we'll leave. Plead a headache the moment dessert arrives,' he chuckled, then kissed my ear.

He did not smooth his hands over the length of my hair as he normally did when we were about to go out. Of course, the length itself was gone.

'Time to go,' he sighed and pulled my hand. 'We'll make it as quick as possible.'

'My necklace!' I raced back in and grabbed the antique necklace he had given me for Christmas. It complimented the vintage nature of the dress. My hands were shaking just thinking about Miriam Beckett. Such a prude, such a bitch. I felt sick.

'Let me.' He draped the necklace at the hollow of my throat and clasped it. Then he kissed the nape of my neck. That spot. It gets me every time. I froze and let the pleasant tickle and tingle run down my spine.

Then his hands were in my hair. Shoving up under the chunky layers along my neck. His fingers slid up to rest below my ears, which made me shiver. He sifted my newly shorn hair through his big fingers and I heard him make a low sound. A pleased sound? I wasn't sure. Then he gripped a fistful of my hair at the base of my head and tugged ever so slightly. I gasped and felt my nipples bead against my silk bra.

'Time to go,' he said again but this time his voice was a little thicker. A little slower.

We went.

Somehow, all through dinner, all I could think about was how it felt when Jacob gripped my hair and pulled. How it was pleasingly painful. When I closed my eyes I could feel it; a phantom sensation of him yanking me by my short stylish hair. By dessert, I couldn't stop shifting in my seat. My panties were damp, I was bored beyond belief and all I wanted was to get home so I could find out what it felt like when he pulled my hair like that with his cock buried deep inside me.

'I have a migraine!' I blurted with only two spoonfuls of sorbet under my belt. What I really had was a soaking wet cunt and an overwhelming urge to run screaming from the boredom.

'I'd better get you home then,' Jacob said gallantly and mumbled his thanks and goodbyes.

I was the only one who noticed his subtle smile. Or the

way his eyes flashed with a hunger that had nothing to do with dessert.

We didn't speak on the drive home. Jacob piloted the car with one hand. The other was perpetually in my hair. Twirling, yanking, sifting. The only sound I made resembled the purr of a content feline.

In the house, he was deliberate. He hung up our coats, checked the door, fiddled with the thermostat. I waited. It was all I could do to keep from hiking up my dress and demanding his services right then and there. I knew better. The waiting made the event more exciting. The waiting was the foreplay.

Without a word, he took my hand and firmly led me up the steps. He bent, removed my shoes and put them neatly to the side. Standing together. The heels aligned as perfectly as if on display in a shop window.

Then the stockings. Then the tie of the dress. When he pulled the second tie, he finally spoke, 'I love taking you out of one of these things. It's like unwrapping a present.'

I didn't say anything. I swallowed and my throat clicked. My heart hurt it was beating so hard. My eyelids shut and I hummed aloud as he dragged his warm hands over the flat of my belly and then hooked my panties with his thumbs and pushed them down. His mouth gave my pussy just enough attention to leave it wanting. Just a few delicate tastes of my sensitive flesh. A few flicks to my swollen clit. Then he continued his trail upward as I shivered and shook and fought the urge to beg. He bit my nipples through the lace cups of my bra as he unhooked it, then, lowering it with dramatic care, he hung it on the knob of my bedside table drawer. Each breast received its reward. Each nipple tortured into perfect tautness. And when I was shifting and breathing in little fits and gasps, he spun me and pushed me to the bed.

'How wet are you now, Annalee? I bet you're gushing. I bet I could stick all of my fingers into that perfect pink cunt. Should I try or do you want something else from me?'

I whimpered.

He pushed me so my upper body was bowed against the mattress, my ass in the air. I sighed, this was how I liked to be. Held down by him. Taken. Overpowered. He slid his hand along my neck as the other was busy with my cunt, my clit. He shoved his hand into my hair and gripped a nice fistful tugging to the precise level of pain I like and slid a thick finger into my ass. I bucked under him, fire spreading from my hair to my ass, flowing like quicksilver into my soaking sex. I wanted to plead with him but I knew better.

'You want something else. I know you do. If I stare at your pussy, I can see it moving. Greedy, greedy girl. It contracts and expands like it's dancing.' Jacob laughed and I heard the smacks echo through the room before I felt them. Then the fire set in. The burn of sharp cracks of open palm to the soft flesh of my bottom. He yanked my hair and with the combined pain I felt a warm slow trickle slide down my inner thighs.

His finger wiped some up. I heard him lick his finger and laugh. With a final tug to the tender roots of my hair he shoved into me. His hips banging me mercilessly, driving me into the mattress as he gripped me with the most fragile part of my body. My scalp sang with pain even as my cunt tightened around him. The agony in my scalp making the pleasure that flowed nearly to my womb that much more sweet.

More smacks and I bowed under him as much as physically possible, my body demanding release even as my soul relished the torture.

'I say three,' Jacob ground out the words. His voice was heavy and thick. His hips moving faster. He was going to come.

I would go with him.

'One!' he shouted out and I could tell he was fighting for control. My body jerked and my cunt grew tighter. 'Two!' The sensation of tension. The heavy feeling of almost release. 'Three!' he bellowed with the final blow and a perfect painful yank to my scalp.

I came. A great spiralling orgasm that had me sobbing under his bucking body. Fire and light and pain and pleasure became one as I let go and fell into it. No body, no time.

Nothing. A single nerve ending singing with unbearable pleasure. That was all I was for that moment in time.

Jacob fell against me, helping me to lower myself flat on my stomach. He lay on me, crushing the breath from my lungs but I liked it. The fingers that had just yanked and tortured, smoothed along my scalp in soothing circles. I felt the mattress wet beneath my face. I was crying. I usually did.

Jacob kissed the nape of my neck. Bare, naked, and on display for him at all hours now that my curtain of hair was gone. His cock had gone soft inside of me but we stayed that way. Connected.

'I owe you an apology, Annalee,' he laughed in my ear. His hand found my breast and gave a possessive squeeze.

'Oh yeah?'

'I love your new hair,' he chuckled again and then gave my nipple a twist.

I gasped and squirmed under him and then I was laughing. 'Thank you. I knew you'd come around.'

All the Boys

'I'd like to take your picture,' he said out of the blue. I was eating lunch at the park. He was walking his dog.

'Oh, I bet you say that to all the boys.' I laughed when he looked confused. I bent to pet the beast he had tethered to a leash. 'Who is this?'

'Her name is Beatrice and she has exquisite taste,' he said. He blinked, looking a bit owlish behind round glasses that were a little too big for his face. His hair, the colour of warm homemade caramel, fell over his forehead. He looked more like a college freshman than a man my age.

'Hello, Beatrice,' I said, addressing the slobbering dog. She seemed to be smiling and I smiled. Even with a palm full of dog drool, I smiled. 'My name is Gilbert and who's your daddy?' Then I realised what I had said and my face flushed, hot and sudden.

'Daddy's name is Simon,' he said. I noticed his face was a flaming shade of raspberry too. I took a breath and relaxed. 'And I really would like to take your picture.'

'For what?' Now I was intrigued. I'd heard the picture line before but usually at a party or a club. Some big daddy in thick gold chains showing tons of chest hair. Or the artsy guy who thought that was the quickest way to a sweaty blow job. Offer me immortality. Capture my look and my ego on film and I will be your slave and suck your cock.

'I like pictures. It's a hobby. I like ... beauty,' Simon said and then his face went from berry to tomato. 'You are beautiful. Even Beatrice can see it.'

Part of me thought it should feel creepy. A young guy offering to take my picture. Worse yet, a young guy who apparently looked to his Saint Bernard for an opinion of beauty. Instead of feeling creeped out, I felt a smile split my face and a hearty laugh snaked out of me before I could stop it. It felt good to laugh like that. The genuine kind of laugh that started somewhere around your belly button and burned a bright yellow trail on the way out of you. An honest to fucking god happy laugh.

'OK. If Beatrice insists.'

Recognizing her name, the mighty dog let out a deep woof that made her jowls tremble and her flanks sway. She really was quite gorgeous in an unusual and terrible kind of way. Sort of the way I felt about myself.

'Will you come with me?' Simon cocked his head, that lovely brown hair shading his face, and blinked rapidly. He pushed his glasses up onto his nose and I grinned. A nervous tic, a habit, whatever it was, his way with his glasses and his boyish habits were charming. It took all of the fear right out of me.

'You won't put me in a pit and force me to slather lotion on myself, will you?' I rose to my full height, gathering my trash. I had a good four inches and twenty pounds on Simon. He was no threat to me. At least physically.

He blinked rapidly again and frowned. 'Dear God, no. That's just … *awful*.' He said the word softy as if *awful* were foreign to him.

I wished I had the same innocent naiveté with awful. 'It is,' I said, trying to keep a straight face. My guess was that he'd never seen the movie. 'I'll follow you?'

We walked together, Beatrice leading the way, to the parking lot. My red sports coupe was parked to the far left. I thought about offering him a ride but where would we put the moose he called a pet?

'I'm the grey Saab. Follow me. Just in case. I'm on Oak. It's the only yellow house on the street.'

I nodded. Yellow for sunshine. Yellow for pureness. Yellow for laughter. 'Got it. I will follow you and if I lose you, I will follow the trail of dog slobber.' I grinned.

He jerked back as if slapped and then, slowly, his face split into a smile. An uncertain shy smile but a smile. He had gotten my joke. Beatrice gave a chuff that sounded almost like a laugh. I leaned in and said, 'I'll see you soon, gorgeous.' Then I got in and followed the charcoal grey Saab to the yellow house.

When I pulled into his drive, it occurred to me that *what kind of pictures?* might have been a wise question. When I climbed out and waited for him to lock his car and unleash his dog, I realised it didn't matter. He couldn't hurt me. I knew it and he knew it. And that was very, very important.

'You have a beautiful face. I've seen you for a few weeks. You seem kind,' he said shyly and walked past me. Beatrice looked back, breathing harshly as if she had run a race. I followed his broad back, swathed in a faded denim shirt. His words echoed in my head *you have a beautiful face*, and my scars itched for the first time in years.

I had been thinking digital. Everything was digital now, right? Digital cameras, digital media, digital music. When Simon pulled out an honest to god camera, I did a double take. It was the equivalent of someone pulling out a typewriter to write a letter.

'Wow,' I said, meaning the camera and his work. The large room was three walls of window and one solid wall of black and white prints: a blond young man in a pair of well loved jeans; Beatrice in a large stream, holding a stick and mugging for the camera; an older man with a scruffy beard and an easy smile; a man my age with tousled dark hair and a chiselled abdomen that made me suck in my gut; a young woman who looked an awful lot like Simon jumping in the air. He had caught her hovering, half floating in the low light of day. Surely in the photo it was dusk and she was joking with her brother. If that wasn't his sister, I would eat my shoe.

'You have a beautiful face,' he said again and his smile was both appreciative and gentle. It stirred a sadness in my chest and a lump formed in my throat. I cleared it to try to make it go, but the lump stayed stuck. 'Don't be intimidated. The camera sees the truth of it all. It will love you ...' He said it so sincerely, I was tempted to believe him.

'OK.' I meant to sound self-assured when I said it. It didn't happen that way. I sounded breathy and scared and I fisted my hands in my jean pockets to keep from punching something with frustration. I would not be afraid. Not of him or the camera. Not of my scars. Not that I had lost all of my beauty long ago and that his antique 32 millimetre camera would spit a monster back at me when the photos were developed.

Simon stared at me as if seeing past the first layer of Gilbert. I felt like an onion. His dark brown eyes were stripping me layer by layer and the fists in my pockets twisted with nerves. Fuck.

'The scars will look lovely in black and white,' he said.

Something dark and hard shifted in my chest and I pushed down the rage. Who the fuck was he to talk about my scars? I swallowed. I would not give in. I would not feel that anger and that grief. This was supposed to be fun.

Beatrice whined and looked at me with drunken hollow eyes. Only a Saint Bernard could have those eyes and look cute. She made a sad noise in her chest like she could read my mind. 'I'm not worried about it,' I lied.

'Will you take your shirt off for me?' he asked softly. His blush returned. As hot and intense as a summer sunset.

I grinned at that and whipped it off over my head. I let the white T-shirt drop around my busted up boots. Every insecurity I had about my face was balanced by a confidence in my chest. Many gym hours had earned me a chest I didn't think twice about showing. A shrink would tell me I was making up for one with the other. That's why I don't have a shrink.

Simon blinked, blinked, blinked and then he licked his lips. He looked nervous and turned on and awkward and sweet. I smiled at him and he smiled back. 'Um, yes. Thank you. That's good.'

He only said good but my cock stirred in my jeans. A subtle pleasure at his soft spoken words of praise. 'Thanks, man.'

Simon laughed at that. A short, deep bark that I would never had expected from his straight-laced self. 'Let's just take a few shots and see.' His voice was much more confident when the camera was up to his eye and his finger was on the trigger.

I didn't know what to do, so I just stared. Stared at the camera and tried to shield my soul. Every time the bright flash strobed I heard the sound of fist meeting bone. I heard the crunch in my head the first time Richard broke my nose. I heard the cuts and digs coming off my loving partner's lips, *whore, asshole, dick, stupid, retard, loser*. I felt the stab of numbing needles in the ER and the bright light blinding me as they stitched over my eye, or repaired my busted lip. I stared at the camera and came unglued.

I took out one, two, three glass frames and Simon just stood there and waited.

I was panting and bleeding and I looked around slowly, coming to the surface too fast like a diver who was destined to get the bends. 'Jesus fucking Christ, Simon. I'm sorry,' I managed and I came apart completely, sinking to his studio floor amid the glass and paper. A bitter taste flooded my mouth and I knew it was fear.

'It's OK, Gilbert,' he said so softly I was half convinced I imagined it.

'No one calls me Gilbert,' I said distractedly. 'It's Gil. Gil. And I will pay for all of this.' I sobbed a little when I said it. The full impact of the anger I had unleashed was sinking in and I felt out of control. The monster somehow unleashed by accident.

'It's OK. Really.' Simon sank to his knees and touched the scar that nearly bisected my face. Not quite in half. It started on the inside of my right eyebrow and ran down the inside of my nose. It tore through my lip and my chin like a line of demarcation.

I flinched as if he'd punched me and Beatrice whined softly, shifting away from me as if I were toxic. I couldn't blame her. I felt a black surge of anger swell in me and I clenched my fists to keep it down. 'I think I should go.'

'Don't go,' he said and put the camera down. When he undid my jeans I muttered arguments. My mouth gave him reasons not to but my hips rose up to convince him to go ahead. His lips on me were a hot peach coloured heaven. His tongue on my cock the best memory eraser I had ever had. Better than drugs or booze or bar fights. Sweet and slow and *there*. He was all there the whole time. No agenda, no manipulation. No nice words backed up by harsh punches and nasty words. Just him licking me until I jittered across the scarred hardwood floor like a maniac.

I was right on that torturous cusp. Hovering on that white hot orgasm and it wasn't enough. The glass whispered around me as I shifted, gathering my strength like a storm as I hauled him around and onto his knees. Gratitude and pleas falling from my lips as I wrangled with his sharp creased chinos until he stilled my hands. Stilled the thing in my chest that beat its wings and demanded its due. Through the niceties and the readying part of me laughed and part of me sobbed and I heard both echo through the big empty room.

Sliding into Simon, feeling him clench around me, hearing his steady and somehow serene breathing was bright yellow. In my mind I could see it, like cleansing rays of the brightest sunlight. When I came it flooded out of me. Light through my fingertips, light out of my toes. I laughed deep yellow laughter when Simon bucked under me. His come coating my fist and warming me all over.

Finally, I kissed him. Hard. I was ready for round two with the camera. I thought it might catch something new this time. Something easier. Something more peaceful.

His warm fingers on my chest made me shiver and he said, 'your scars will look lovely in black and white.'

The scars were far from faded. The ones the camera could see and the ones it could not, but I felt easier about them. I laughed and grabbed him by his warm brown hair and kissed him some more. 'I bet you say that to all the boys,' I said. In the corner, Beatrice chuffed as bright buttery sunshine flooded the small room.

Spank Pants

I saw them in the store. I was there to get pantry items and dog food. All the boring stuff that makes the home complete. I was not supposed to be buying clothes. Not. But I needed new ones (I told myself) as I had lost a good amount of weight. Working out, eating healthy, I *deserved* them. And what better piece of clothing to buy than new work-out pants. They were a necessity, just like the dry goods and dog food. Plus, they were on clearance. How can you pass up clearance work-out pants that are to die for? That's easy. You can't.

Then I had a problem. I bought them. I loved them. Should I wear them? I turned it over in my head after my shower, while examining my new pants. They were a nice shade of blue, meant to hug the tush and the curves. Both my tush and my curves were looking spectacular these days. They sat low on the hips, had a drawstring, and right in the middle of the seat (right above the middle of my ass crack) was a teeny tiny decorative flourish and a little skull. Both girly and kick-ass. They were perfect.

I would wear them and I would hope that Grant wouldn't notice. He's a guy. Guys do not notice new pants. Do they?

I put them on. I took them off. I did this several times. Every time I put them on I would sneak a little peek in the full length mirror. I would turn my ass to the glass and gaze over my shoulder at my own bottom. My own bottom that looked (not to be conceited) ravishing in the pants. Then I would hear Grant in my head, *Not a penny, Marcy. Not one penny that you don't need to spend. Let's get our finances in order and then you can buy your shoes and your clothes and all that stuff. Promise me...*

87

And, dammit, I had promised. I had promised to keep wearing my baggy clothes until everything was in order. I climbed into my baggy yoga pants and looked. rubbish. You couldn't even see my ass. A potato sack would be more flattering.

Fuck it. I put them back on. This time I would stay in them. I would deal with Grant if need be.

An hour. It took an hour. What with the Military Channel, the crossword puzzle and the magazine that had come in the mail. I thought I was home free. Giddy with the fact that I had bought new sexy pants and he didn't notice. I was carrying my final load of laundry through the living room when it happened.

'Marcy?' That tone. I knew that tone. That was the oh-missy-you-are-in-trouble tone.

'Yes?' I kept moving. Maybe if I went upstairs he would forget.

'Come here, Marcy.'

Fuck.

'Why?' I tried to sound nonchalant. I tried to sound sure of myself. Defiant. I tried it all. What came out of my mouth was a high-pitched tone that basically screamed, *I'm sorry!*

'Please come here, Marcy.' He was smiling but, damn, I didn't trust him.

I set the basket at the bottom of he steps and went to him. Slowly. I hated feeling like a naughty little girl. All I had done was spent fifteen dollars on a pair of pants! The feeling was there nevertheless. I had lied. I had promised I wouldn't buy anything that was not a necessity and I had lied.

I stood in front of him and he took my hands in his. You would think with him seated on the sofa and me standing, I would feel a little less nervous. I would at least have the illusion of power. Wrong. It didn't matter that physically I was in the dominant position. I had guilt coursing through me like black poison and he knew it.

'I thought we made a deal.' He said it softly. Then he directed his stare at my gorgeous new pants.

'I–'

'Marcy?'

'Yes?'

'Are those new pants?'

'Well, they–'

'Marcy!'

'What!' I jumped at his harsh tone and my fluttery response. What the hell? Grant counted on me to do right but he was treating me like a child. To make matters worse, my body was responding to his tone in the most bizarre way. My nipples were hard and sensitive under my T-shirt and the crotch of my lovely new pants was…wet.

'Are those new pants?' He enunciated each and every word, letting them fall from his lips like heavy stones.

'Yes,' I sighed and hated myself for my grovelling tone. 'They were on clearance. They didn't cost much. I've worked so hard and I just wanted to have *one* pair of pants that actually fit. So I can see all my hard work,' I rushed on. I had to make him understand that it was only a small break in my promise. I really was on board with getting our finances straightened out.

'Turn around.'

'What?'

'You heard me. Turn around.'

It was the tone. That tone. A disciplinarian's tone. It transported me back to my Catholic school days and without thinking, I promptly turned my bottom to him and stood ruler straight.

What are you doing! My brain was protesting but my body was humming. I could feel little blips of excitement and dread and what could only be arousal pulsing under my skin. My cheeks were hot with shame and something else. I could feel my heart beating at the base of my throat, so hard it hurt a little.

He smoothed his hand over the skull that hid the treasure of my ass crack. I flinched a little even though it was a gentle touch. Something was coming. I could feel it. The air in our generic, homey living room felt thick and charged. It felt like the air before a violent thunder storm. I shivered and his hand smoothed lower, running over the firm underside of my left buttock.

'You made me a promise and you broke it,' he said softly. His hand roamed over to my right buttock and took a gentle tour of the soft fabric.

At first I thought the soft sound I heard was the sound of his work-callused hand on cotton. I realised when I heard the sound a second time, it was me. Sighing.

Grant placed his big hands on my hips and turned me. I went willingly. I had a quick mental flash of a ruler being brought down across my knuckles for writing on the white part of my saddle shoes in high school. I had been in Catholic school before they had outlawed the nuns doling out corporal punishment. This felt that way. I was about to be punished. Somehow the thought of being punished by my husband's large, warm hands made me squirm in my pretty blue pants.

As I faced him, he took my hands again and gazed up at me. The look on his face was both stern and sorrowful.

'You know how I feel about lying. I don't lie to you. You don't lie to me. That's been the deal. It always has been.'

I nodded. Part of me wanted to plead my case, remind him it was only a *little* money, apologise. A bigger part of me very much wanted what was coming to me. I remained silent.

'You broke your word to me, Marcy. Now I want you to lie across my lap.' He indicated his denim clad legs. He did not smile. There was no indication that this was a joke.

'I—'

'Now,' he said, quietly but there was clearly no room for argument.

My knees were shaking and my legs tingled. I positioned myself over his lap and fought the urge to raise a stink. This was ludicrous. It was insane. It was also clearly turning me on. The cotton crotch of my pants meant to absorb sweat was now flooded with my own moisture. A flutter had started low in my belly and my pulse was slamming so hard my ears were ringing.

I lay with my lower belly and pubic bone over his lap. My head hung down and the blood immediately rushed to it making me feel off balance. My legs dangled, my toes touching the floor.

'How much were the pants?' he asked. Finally!

'Fifteen dollars,' I said contritely.

'Fifteen it is,' Grant said. 'Count them off.'

Again the urge to climb off of him and give him hell surged through me. Again I let myself feel the growing urgency in my sex. In my breasts. Way up in the deepest part of me that made my belly feel achy and hollow. I nodded. I would count.

He smoothed his hand over my ass and when the hand withdrew I braced myself. Nothing. A moment when there was no contact and then his hands were caressing my bottom again. Gentle. Lovingly. I relaxed into it, enjoying the sensation. Then too fast for me to register he brought his hand back and the first smack rang through the room.

'One,' I bellowed as my head shot up and the pain registered. Great coursing sizzles of heat ran through my flesh.

Another stroke and a second smack. This one a little harder than the first. He'd aimed to criss-cross the spot that was already flooded with heat and blood. 'Two,' I blurted and squirmed a little.

The pain had bled into the pleasure I felt and I was left with a confusing sensation of shame and arousal.

I sang out for each smack as it landed. Sometimes softer, sometimes harder. Each one ratcheted my pleasure up a notch. Each one made the heady feeling I had a little worse. When we hit ten a light sheen of sweat had broken out on my skin and I was gasping from pain and pleasure.

'Stand up,' Grant said.

'But that was only ten,' I protested. I damn well wanted my full punishment now.

'Stand up!'

I stood, resisting the urge to balk. He spun me roughly and yanked the drawstring nestled below my belly button. The pants loosened and slid to the floor with a soft sigh. Knickerless, ass singing with pain, I stood before him. This time when he turned me, it was slowly.

I held my breath. What now? Grant was keeping me off balance and that was both strange and amazing.

'You should see. Lovely. Every single one is gorgeous. All criss-crossed and red with little flecks of purple.' As his blunt fingers traced the imprints of his hands, I started to sag. His gentle touch on my tender skin was overwhelming and felt so good. I stood there and let him admire. He kissed along my right cheek first. His tongue hot and soothing on my skin. When he moved to my left cheek, I thought my legs might buckle and I would fall to the floor. Visions of his hard cock sliding into me filled my head.

I was not expecting it when he said, 'I think the final five should be on your bare bottom. It's only fitting, don't you think?'

First fear shot through me. My ass was already stinging and raw, now he wanted to spank my naked flesh? Then I felt another fresh rush of fluid between my thighs. That was it. My body had made the decision for me. I nodded.

He didn't even tell me to count but when the first blow fell I yipped, 'Eleven!'

'You should see what this well toned ass looks like when I hit it,' he whispered and then cracked me again before I could prepare.

'Twelve!'

Thirteen and fourteen had me at the point of dripping. My cunt was constricting impatiently against nothing, my nipples little painful nubs of desire. I felt his hot tongue dive the length of the seam of my ass and pushed back against him eagerly. Soothing. Hot. Warm. Wet.

Crack!

'Fifteen!' I sang and started to sag.

He caught me. Suddenly the disciplinarian was gone and my loving husband was back. He cradled me, lowered me to the sofa.

'Take off your jeans,' I pleaded.

'I'm halfway there, darling,' he laughed softly, popping the buttons one by one. I watched, transfixed as the little silver buttons parted to show me a pair of blue boxer briefs.

I wanted to reach out and shove them down and be aggressive the way I sometimes could be when we had sex, but I was too tired. I felt stripped and exhausted and raw. Used and abused, but in the most delicious manner.

I parted my thighs willingly, eager to have the length of him fill me. To make good use of the fluid and need my body had generated. He slid into me with one long stroke and I felt the first flicker of orgasm from that single thrust. The flesh of my bottom burned, the pain coursed up my spine, making my scalp tingle and ache. But the pleasure he filled me with blended perfectly, accented the pain. Or the pain accented the pleasure. I wasn't sure. I didn't care.

Each thrust was heaven and I hung on tenaciously. I did not want to come yet. Not yet.

Grant watched my face, his face soft and sensitive again, then he pushed into me brutally hard, and barked, 'Come for me, Marcy.'

I obeyed. Unclenching my jaw and giving myself over to the intense stabs of pleasure that echoed through my body, I rode out the lovely, fluid waves of my orgasm as his tempo increased. A small sadness bloomed in my chest. I had wanted it to last longer. Once I came, Grant was always right behind me. My own release triggered his.

But not this time.

His face, once again dark and intense loomed over me. He fucked me roughly now. His movements a little frenzied, his breathing hard. He yanked my knees high and wide, leaned back to watch himself thrusting into me. I looked, too. Watched his long, rosy cock being swallowed by my body.

His eyes were on me again. Normally bright blue but now the colour of a storm over the ocean. 'I want you to come again,' he said, his thrusting so forceful I was being shoved against the sofa arm.

'I don't think I—'

He pounded into me and then pinched me. Hard. Right on the sore, recently abused flesh of my ass. I came. As Grant emptied into me I came long and hard for the second time, my body milking and working his cock.

When he collapsed on me, all the breath rushed from me. I couldn't breathe. The flickers of my orgasm were working through me like tiny strobe lights. Winking on and off throughout my body. My ass burned and hurt. I didn't care. I wrapped my arms and legs around his warm body and sighed.

'Bet you won't do that again,' he chuckled in my shoulder.

'Nope.' But the truth was, I was already picturing the other workout pants I had admired while shopping. Each and every pair on clearance. And, in my humble opinion, they were a necessity.

Flexible

'You need to be more flexible, Ellen,' Rick said.

To be honest, I felt damn near panicky. Every day I rode my exercise bike for an hour. Every day. It was my built in me-time. Time to ride hard, break a sweat and read a really good book. And I didn't get to continue in the book until I rode the next day. 'I am very flexible. But I want my damn bike,' I said. I swallowed hard. I did not want to cry. Not over a bike. However, I was feeling very irrational at the moment. I was ready to get on my bike and ride and it was broken.

Rick rubbed my back. I could tell he was torn between frowning and laughing. He loved me, but I could be a bit on the uptight side. 'Come to the gym with me.'

'I hate the gym. It's too full of people and music and TV's blaring and people shouting. God knows who's been on those bikes. And people try to talk to you to pass the time.'

'Put on headphones, take your book and we'll wipe down the seat.' He did smile this time and kissed me on the nose.

But I wasn't done. 'Rick, there's no guarantee that I'll even get a bike. You know as well as I do that I could sit there for ever just waiting to get a turn.'

My husband shook his head. 'Always borrowing problems.' He pulled his phone out and punched in a number real fast. 'Andrew? Can you stick a sign on one of the bikes for me? Thanks, man. Appreciate it.' He punched the button and picked up his duffel bag. 'There I called in a favour for you. Let's go, darling. Your bike awaits.'

Well, damn. I couldn't argue with that, could I?

You'd have thought he had a limousine waiting for me. Rick

ushered me into the cycle room with a flourish. And just as I had thought, wall-to-wall people, racing to nowhere on bikes that didn't move. Talking on cell phones, jacked into iPods, one guy was dictating a report into a recorder. I sighed. Mobbed. Not a single bike free. Except the broken one.

Rick followed my gaze and pushed me gently toward the bike with the *OUT OF ORDER* sign taped to it. 'Climb on, Ellen. Here you go.'

'It's broken!' I said and swatted his arm.

He pulled the sign off and shoved the paper in his pocket. 'Now it isn't. Andrew put it up for me. We saved it for you. Ah, and here he is. Speak of the devil.'

I was grinning over the bike when I turned, but my stomach did a nervous roll when I saw the man in question. Andrew. Rick's friend Andrew. Tall and lean and spectacularly muscular without being overdone. He looked like an athlete. Not like someone had blown him up like a tire pump. Not a gym rat but an honest to god athlete. Short dark hair, cut close to his scalp. Ice blue eyes. Nice jaw. Great smile.

'You're the lovely wife and I am the owner. Glad you finally came in to work out.' He shook my hand and my heart gave a little jump and my body grew warm. Way too warm. I was hot and flushed and I had somehow forgotten how to talk.

'Yes.' They both stared at me, smiling slightly. 'I mean, yes, glad I came, too. Nice to meet you. And thanks for the bike.' Now I was talking a bit too fast and my heart was revving up with it. 'I'd better ride now. I seem to be a bit wound up. I don't like anything to be off on my schedule. Or my routine. Or my bike, as you can tell.' I bit my tongue so I would shut the fuck up. God. Why was I still talking?

Andrew finally let go of my hand. That was why I was so damn warm, he had been touching me that whole time and the effect was similar, I assume, to being mildly electrocuted. I climbed on my bike and when I turned to wave them off I caught them both staring at me. My husband and my husband's friend. Andrew.

My feet took to pedalling and Andrew grinned and

winked. It wasn't a cheesy wink. It was a nice friendly wink that made me wet between the legs. I pedalled faster. Rick came toward me and like a light bulb going off over my head, I got it. We hadn't met another couple for a while. That was how we worked. We found some people we liked, we stuck with them, we stopped dating, we lay low for awhile.

He opened his mouth to speak as I turned the bike up a bit higher. I really needed to expel a fair amount of energy. My belly felt like I had swallowed a beehive and my head was buzzing with excitement and nerves.

'I know. You want me to have the hots for Andrew.'

He grinned and leaned in. He was so tall that he was face to face with me despite the height of the bike. His dark blond hair fell across his forehead, dark brown eyes regarded me calmly. He laughed a little and kissed me softly. When I opened my mouth to him, he kissed me harder. 'I just thought you might think he was a bit ...'

'Yummy?'

'Yummy does it,' he said and laughed. His eyes were shiny with humour and his stubble was making the situation between my legs that much worse. I knew when we got home later he would fuck me until I could barely walk. And I could hardly wait.

'What's the missus look like?' I teased. We played nice and we played fair and we played as a couple. I wasn't jealous but I wasn't above giving him a hard time. If I could torture him just a little over this situation, I would

'Enh, you know. Ugly as sin, one eye, a hump, some stitches on her face, bolts in her neck.' He imitated Frankenstein's monster.

I laughed and put my head down. It was time. I was ready. I could use a very good dinner and some very good wine and a very good fuck with a man like Andrew. And I knew Rick could use the same. I was excited now. Good. It felt good to be worked up over something. My legs circled faster and the friction rubbed my clit and I clenched up my insides creating a burst of pleasure. 'Set it up, OK?'

'I thought you'd never ask, baby.' He kissed me again and

off he went. To play squash with Andrew and set up a nice dinner and hopefully a spectacular dessert. For four.

The missus, aka Chandra Jackson, was gorgeous. Tall to my petite, dark hair to my blonde, deep green eyes to my sky blue. Her breasts were full, her waist tiny, her legs long and she was dressed like a model. She was spectacular. I leaned into my husband and said softly, 'You might have to fight me for her.'

'I can share, baby. What's mine is yours. You know that. But I get first dibs.' He patted me softly on the ass and I swallowed my laughter. I didn't want to make her nervous. That would be rude and possibly a catastrophe.

'Careful, I might take you up on the sharing part.' Then I rushed forward to meet her. I took her hand and leaned in for a friendly kiss. Instead of turning her head and offering her cheek, she leaned in and kissed me very, very softly on the lips.

So softly that at first I wasn't sure it had happened. I thought maybe a very vivid fantasy had overtaken my mind, but I heard Rick give a low chuckle and I knew it hadn't been in my imagination.

'Thank you for having us,' she said. Her eyes up close were bottle green and completely stunning.

'We're so glad you're here.' And I meant it. She seemed very nice even with the prospect of sex on the horizon, which could muddy the waters sometimes. Hard to tell if you really liked people when you were physically attracted. But I liked her instantly. I could use a woman in my life on many levels. I was a bit of a loner and Rick was my best friend. Someone to do "girl things" with would be great. And of course the sex. That was important, too.

'What are we having?' She looked around and dropped her black jacket on the sofa. Andrew watched her, his eyes pleased and proud and impossibly sexy. A smoky gaze and a cut jaw. I wondered what he looked like naked. But I would have to be patient because it was usually nice to chat and eat first.

'We have some nice steaks ...' Before Rick could finish, Chandra was undoing the tiny pearl buttons on her black sleeveless blouse.

'Because I always like to fuck first when it comes to these things. Then dinner is so much easier and more friendly. People aren't so uptight, you know? The sex has been had and then it's wine and laughter and food. Providing we get along of course. But I know we will. I can feel it,' she said, dropping the blouse on the sofa and unsnapping her pale pink bra in the front.

I opened my mouth and Rick's voice came out. 'Whatever makes you the most comfortable.'

'Oh, she has no patience,' Andrew said, waving his hand at his wife. His face amused and completely full of an easy kind of adoration. He came toward me and took my face in his hands. More laid back than his wife, he started with a kiss. Deep and soft. His tongue tasted like peppermint and he smelled like wood smoke. He was a good kisser. I relaxed into his hands and felt my body soften. I was beyond turned on.

I opened my eyes and found Chandra unzipping her skirt. The slim black garment puddled at her feet. She looked like a pin up girl. Pale pink lace panties on her pale white skin. Just the slightest hint of a belly and just a shadow of dark pubic hair through the lace. 'Can you help me with these?' she asked my husband, but I didn't see his face because Andrew's fingers were drawing down the zipper on the front of my dress. The halves fell open revealing my bare breasts. I had gone braless for comfort and, secretly, for speed.

'You are a beautiful, woman,' Andrew said and I could tell he meant it. It wasn't a line to loosen me up. The look in his eyes matched the tone of his voice. I smiled. 'Truly,' he said. I started to thank him but he dipped his head and sucked my nipple into his hot mouth. I forgot all about thanking him then.

My dress hit the floor and he was pushing at my panties. I palmed his hard-on and spread my legs to help him along. Panties snagged around my knees and I swayed off balance.

But he steadied me easily, one hand on my hips, one hand parting my thighs more and then stroking the inside of my legs, while his lips grazed and bit along the slope of my throat. I moaned, finding Rick with my gaze just as he was finding me. Our eyes met. We liked new but we liked to share new as a couple even if it was just a glance. A sound made that can be heard from another room. The lovely Chandra was on her knees, taking my husband's hard cock deep into her throat. He smiled and the sight of her lips on him made my pussy that much wetter. Made my heart beat faster. Andrew pushed his fingers into me. Slow and easy until he was deep, then he curled, curled, curled his fingers until my knees started to let go.

'Can we move to the sofa?' he said in my ear. He bit my earlobe hard enough to make me cry out but my nipples pebbled against his soft blue sweater. The gentle caress of the fabric against me nearly unbearable. I nodded and off we went, me trailing a pair of panties on my ankle. We met as a group there. Something Rick and I had never done. But I liked to keep track of him and him of me. It seemed Rick and Chandra were the same. Our big brown sofa was a flurry of limbs and rustling sounds and sighs. I parted my thighs wide for Andrew and he slid a condom on, rolling it down his hard cock. He fisted himself and I purred. I loved to see a man touch himself. There was something nearly primal about it for me, the handling of a hard dick by its owner.

He pushed against my pussy, pulling me up a bit and sinking into me slowly. At the very last second, Chandra reached out and stroked my breast. Her long thin fingers played up the sensitive side swell. Up over my nipple. Rick was rolling his own condom on and he stopped to watch her. She ran her fingertips along my skin and goose bumps rose on my chest. 'Oh, baby, is it good?' Andrew asked, but he wasn't talking to me. He was watching her fingers and I was watching Rick push his cock deep into Andrew's wife.

Pleasure uncurled in my pussy, beating low through my belly as I watched him move and watched her respond. Andrew's thumb rolled over my clit and Chandra's thumb rolled over my nipple and I closed my eyes. I soaked in the sighs and moans and slippery sounds of sex. Andrew's mouth covered my other breast, sucking hard until the pleasure and the pain mixed and swirled. His fingers dug into my hips as he moved faster, deeper. His cock banged my g-spot and I heard my husband grunt in that excited way he does when he is getting close. That did me in. That desperate, excited, frenzied animal sound that Rick makes.

'Rick?'

'Baby?'

'Touch me.'

He did. He rolled his hand along my flank, moving faster inside of the lovely Chandra. His hipbones banging the edge of our sofa as he kneeled on the hardwood floor. Andrew shoved my thighs high, angled his head so he could watch his cock slam home inside of me. He slung my legs over his shoulders and fucked me faster. I was tilted and his cock banged my g-spot over and over again until I was no good.

'I told you I could be flexible,' I said. Rick laughed at our inside joke and I felt a wave of overwhelming love for him. No one else understood what I meant.

Hands were everywhere on me. Somewhere in there, I lost track of whose hands they were. I sank into the feel. The feel of hands stroking me on the outside, Andrew, unfamiliar and gorgeous stroking me from the inside.

'I'm going to come,' I said, softly, not sure anyone could hear me. Possibly I was talking to myself. But the hands moved faster and slower and softer and harder in unison. Andrew gripped my bottom, levering me more and fucking me faster.

I fell into my orgasm. Let the pleasure and the warmth and the spasms suck me under and then push me up. Rick was next, set off by the sound of me. Sounds he had heard a thousand times. And then Andrew, maybe because there is nothing sexier than the visceral sound of the male orgasm. Chandra was the grand finale. She came with my husband's cock slamming into her on the last waves of his orgasm and my lips on her nipple.

We were suddenly a pile of bodies. Hot, wet, flushed and pleased.

'So, dinner, anyone?' I joked.

Chandra turned and smiled to me. 'Yes, please.' We were still naked. Husbands still buried to the balls in the wrong partner and I smiled back at her. Odd maybe but not too odd, I guess. 'I am famished.'

And then it was a sorting of clothes and men discussing the grill and me asking Chandra if she'd help me make the salad.

'You're right, that was nice.' I poured her a glass of wine and pushed a stray tendril of hair behind her ear.

'What?'

'You know. Having sex first and getting it out of the way, so to speak.' I cut chunks of ripe tomato, slivers of cool cucumbers, orange discs of carrots.

'Oh, not out of the way. A bit of an appetizer.' She tore the lettuce into tiny little pieces, uniform but unique. Bright green confetti in the bowl.

'Oh?'

'I'm not done. God, I hope you're not, either. I would like to have some time with just you. The men with us at some point, obviously, I like it that way, too. But I'd like to have my time with you. I've heard all about you. I never thought they'd get you into the gym,' she smiled and then surprised me by leaning in and kissing me again. I could taste Rick on her. The heady scent of my husband's cock.

'What do you mean get me into the gym?'

'Rick said you refused to come in. That you loathed the gym.'

'That's true. How did they get me in? I only came in because my bi ...' I stopped and she grinned. Her pink petal lips curling up like she had a secret. She bit her bottom lip and I thought of those lips, that tongue on me some time after dinner. I pushed my thighs together but the pulse in my cunt only grew heavier. 'You?'

She rolled her eyes and laughed, tearing more lettuce. 'Two men conniving to get us all together and it took me to tell them to disable your bike.'

I giggled and then I outright laughed. 'You're one smart cookie,' I said.

Chandra leaned in and I could smell her shampoo. She smelled like sugared pears. I made a soft noise as her scent filled my head and her soft pink tongue licked along my lower lip. 'I'm a tasty cookie, too,' she said.

I couldn't wait to find out.

Black and White Photos

'What the hell is that,' I giggled into Charles's shoulder.

We stood together, arms linked, staring at the monstrosity in charcoal. Maybe that was the title, 'Monstrosity in Charcoal'.

'It's clearly... um. It most definitely is a,' he paused, stroked his chin and set his face in a scholarly mask. 'A flaming baby with three heads and a tail.'

I hid my face against his shoulder and gave into the laughter for real until he nudged me. Someone was coming. I could only guess it was someone who shouldn't see me laughing my ass off at the art.

'Ah, I see you found Caroline's charcoal of her father.' Hank slapped Charles on the shoulder and guffawed. 'Isn't it wonderful? So stark and yet inspiring such hope.'

I glanced back at the flaming, three-headed baby and smiled politely. 'Absolutely. Is Caroline here tonight?' I asked, praying the answer would be no. I most certainly hoped she hadn't witnessed our juvenile display of humour over her work.

'Sadly, no. She had to work. Even us artists have to eat. God knows, being an artist rarely pays off,' Hank said and took a healthy swig of his martini. Already his face was florid and he had that dazed, fish-eyed stare of someone well on their way to be full-on shit-faced.

'A shame,' I said and took Charles's arm. Hank was his friend and I had never kept my distaste for the man a secret. He had promised me the moon just to come tonight. 'We don't want to dominate your time. I know how much these art evenings mean to you. Not to mention, I saw some beautiful

104

black and white photos over there I want to get a better look at.'

He nodded and smiled his big I-am-the-host smile. 'Ah, those were done by a new fellow. I've never invited him to art night before. Met him at a gallery opening down town. Jude Belmont. Nice boy. He's over by the shrimp puffs.' With that Hank disappeared back into crowd.

'I love how he slid in his 'art night' plug right along with calling attention to the fact that there are shrimp puffs,' I snorted as we wandered over toward the wall that displayed the black and whites.

'Be nice. He thinks he's helping his fellow artists by hosting these evenings. Who knows, he might be.' Charles patted my lower back and then surreptitiously slid his hand down for just a moment and gave my ass a squeeze. 'If you behave, I'll do something nice for you later.'

I caught his wink and grinned. It wasn't as if I had to convince my husband to have sex with me. I didn't even have to remind him to give me my due pleasure. It was him plying me with promises of sex that got me worked up.

'Well, I don't see how showing artists the work of other artists furthers anyone's career, but I will behave. Plus, I really do want to see these. I only got a quick glimpse on the way to the flaming baby, but they look like they might be rather good. Worth standing and staring at,' I said.

'Worth stroking our chins knowingly and tilting our heads?' he teased.

'Maybe so, my dear. Let's go see.'

There must have been a mad rush for the shrimp puffs then, because a wide space cleared in front of the three framed black and whites.

'I don't know,' Charles whispered close to my ear, 'if they're all dispersing that quickly, maybe it's black and whites of road kill.'

I started to laugh but then we were standing right in front of them and my breath caught in my throat. My pulse felt like a living thing trying to break free of my skin.

'I don't think so,' I heard myself almost sigh. 'They are

gorgeous. My God, Charles, he has real talent on this wall.'

And they were gorgeous. Most certainly unexpected. In a room full of flaming babies, and still lifes of oddly shaped fruit and a few Dali-inspired melting objects, they were bright like a flame. Simple, stark, beautiful. Each was an eight-by-ten print set with a plain white mat and then framed in a brushed black frame.

The first was titled, 'Elle'. In it a tall blonde woman straddled a plain ladder-back chair. Her legs from the knees down were encased in patent leather boots. Kick-ass boots. Her wrists were encompassed in handcuffs but the chain had been broken. Her thin hands gripped the back of the chair. Her head was down, blonde hair hiding her face. With all the hair, the viewer could barely make out the studded dog collar around her neck. She looked both broken and free. I heard myself sigh again.

I moved to the second, nearly oblivious of anything but the photos. I heard Charles moving with me but even he seemed distant to me now. The middle photo was titled 'Jane'. In this one the only thing visible was the woman's face. Clearly in mid orgasm she was ugly and sensual and radiant all at once. From one angle she looked angelic, from another demonic. The distortion of her features was art in itself. Her hair was neither blonde nor overly dark. My guess was red hair. The only thing visible besides her and a swatch of nondescript bed linens was the edge of one wrist. It looked to be wrapped in fabric. Most likely a scarf. This time the sound that came out of me was not a sigh. It was more like a whisper.

As I moved on to the final frame, I noticed how damp I had grown and when Charles touched my bare wrist it was like having a match held to my skin. Every nerve was awake and alive and singing. I hissed.

'Did I hurt you?'

I shook my head, didn't look at him, and moved to stand directly in front of the final photo. 'Anna'. She was my favourite. I might have said it out loud. I don't know.

Anna had chin-length hair like me. Teacup sized breasts overrode the black lace half-cup bra she wore. Her nipples, so

106

light in the shades of black, white, and grey, that they could only be petal pink in real life. Her hair fell around her face, hitting her jaw in a way that reminded me of a flapper. The majority of her face was swallowed by the blindfold she wore. The tip of her thin regal nose was tilted up, her lips parted in what wasn't a smile but was well on its way. She looked serene and satisfied. Behind her hair was a white pillowcase. Nothing more. Her face. The mask. The nondescript white pillow. Anna.

Charles squeezed my shoulders in his big hands and the moisture between my legs gave way to a pulsing that demanded one thing. 'I wonder what was happening to her when he took this,' I said softly so only he could hear. 'What he had done to her or was…' I let my heart still a little before I finished, 'about to do.'

'You've never been into this sort of thing,' he laughed softly in my ear. 'I think you've even used the word 'perverse'.'

'That was before I realised it was beautiful,' I said more to myself than my husband. 'Look at them. It is beautiful.' I stared at Anna again and went so far as to reach out and brush my fingers over the black frame. Could I touch what she was feeling if I touched the art? 'I wonder what was happening?' I said again and even I could hear the want in my voice.

'What do you think?' Charles asked and then his hands were around my waist. His fingers played low over my belly. A very appropriate and marital public display of affection for anyone paying attention. Only I could feel his hard cock pressed against the seam of my ass. Only I could tell that the very tips of his long fingers brushed the very top of my pubic hair, sending tingles and frissons of energy shooting from where his fingers touched me to the tips of my toes.

'I have no idea,' I said, my voice a little harsh from the sudden overwhelming urge to fuck that had been set off in me. I loved sex, don't get me wrong, but what I was experiencing right then was the urge to rut like an animal. Irrational. Consuming. Insane. 'I wish I knew.'

'I think I know.' Charles words sent a shiver through me.

107

Not just up my spine but through my entire being.

'Do you?' I pressed back against him. I was subtle but I did it. The feel of his cock made me close my eyes for a moment, even if it meant losing sight of the photos for an instant.

'I do. Let me take you home and I'll show you what I think.'

I nodded because I thought if I opened my mouth I might start laughing. Joy and desire and peace. That was what I saw in these photos. I didn't want to look away but I wanted to know what Anna was feeling. I knew Charles would do his best to take me there.

He broke our contact and walked away. I would simply look at them until he returned with our coats. I saw him talking to Hank. Hank pointed, chucked my husband on the shoulder and then turned to wave at me. I waved back. Then Charles was talking to another man. A younger man. Tall and thin with nearly black hair and nearly black eyes from what I could see. The man handed him a card as Charles pulled out his wallet. I saw a bill pass hands and then my husband was heading my way holding my coat and smiling.

'Who was that?' I asked as he helped me into my coat.

'That was the artist. I gave him a hundred dollar bill and told him to hold the photos until tomorrow. I'll go pick them up and pay him the balance.'

'How much did you pay?' I asked as he turned to me and kissed me quickly.

'Not nearly enough, I suspect,' he said and led me out.

The moment we arrived home, Charles put the blindfold on me. Technically, it was a sleep mask but it was black and it accomplished the same task. I was left on the bed, naked and in the dark. With each passing moment, my body tightened. Not with fear but with excitement and desire and the delicious feeling of being at someone's mercy. Blind to the world, my other senses were heightened. I could hear Charles's big feet padding across the hall carpet. I heard the distinctive creak of the closet in the guest room. I heard the ticking of the grandfather clock in the living room. When the chimes announced ten o'clock, it was deafening in my personal darkness.

Charles entered the room but didn't speak. That alone made my nipples rigid and the sudden harsh hardening spurred a shower of warmth through my body. I was having trouble breathing, the air seemed to have solidified. What would he do? What did he have? Would he fuck me? Eat me? Spank me? The more I thought of what he might do, the more my body responded. Becoming one hot liquid nerve.

He was at the side of the bed. Right there. I could feel him. The energy of him, and yet he didn't speak. That alone was unusual for us. Our sex was full of words and laughter and noise. His silence broke me out in goose bumps. I swore I could feel his gaze on me. Feel it like the strong stroke of hand on flesh.

My husband touched my wrist and I sucked in a breath that left me heady. My arm was raised above my head and I heard the swish of fabric before I felt the cool silk touch my skin. My wrist was bound to the maple headboard tightly but not tight enough to hurt. So, that explained the creak of the guest room closet door where I stored my rarely worn clothes and shoes. His warm hand took my other wrist and this one was also bound. Not silk this time but suede. I heard a tiny clink when he secured it. My suede belt. Thin enough to tie but the buckle gave a merry tinkle when he pulled.

'Charles.'

'Shhhh.' That was it. All he said. The muscles of my stomach tightened, fluttered, and sent a nice slow wave of warmth through my cunt. Charles never hushed me.

What had I been about to say, I wondered? Nothing. I had said his name and that was it. For reassurance? I had no idea.

His fingers started at my lips. Tracing them, pushing past gently, then forcing into my mouth and I responded. In my darkness, I responded without thinking. I took them into my mouth and sucked. I licked and nibbled and did all the things to his broad digits I might normally do to his stiff cock. He moved and when he did his erection brushed my thigh leaving a small trail of pre-come on my hot skin. The moment he moved again, I felt it start to dry.

His now wet fingers trailed down my throat. He explored the hollow of my collar bone and the sensation was overwhelming. Cut off from vision, each touch was distorted. His fingers dipped back in my mouth but only for a moment and then his wet fingertips pinched my nipples. Already erect, the sudden assault was enough to make me yelp and squirm but the dampness between my legs grew in proportion. My clitoris danced, my inner thighs grew slick.

I wanted to beg right then and there. I wanted to beg him to fuck me and fuck me hard. I knew he would. My husband would do anything and everything I asked. In my newfound darkness, Anna's ecstatic visage flashed before me. I wanted that. To feel what she felt. To see what she saw in her darkness.

I did not beg.

Then he was pushing his big hard cock between my lips. I gulped at it. I chased it as it bobbed before me, unable to use my hands. My mouth never stopped. Lips, tongue, teeth. I felt like I was starving and he was the only sustenance in the world. I had never wanted to have my husband in my mouth as badly as I wanted it right then. I felt greedy and ravenous and I only stopped my wet work on his cock when he pulled himself from my mouth.

The sound I made was primal. I settled only when his own wet mouth found my clit, parted my vulva, suckled and nibbled until I yanked my wrists against the gentle bonds that held me.

This is what a caged animal in heat must feel like. The thought was like an echo deep in my head that flitted out of range when his rigid tongue shoved deep into my pussy, his hard white teeth grazing my engorged clit and I bellowed as the orgasm claimed me. Behind the blindfold a kaleidoscope of colours bloomed. I yanked against my binds without thinking and the thin flesh of my inner wrists screamed with agony.

I didn't care.

And then he was in me. He had probably planned more

torture but that sight, that sound. I knew my husband well enough to know that he had been pushed too far. Now he pushed into me, roughly. Stretching me, filling me and behind the mask he was all that existed. His body in my body. His cock in my cunt. His breath on my face. His hands clutching my hips and yanking me up even as he plunged into me.

I couldn't hold him, couldn't pull him closer or deeper. I was at his mercy for my pleasure and that thought started me off again. A building heat. A tightening deep inside that made me want to squirm and pant and yell. I didn't, I received. I took each harsh thrust. I absorbed the feel of his eager fingers digging into the soft flesh of my hips. Breathed and cooed and grunted as his hairy chest slammed against my breasts and tickled my over-sensitised nipples.

'More beautiful,' he grunted and I didn't question him. My body was lighting up, flickering and moving around his. Each thrust drew me closer, each sound and grunt lifted me up and I felt it coming like a storm. I was going to come. Again. With him.

'More beautiful than Anna,' he almost yelled. His urgency was like the feel of the air after a lightning strike. So intense, so charged with energy I felt the hair on the back of my neck rise up. 'You should see yourself like this,' he growled and went rigid against me.

I came. Sobbing, babbling, pulling against my bonds to try to reach him. When he emptied into me, jittering against my body, he sounded like a stranger. Like a beast. Insane.

I shivered under him as he settled on me. Warming me.

Colours danced in my darkness. After kissing my face from forehead to chin, Charles took off the mask. I blinked feeling disoriented. He untied first the scarf and then the belt. I watched. Not speaking. Focusing on breathing.

When he turned back to me he looked worried. When I started to cry, he looked terrified.

'Did I hurt you?'

I shook my head and wiped my eyes. I felt thoroughly used and exhausted and… sacred?

He wasn't buying it and he gathered me into his arms. He

smoothed and rubbed and shushed in my ear as I sniffled. 'I must have hurt you. You're crying.'

'True, but not because you hurt me.' I curled around him, feeling the pull of sleep.

'Then why.'

'It was beautiful. I can't explain.'

I felt him exhale with relief. 'It was. It really was. If you could have… you were…'

'The pictures,' I mumbled, already feeling myself drift off, 'the black and whites.'

'What about them, baby,' he whispered.

'I want to hang them in here.' My eyelids descended.

'Of course.'

'And I want to…'

'What?'

'I want to try them all,' I said, struggling.

'OK.'

'And then, I want to take our own,' I yawned. I slept.

Just Like Your Father

'And this is Carlene. She worked with your father for five years. She'll be able to give you just about anything you need.' Zoey smiled at Eli. Eli felt nothing but panic.

He smiled, swallowed it down and shook hands with the woman he guessed to be about five years his senior. 'I hope that means you make magic happen.'

Carlene laughed, long, cool fingers playing over his as she withdrew her hand. 'I try. I don't think I make magic, but I do make things happen.'

'I can attest to that!' Zoey said. 'But now I'll leave you two to get to know each other. I have a presentation to give down on the third floor. Nervous is not a big enough word to cover it.'

'You'll do great, Zoey, just remember the most important thing.'

'Drink?'

'Breathe!' Carlene touched Zoey's arm and off she went, into the wild workplace.

'I hope that goes for me too,' Eli admitted.

'You'll do great too, Eli. What seems foreign today will be second nature in a month.'

'From your lips ...' Eli said with a nervous laugh.

'When you laugh you sound just like your father. Now let's start easy. Phone system?'

'Hey, might as well.'

When he sat in the chair he felt like an impostor. A little boy sitting in his father's place, playing make-believe. When Carlene leant across his back and started to push buttons, he felt giddy. With the smell of her perfume – sandalwood and peaches – his body hummed to life. She was gorgeous – lush and ripe with dark brown hair that glowed with good health and a sturdy brushing. He imagined she could give a really good ...

'– this one puts you right back to me after,' she declared and he looked up into her smiling face, her bright blue eyes twinkling with good humour.

Eli felt his eyes do a fast detour down her slender neck to the swell of her cleavage – tasteful, but present – the pinch of her waist, the flare of her hips. The decadent way her body curved that made his tongue feel about two sizes too big.

'Sorry?'

'I said if you want to put someone on hold and then talk to me you press this one,' she pushed a button gently using his finger instead of her own. Her hand wrapped around his and Eli felt his cock tent his charcoal grey pants.

Great. Offend the woman who runs the show by getting an erection because she touched your hand. Because you are ... oh ... 14, Eli!

He gritted his teeth and tried to focus. He caught Carlene watching him and nodded as if it made all the sense in the world. 'I push this and then ...'

Carlene moved his hand to another button, this one green. 'This one,' she said.

'Right.' He pretended to push the button, which made him think of her clit, which made him think of burrowing his head beneath that proper skirt to see if she had on full stockings or thigh highs. Or was she old school and sporting garters and panties and ... This wasn't helping.

'When you get flustered, you look just like your father,' she said right up to his ear and Eli felt a rush of goosebumps across his neck and shoulders.

'You worked a lot with my dad?'

Carlene nodded, and moved to the other side of his desk. There. That was good. He was safe now. She was *allllllll* the way over there.

'We worked closely. Especially on a few big projects. Penski, Stewart, Toye ...' she rattled off names that meant

114

nothing to Eli. Aerospace might as well be gene splicing for all he knew about it.

'Good, good. I'll need help.'

Carlene smiled and said, 'I'll give you anything you need that you think will help, Eli.'

Blowjob? ... no, no, no! You perv. Stop!

Eli cleared his throat and tugged his collar. 'Erm, thanks, Carlene. You're a gem.'

'No problem. Now I'll just go and get–' Her sleeve, a festive bell-shaped sleeve that made Eli think of fancy women dancing in big ballrooms, caught his pencil cup and tumbled the contents to the ground. 'Oh!'

'Let me help,' Eli said. He felt so much better now that she'd done something imperfect. It helped him breathe and be calm. She was not infallible and he didn't have to live up to his father's shadow. He just had to be himself. He was running the sales and overseeing for Richardson Aerospace, not building the parts.

Together they crawled around on the floor, picking up pencils. Eli's eyes would stray to the gorgeous swell of Carlene's ass and then he'd bite his tongue to focus. He saw a flash of thigh, a flex of calf, and yes – sweet merciful Lord – a garter and the lacy top of a stocking.

Awesome, now I can drive nails with my dick ...

'There. I think that's all of them,' she said, brushing the fluffs of dark hair from her face. 'I'm sorry. I'm really clumsy sometimes.'

'Me too,' he admitted.

Carlene touched his hand and said 'Just like your father ...' and shook her head with a smile. 'He spilt more coffee than any man I knew. And dropped pencils. Papers. Everything!'

So he could watch your fine ass when you bent over to pick them up. He's no fool, the old man ...

'It must be an inherited trait.' He swallowed hard and averted his eyes. This woman was going to be the gateway to his success. Not a good thing to take pleasure where you should be doing business.

'I'll leave you to look over paperwork. I'll be right out

here. I have some reports to type up and some files that need attention. A recent temp put financials for one vendor in another's file and so on. It's a mess.'

'Right. Good stuff. Carry on. I don't mean to hold you up.'

She blinked, looking sorry for him and then bent to retrieve one more stray pencil. Eli got a dizzying glimpse of a valley of creamy cleavage and he thought he might actually expire in his father's big, poufy swivel chair. He shut his eyes to stop his heart-rate from climbing.

'You're no bother and no hold up. Such a worrywart,' she said. 'And handsome. Just like your father.'

Hmm. What else has this little minx done with my father?

But he shook his head and shooed her. 'Go on, be productive. One of us should be.'

She went with a healthy swing of her luscious ass and Eli briefly considered locking the door and beating off, but then thought better of it. Probably not a good idea your first day "in charge" to get caught spanking the monkey, so to speak.

He sat and pored over thick important documents and spreadsheets that glowed gruesomely on his screen, mocking him for not understanding. 'Might as well be written in Greek,' he growled, feeling frustrated and impotent and like he wanted to just hit someone, or something.

'You'll get it,' she said from the doorway, looking like a vision. 'Brought you some coffee.'

Her nylons whispered secretively as she crossed the room and Eli had a brief flash of peeling them off of her long, long legs. Carlene made him a cup of coffee without asking his preference and when Eli tasted it, it was the best fucking cup of coffee he'd ever had. Probably because she'd made it, but that was neither here nor there. 'Thank you.'

'You just need to relax,' she said. 'May I?' she nodded toward the empty visitor chair.

'Oh, please!'

Carlene wrestled it close so that her chair pressed his and Eli was wildly aware of the warm scent of her and her outrageous body that seemed to push against the restrain of her proper clothes. 'You just need to highlight the intended amount and that shows you how much has been ordered and for what quarter ...'

He lost her voice then because his pulse had jacked up so high all he could hear was his loud heart and the dry click in his throat when he swallowed. She caught his gaze and said, 'You really do need to calm down.' She sounded like she was at the far end of a long tunnel.

'I don't know how,' Eli said, giving himself fully to the panic.

'Hmm. Let's see.' She dropped to her knees right there, pushing him back on his wheeled chair. Eli was thankful for that chair because, without it, he surely would have fallen on his ass and he had finally − it seemed − started to hallucinate. 'What can we do about that?' Carlene asked and undid his zipper.

'The door?' he said numbly.

'Is locked,' she answered.

And then his cock was in her hand and her lips followed swiftly. Glossy pink lips that sucked the head of his cock deep and a warm, wet tongue that swirled in dizzying loops around his shaft. She sucked him deep and her fingers played along the base of him with cool efficiency. She handled his balls gently but sucked madly and within moments a load of stress rushed out of him and he was touching her soft, soft hair.

'Stand up.' Eli's voice finally sounded commanding and her big blue eyes found his. She smiled, his cock still in her mouth, and he thought he'd come if she didn't stop right then. 'Now.'

She stood in front of him and Eli ran his hands along the valleys and peaks of her body. He pinched a nipple through her crisp white blouse, feeling the lace of her bra underneath. But her nipple rose up and she made a soft sound that made him feel a bit crazed.

Eli hiked up her skirt and pushed his face to the cream-coloured knickers underneath. He felt the warmth of her sex on his cheek and she pushed her fingers into his hair. Oddly, he found that he had the urge to stay right here until his body and mind calmed. Instead, he pressed his lips to the gusset of

117

her panties and breathed out, while worming a finger under the elastic and testing her cunt.

God, she was wet. God, how he wanted her. This was *so* much better than masturbation in a locked office.

He made a slow ritual of undoing her garters, peeling her panties down, leaving her garter belt in place so that the elastics swung festively. As he rolled down her stockings, she said, 'See, you can do a meticulous job when you calm down.'

'Good point.' Her pussy lips were slick and soft and he sucked one and then the other before locating the swollen nub of her clit with the tip of his tongue. Eli drove two fingers deep and curled the tips against the wet suede flesh deep inside her.

'Oh,' she said as if in mid conversation.

'Yes, oh.' He sucked and licked until her body grew taut and her fingers bit into his scalp and, when she came, he felt the ripple work through her cunt and her body shivered with it. 'Now, about bending over that desk.'

'Yes, sir,' she said, her laughter sweet to his ears.

Eli parted her legs, studying the swell of her ass, the puckered star of her anus, the wet split of her pussy and he drove himself deep into her inch by inch, his fingertip playing her back hole until she squirmed under him like a cat in heat. It was the hottest thing he'd ever seen. 'You're so wet.'

'I am.'

'And tight.'

'Good.'

'And hot.'

'Yes,' she said.

'I'm going to come,' he admitted.

She worked a hand under her and Eli watched her tendons flex as she rubbed her clit in time with his thrusts. He gripped her flared hips tightly, relishing the jiggle of her bottom as he fucked her. When her pussy clamped up around him again, he let himself go. Dropping backwards into his orgasm like a man dropping into a pool.

The orgasm ripped through him and when it had passed, he

dropped to his knees, feeling a bit weak. He kissed the back of each of her pale thighs and then watched her calmly put herself back together.

She dropped into his lap and kissed him softly. 'Feel better?'

Eli nodded. 'I do. And let me guess. I did that just like my father.'

Her face clouded. 'Oh, I wouldn't know. I never did *that* with your father.'

'So just me?' So sue him, he felt a rush of glee at the information.

'Yes. Just you. I have to admit, I found you attractive from the get-go.'

Something swelled in his chest and he nodded, ready to tackle his difficult first day. 'Great. I'm thrilled.' He gave her a kiss and said, 'Now about ordering lunch?'

'I'll get right on it.'

'And then I'll need your help with this database. So I can decipher it.'

'No problem,' she said, all business again.

'Oh, and Carlene?'

'Sir?'

'When you come back with the food, lock the door. I have a feeling this database is going to stress me out a lot.'

She smiled and it went straight to his dick. 'We can't have that now, can we?'

'No. No, ma'am, we can't,' Eli said and sat back in his poufy swivel chair. It was good to be the boss.

Picket Fence

Nick found the Polaroid camera while we were doing our Spring cleaning. We had devoted our entire Sunday to lightening our household load. He waved it around with a grin. "Think they still make film for these things?"

I glanced up from a box stuffed full of knick knacks that I hadn't seen since I packed them. When we moved in, they went directly under the bed to be dealt with later. I wouldn't even unpack the box. The whole thing was going straight to charity.

"Actually, they do. I was at the pharmacy the other day and they had it hanging behind the counter. I guess enough people still have them that they continue to make film. Why?"

"Just curious," he said still grinning. Then he started holding up items from an old bag of clothes.

"Ditch it... ditch it... ditch it..." I sighed. "Put them all back in the bag and give the whole bag away."

"What if there's something good in here?" he joked, tying the bag closed.

"If we don't miss it, we don't need it. Time to get the clutter out of here. Then we can paint and redo the floor and actually have a home. Not a messy fixer-upper. A home."

Nick nodded and smiled. "Fine. But I'm keeping the camera."

"Keep the camera," I laughed. "I don't care."

Then I forgot about it.

Two days later he called me at work to tell me not to cook. He'd be picking up dinner. Fine by me. Any night I can eat without cooking is a fine night in my opinion.

When I got home, I poured myself a glass of wine and

settled on the sofa, relishing the freedom from figuring out what was for dinner. He came through the door a few minutes later with a takeout bag in one hand and a small paper bag in the other.

"What's for dinner?" I asked, sipping my wine.

"Charlie's Bistro. We have roasted chicken, corn pudding, fresh bread and steamed green beans."

I loved Charlie's. The best take out around. There food was like mom's home cooking. Or in the case of my mom, better. "And?" I knew him too well.

"And just because I love you, half of a Sin Cake. I pointed to the one with the extra chocolate shavings on the top. Do I take care of you, or what?" Nick walked into the dining room and set the bag on the table. "Don't you want to know what's in the other bag?" he called.

"I hadn't even give the other bag a thought," I teased, following him. "Once you mentioned Sin Cake my brain short circuited."

I unpacked the bag from Charlie's and revelled in all the tasty smells. Nick shook the little paper bag at me. OK, I would play.

"A pregnancy test?" I said, reading the name on the bag. It was from the pharmacy up the street. "Are you pregnant?"

"Nope. Try again?"

"Condoms? That would be a waste of money, though, with me on the pill." I popped open the chicken container and then the containers of side dishes.

"Nope."

"I give up," I sighed. I was starving and ready to eat. No more 'what's in the bag' game for me.

Nick tossed me the small bag and I barely caught it. I peeked inside and was instantly confused. "Film?"

"Polaroid film," Nick corrected, filling our plates with food.

"How very exciting for you," I laughed. "You bought film. For an ancient camera. Did you forget that we own a top of the line digital?"

"Of course not," he said softly and then handed me my

plate. "But digital doesn't have the panache of the old Polaroids. All vibrant inside their little white borders."

"Ooh-kay. So what's it for?"

"I'm going to take your picture," he said.

As we sat and ate on the sofa and sipped our wine, he wouldn't say anything more. He was going to take my picture. No matter how much I bugged him he would only shake his head, smile and say, "later".

When later finally came, I was on my third glass of wine. I was feeling no pain and in a rather relaxed mood. No dinner dishes to do. Nothing to do but settle in for the night with my husband. My kind of evening. Nick came out with the camera and slid the large film clip into the slot. Then he looked at me and said, "Take your blouse off."

"What?!" That woke me up. My warm wine buzz flitted out of reach. I stared at him. Certainly he wasn't serious.

"You heard me, Noel. Take your blouse off."

"How much have you had to drink?" I laughed nervously. I felt very uncomfortable but way down deep, I noted, I was also feeling sort of... turned on.

"One glass of wine. That's it. Come on, babe. Play with me. Take your blouse off." He stood patiently. Waiting.

"Fine." I proceeded to unbutton each of the tiny white buttons on my silk blouse. I pulled it off and laid it on the sofa. My hands shook a little as I did it.

"Now the bra."

"Nick—"

"Just do it, babe."

I did. I unhooked my bra and pulled it off slowly, watching his face the whole time. His expression was a mix of excitement and intensity. I laid my lacy white bra on top of my proper white blouse and straightened my spine. My nipples were dusky hard peaks but I would not comment on that. It could be the temperature change. It did not mean I was aroused by this odd shift in evening routine.

"There." I said almost petulantly.

"Thank you," Nick said. This time he gave me a small, reassuring smile. "Now hold them in your hands. Hold those beautiful tits in those elegant hands."

A shiver ran through me and I obeyed. His words and requests were so strange, but also intoxicating. I hefted my breasts in my hands, letting my fingertips stray over my deep pink nipples. His commands and my capitulation serving to heighten the pleasurable sensation. Excitement coursed through me, shooting straight to my sex.

Nick made a small sound and raised the camera. The flash was blinding, the noise so loud after having grown used to the quiet ways of a digital camera. The photo ejected like a broad, square tongue. Nick pulled it out, set it on the side table and watched me. Just to torture him, I lifted my breast to my lips and sucked my own nipple.

His voice hoarse, he said, "Now the skirt, Noel."

I stood, unzipped the side zipper of my work skirt and let it fall. I stood there, suddenly sure of myself in my black panties, garter and hose. Another flash, another whine. The second photo shot out of the camera. He set it with the first and nodded. He didn't have to tell me. I unhooked the hose, rolled them down and placed them with my other clothes. Next the garter. I folded it in half slowly and then turned to add it to the pile.

Flash. Whine. A third picture had been taken.

"Nothing like that perfect ass in a nice pair of black, lace panties," my husband said.

When I turned he gave me another nod and I shucked the panties. Completely nude I stood before him. He took the fourth picture and then eyed me warily. He seemed a little unsure. What would he ask me to do now?

"Lay back on the sofa for me, baby. Spread your legs."

I did and the flash blinded me yet again. I wondered what the photo looked like. I could feel my cunt swollen and wet. How did it look? Rosy red with shades of pink? Did it look as engorged and slick as it felt? Did my arousal show up on film? Were there glistening slicks of my own fluid between my thighs? I sighed and without him asking, ran a finger along the seam of my cunt. I rubbed my fingertip along the hard knot of my clit and shuddered.

Flash. Whine. The fifth picture ejected with a triumphant sound.

I slid two of my fingers into my cunt and flexed them, pushing and probing. I stroked my G-spot and continued to stroke my clit. My pussy clenched around my fingers and I arched my back to stroke deeper. I heard Nick take the sixth picture and when the flash flickered I came, contorting on the sofa as spasm after spasm coursed through me.

Then he was on me. Discarding his work pants and shirt. His face dark and serious. He still held the camera and he set it on the back of the sofa as he pushed my legs up and settled the swollen head of his cock against my opening.

"You are beautiful. Gorgeous. Thank you," he was almost babbling as he thrust into me.

I was still feeling the effects of my first orgasm. My husband's swollen cock sliding into me, stretching and filling me was enough to make me hum my pleasure against his warm shoulder.

"My pleasure," I sighed and laughed.

Nick fucked me slowly at first. Drawing out almost all the way only to slide slowly back in to the root of his cock. He pushed into me slowly but thrust high inside my cunt. I would come again, I could feel it already. Then he pulled half way out, propped on one arm and aimed the camera at our bodies where they joined.

"I want you to see this the way I see it," he murmured and then pressed the button. Without removing the photo he set the camera back down and began to fuck me in earnest.

His movements grew faster and jerkier. His breath tearing in and out of him loudly. I pushed up against him, after flashes going off behind my closed eyelids. In my mind's ear I could hear the camera capturing what I had done. When he stiffened against me and came with a groan, I came right along with him. My pussy sucking eagerly at what he had to give.

We lay there listening to the silence for a few minutes. No sounds but our breathing. When I could stand it any longer, I swatted him playfully on the shoulder.

"Enough of this. Let me see them!"

When I flipped through the stiff little photos, was both surprised and pleased. They were beautiful. Sexy. Raunchy in a classy sort of way. I handed them back. "Nick, my face isn't in any of them."

"I know." He opened the side table drawer and put the pictures inside.

"You don't like my face," I teased, but I was half serious. Not a single photo showed me above the neck.

"I love your face. Your face is beautiful, you know I think you are beautiful. All of you. Head, body, brain, soul." He smiled and kissed me.

"Then why?"

"There's a very good reason." That's all he would say.

The following day, I came home to another take out bag on the dining room table. The Archer. I smelled roast beef. I smiled and headed to the kitchen for a drink. I found Nick at the large kitchen window that overlooks our backyard. Backyard is a stretch, really. It's more like a post card sized swatch of grass and a small concrete patio that has gate access to the wide alley that runs the length of our block. On the far side of the alley, the county had put up a tall picket fence to block off the small area of woods beyond. It looked like Nick was staring at the fence.

I poured a glass of wine and walked up, resting my head on his shoulder. "What are we looking at?"

"Them," Nick said. His eyes met mine for a second and I detected a tiny flicker of what looked like fear.

I looked out to see four men standing in the alley. They were spaced several feet apart, each gazing at a section of the fence. I saw tiny squares, so tiny from my vantage point, I couldn't make out what they were.

"And why are we looking at them looking at the fence. Or whatever's on the fence. *What is* on the fence?"

"You are on the fence," my husband said and wrapped his arm around my waist, pulling me close.

"What?" I yelled and stiffened under his arm. I tried to pull free of him but he pulled me closer and held me tight.

"Before you get all upset, just listen to me."

I was torn between punching him in the forehead and staring at the men who were in the alley gazing at my naked body... and me touching myself... and my husband fucking me!

"I don't think there's anything you could say to make me not want to kill you right now," I hissed.

"OK, then just watch them."

I turned my attention to the gathering below while I fumed. I wanted to march out and tear them all down and shoo away the perverts staring at me, but I knew that would give away that I was the object of their attention. So, I watched instead. The tallest man reached out and touched his fingertip to a photo. Just a fingertip. Then he withdrew it and stuck his hands in his pockets. I wondered if he was fondling himself through his pocket as I had seen men do. A hot white spark of excitement rolled through my belly and my face burned with shame. Now who was the pervert?

"Watch him," Nick said, pointing to the small dark man closest to us. I watched fascinated as he first touched himself through his khakis, and then, to my surprise, unzipped his pants.

"He's..." I trailed off as he pulled his stiff cock from his pants and started to beat off. His hand a blur over the purplish flesh of his member. He stared straight ahead at whatever picture he was viewing and continued to stroke himself ferociously.

Fluid flooded into my panties and I shifted my stance, trying not to show exactly what this was doing to me. There was no way I would give Nick's betrayal any kind of approval.

"He's in his own little world," Nick sighed, running his hand over my bottom absent-mindedly. I shifted my footing again as his gentle touch added to what I was feeling inside. "He's locked there. Him, his dick, and you." Then he turned to me and touched my hair. "This is why your face isn't in

126

there, Noel. I've wanted to… share you for a very long time. I didn't' know how. Then I figured this out."

"And?" I tried to keep my voice steady, angry. How dare he without asking me first? But his soft words and obvious sincerity loosened some of the tight anger in my chest.

"And their reaction is just like my reaction is when it comes to you. How it has *always* been when it comes to you." He turned his attention back to the men so I did the same. Just in time to see the man who was so oblivious to anything but my image come in long, ropey white streams. Nick sighed.

"And what's the reaction?" I asked. Fascinated, I watched his come coat his hand and drip, as if in slow motion, to the alley floor.

"You're like a drug. To me, being with you is as high as I can get. They're only feeling a small part of what I feel every day."

Forgetting my anger and my urge to hide my arousal, I slid up against him. I watched as another man, not as brave as the one who had just brought himself to orgasm, stroked his erection through his slacks. I pushed my hips against Nicks and quickly he got behind me. He yanked up my skirt and pushed down my panties. I heard his zipper and it only increased my need and urgency.

Then he thrust up into me, my upper body pinned against the thick glass of the window. I braced myself, face and breasts smashed against the cool, smooth surface. He fucked me fast, both of us watching out the window as my pilgrims stared and touched and stroked. Nick reached around and gave my engorged clit a few slippery strokes and I came so loud I sobbed on my own release.

He stayed in me, growing softer inside my body. We watched quietly, panting in the dimming light, as they filed off one by one. When Nick pulled his cock from me and smoothed my skirt back down over my hips, the final one walked off.

"Why didn't they take them?" I asked.

"I have no idea. Maybe they're afraid if they do, there wont' be any more." He stared at me and hesitantly asked,

"Will there be any more?"

"Let's eat and we'll think about it."

Our next photo-shoot was in the basement. Nick had always wanted to tie me up and he asked rather shyly if he could. I agreed. The thought of more photos of a second pilgrimage of men to our back alley was enough to rev me up. The thought of being bound forced my pulse into a high, faltering gait.

"This is perfect," Nick said, running his fingers over the headboard of an antique bed.

The bed had been in my family for years but it wasn't my style. The brass scrollwork was oxidized and overly feminine for my taste. It had been propped on end against the basement wall since we moved in. I looked at it in a whole new light now. Standing on end it was taller than me. Maybe a little more than six feet tall. The intricate scrollwork was perfect for looping bonds through. I pressed my back up against it and put my wrists to either side of my head. Nick stared for a moment.

"Put them out to the sides more. That way I can capture your bound hands but not your face," he said softly. I did, spreading my arms like wings.

Nick bound one wrist with a bright paisley scarf. The other with a black scarf. The feel of the silk sliding against my skin, pressing the tops of my wrists to the cold brass worked a shiver through me. My nipples stood out from my own excitement and the chill of the basement.

"Spread your ankles wide," he muttered, bending down between my legs.

I wondered for a moment if a rush of fluid would escape my body when I did. I was growing wetter by the second. I spread my legs wide and watched him fasten first one ankle, then the other. I stared at my left ankle encased in yellow silk, my right bound with purple. When he raised his head and smiled, I smiled back. Then he lowered his face to my parted thighs and pushed his tongue warmly between my damp folds. I threw my head back and moaned. I was so worked up that one slow drag from his tongue sent the muscles in my belly galloping.

Nick inched closer on his knees and buried his face in my pussy. He licked and nudged and probed until I had inadvertently tested each and every bond with my restless movements. I hovered right on the edge of orgasm and my husband knew it. He knew my body like his own. He moved back on his knees and aimed the camera at my swollen cunt. The first image was captured.

I panted and pleaded for him to forget the photos and come back, but he moved around while I struggled and took pictures. When he had seven shiny photos lined up in a row he laughed.

"You were very good, Noel."

I was furious. Bound, aroused and very ready to come, he had made me wait. I pouted.

"Come on, don't be mad, I'm not done with you." Then he picked them up one by one and held them before my angry gaze.

My swollen red pussy, shining with moisture. It looked like an exotic flower. My lower belly taut as I thrashed, a blur of movement in the photo. My bound wrists straining in my bondage, hands tight little fists. My breasts, nipples stiff, swaying with my impatient movements. My feet on tip toe as I struggled, my ankles swathed in bright fabric, my calf muscles standing out proudly. A side angle of my ass and thigh. And my throat. Head tossed back, a bright rosy ring along my throat and collar bone from my anger and arousal.

When he put the last photo down I was panting. Breathless. I wanted him more than I could ever remember. He dropped back to his knees and drank from me. Softly this time. Slowly until I was one taut muscle from head to toe, straining as I came against the dusty brass.

When he fucked me, it was slow and sweet. The fact that I couldn't touch him but he could touch me pushed me head over heels into another bright white climax.

The next day, I left work early. I was that eager to get home and watch with Nick. I knew he was getting home before me and I knew he would go out and place the pictures along the Picket Fence.

He wasn't in the kitchen when I arrived, so I called out and he answered me from upstairs. I found him in our bedroom, kneeling on the chaise lounge under our largest window.

"Higher point of view?" I joked but joined him there, kneeling next to him on the sage green fabric.

"Yes. And they are already here. You missed a guy. Reached out like he was going to take one and one of the men from last time chased him off. Four of the five are from last time."

I scanned the men, recognising the four he spoke of. The fifth was younger. Possibly mid-twenties. We watched for a few minutes. A furtive stroke from one man. A shift of feet and pants from another. The young man pulled out a cell phone and dialled. I felt Goosebumps rise up on my body.

"What do you think?" I asked.

"Don't know but remember, baby, your face is not in there. Unless they get you alone and naked, no one will ever know. And I always space them out evenly so you can't tell which house they came, if any." He stroked my lower back and I pushed myself against his warm hand.

Nick worked his hand over me. Pinched my nipples, ran his palm up the inside of my thigh as we watched them. My body was humming with excitement as I gazed at the men who had gathered to see me bound and naked. I was a voyeur to their voyeurism. After a few moments, a woman strolled down the alley. She went immediately to the young man and he directed her to the Polaroids. At first she looked angry, then flushed, then as if she were calming. When he turned and spoke to the other men, she stood at his side. He pointed to his watch, made some hand gestures and all the men left. They seemed reluctant but willing.

"I think he just told them when they could come back," Nick whispered.

"Why would he do that? And why would they listen?"

"A man understands another man's needs."

"What do you mean?" I was confused.

130

"Shhh. Just watch."

So I watched. I watched the young man walk his girl forward. I watched him look at each photo of me. I watched him stop in front of the one I could only assume was his favourite.

"Your pussy," Nick told me. "All perfect and swollen and ready," he sighed, stroking the back of my thigh through my skirt.

I watched him push her face first against the fence, watched her pale forearms brace against the light wood. I watched him lift her little plaid skirt and push her pale pink panties to the side. And I watched him fuck her with almost animalistic movements as they both stared at a single picture. I watched her come and clutch at the fence. I watched his ass tense up and his jittering movements as he came inside her.

My face was hot and I peeled my own skirt off without being asked. I continued to watch out the window where he was now kneeling before her. Her slim back braced against the fence. My photo over the yellow halo of her hair. I watched him lick her clean and I watched her come again. I did all this with my hands braced on the windowsill and my ass in the air as Nick watched over my shoulder. As he rode me and stroked from the inside out. And when the young woman below came again and clutched her boyfriends black hair in her little fists, he smacked my ass really hard and drove into me.

I came with my breath fogging up the window and my knuckles white from clutching the sill. I came with my husband whispering my name like a prayer as he shot into me.

Over dinner, we held hands. After a glass of wine, we kissed. When we sat down on the sofa and I curled up around him, Nick turned to me and touched my face.

"I'm thinking Wednesdays," he said with a smile.

"Sounds good," I laughed.

"Wednesdays can be picture day," he said, running his hands along the undersides of my breasts. Cupping me there, his hands big and warm.

"And Thursdays can be the viewing day."

He laughed. "That is fine by me as long as it is fine by you."

I nodded. "It is. I don't know how it turned out that way, but it is. Nick?"

"Hmm?"

"Why do you think no one has taken them? Not a single one?"

"I have no idea, babe," he said with a little shrug. "I'm glad, cause I get to see what happens to them when they see you and then I still get to keep the pictures." He pulled me so I was lying in his lap. He stroked my hair and I made happy noises at the attention.

"What if they do?"

"It's OK. We can take more."

I smiled. I couldn't help it.

Worship

No matter what I did, my perspective was off. The woman was too large, the background too small. Disgusted, I threw down my paintbrush and walked away. This was Patrick's fault. Dick.

The tea I made tasted like dried grass, the toast I nibbled tasted like ashes. Nothing was right and nothing made me happy. I glanced at the bottle of wine and then at the clock. Two o'clock. Technically early morning. Could be viewed as late night. I shook my head. No. I wouldn't stoop to that.

Patrick was not worth drinking over.

I whitewashed the canvas, erasing the image. Stared at the gaping white maw. I hated the white in its blankness. It looked like failure. I took his CDs off the shelf, walked over them as the cracked and popped in protest. Threw the mess in the trash.

I didn't feel any better.

Why would I? Six months of my life down the crapper. Alone again. Not that I didn't prefer being alone to being with someone who didn't love me. Someone who treated me like shit. Ran around behind my back. Fucked anything that couldn't get away from him fast enough.

I preferred to be alone to that. But alone was bitter and the taste was in my mouth again.

I heard the crash and looked at the clock again. Almost three. What the hell.

I opened the door slowly aware that things such as odd noises at odd hours had been used to get a tenant to open their door. Home invasions had been all the rage for the criminals in these parts once upon a time. Even as I pulled the door slowly open my left hand was behind it, touching the baseball bat my dad had given me when I moved in.

I saw the source of the noise and let go of the bat.

'Todd? What the hell are you doing?'

My next door neighbour was staring despondently at what used to be a rather large antique mirror. Now it was a rather large antique mirror frame surrounded by shattered reflective shards.

'I couldn't sleep,' he muttered, running a hand through his hair. 'Thought I'd load some stuff in the truck for the morning haul to the antique store.'

Todd finds and sells antiques to the locals on antique row. A five-mile strip of road in western Maryland that is peppered with shops. At first I thought he had to be gay. Then one night I heard him through my bedroom wall. His bed butted up against the wall. I let go of the gay theory after four hours of headboard banging, female cooing and orgasmic sounds that rivalled any porn movie I had ever seen.

'Are you hurt?'

'No. Not hurt. Fucking stupid but not hurt. I should never tried to have moved it alone. It weighed a good hundred pounds.'

'Why didn't you knock? I would have helped you.' I squatted down and inspected the remains of the mirror. We'd need a broom or we would cut our hands to bloody ribbons.

'And why in the world would I think you'd be up at almost three in the morning?' he asked. His blue eyes looked weary but when he smiled they still crinkled in that appealing way I had always admired. Todd had a smile that touched his entire face. When he smiled at you, you instinctively smiled back.

'You're up,' I joked. 'I'll go get a broom. And a trash bag,' I added.

While I gathered the broom and the bag, I considered my outfit. Faded jeans and oversized sweater. Barefoot. I slid my feet into a pair of sneakers, not intent on having to pick mirror shards out of my feet.

'Why are you up?' he asked and I let out a shriek.

'Jesus! Don't sneak up on me. It's late, I haven't slept in

days and damn you are quiet! I could have gone all kung fu on your ass.'

This made him laugh. 'Now that, I would like to see.'

I snorted and handed him the trash bag. 'If you must know, nosey neighbour man, Patrick left me and I am way too pissed off to settle head on pillow. I can't paint, I can't sleep, I can't do anything basically. I pace, I break stuff and I try to paint. Then I start all over again.'

'Can't paint? You?'

'True story. It's all shit. And I can't settle for shit. Then I paint it white and I hate the white more. More than the shit,' I sighed. 'Now, let's go clean that mess up before another tenant cuts themselves and decides to sue you. This is the most excitement I've had in days. Let's get cracking.'

'You shouldn't hate white. It's divine. It's renewal,' he said very softly, but then with a mock salute, he followed me into the hall. I set about carefully picking up the larger pieces while Todd swept. I could feel him watching me and I knew he wanted to ask. I didn't give him the opening but I wouldn't shut him down if he gave into his curiosity. I bent to get a piece of glass roughly the size of a dinner plate and heard him sigh. It was barely audible but I froze. My ass was to him, I was stretching, I could feel the faded jeans I practically lived in stretched taut against my ass. Could that be why he was sighing? I shook my head. Now I was desperate. I was imagining an attraction that wasn't there.

'Can I ask why?' he said so softly I barely heard him over the whisper of the broom and the tinkle of glass.

'Sure. He's an asshole. That's why,' I said, then laughed outright at his shocked expression. 'I'm sorry. Still very fresh, I guess.'

He nodded and focused on his broom. 'Sorry, I asked. Really not my place.'

'It's fine,' I sighed. 'I'm sorry. I just hate to think about the six months I wasted on that loser. The sad truth is, I am apparently boring. I don't like to take risks. I think in this case risks are defined as being open to him fucking anything female and possibly a few males. Also, I take responsibility

135

seriously and I like to focus on my dream. Like to focus on my painting and continue to try to make myself as successful as possible. I don't run around and do whatever the fuck I want and blow everything off. Oh!' I could hear that my voice was raised but I couldn't help it. 'I almost forgot. I am very plain. Not much to look at. I think those were the exact words.'

I dropped the black garbage bag and burst into tears. The tears were from anger and frustration. Todd didn't know that, though. On top of it all, now I was mortally embarrassed. Then I was encompassed in big strong arms and I cried a little harder.

'Come on. We're done here. Lock up your apartment and I'll take the bag to the trash. You can help me move the frame into my place and I'll pour us a glass of wine.'

'We have to share one?' I sniffled and we both started to laugh.

'Okay, we'll splurge. We'll each have our own glass,' he whispered. I could hear the smile in his voice as he smoothed my hair. 'Go on, lock up and I'll be right back.'

I was too tired and too upset to argue. It was nice to just follow directions. Plus, I trusted Todd and it seemed painfully clear all of a sudden that I could use a shoulder to cry on. Even if it was embarrassing to look a little vulnerable.

We met back in the hall and managed to haul the enormous frame into his foyer. He led me to the sofa, sat me down and put a chenille throw on my lap, muttering, 'Chilly in here.'

When he came back with the wine, I stared into my glass for a moment. 'Technically, it's morning and only alcoholics drink in the morning,' I muttered.

'I think that it's technically still night because it's dark out and will be for a few more hours. Plus, I'm not an alcoholic and neither are you.' He took a hefty swig of his wine and grinned. 'There, I went first. It's safe. No one's looking.'

I took a sip, swirled it around on my tongue and exhaled loudly. 'Good.'

'Only the finest bottle that seven dollars can buy.' He

settled back on the sofa and looked at me. For just a moment I heard the phantom sounds of that satisfied female echoing from his bedroom. I felt a shudder work through me and shook it off. This was no time to get horny. Sure, it was obvious that he must be good in bed, but he was my neighbour and my friend.

I took another sip and felt some of the tension drain out of my body. His apartment was full of antiques and throw rugs in warm earth tones. Unusual and colorful art hung on the walls. Antique tin signs, a picture frame made from an old barn window. Nice.

'I'm sorry about the water-works,' I mumbled. I felt stupid and lost but strangely comfortable with him witnessing my disintegration.

'Hey, no big deal. It happens to us all at some point. It sucks to put time into some asshole who can't see how good he has it.' He touched my hair for just a second.

I felt the urge to kiss him and again shook off the impulse. I was being crazy. Seeking comfort in the arms of a man I truly liked to make myself feel better about getting dumped by a flaming, gaping asshole.

'Thanks. Maybe he was on to something, though. Maybe I'm not much to look at. Maybe I am too stuffy and uptight and what was the word? Oh. Driven.'

This time when he reached out, he stroked my cheek. With one finger, he traced the ridge of my cheekbone. I went liquid. Just being touched was soothing. I closed my eyes and let him touch my face. 'First, there is no such thing as being too driven when it comes to your dreams,' he said softly. His fingers brushed along the slope of my nose and I had to force myself to breathe. 'Second, you are most certainly something to look at.' When his fingers slid along my bottom lip I felt it go lax under his touch. When he swept it back the other way, I touched his finger with my tongue.

He made a low sound. It made me want to kiss him more.

'Third,' he said right in my ear and my nipples grew rigid under my sweater, 'you are not uptight. You are fierce. You are funny. You are beautiful. And you don't deserve to be abandoned. You deserve worship.'

I let out a big guffaw and opened my eyes. He was right there. His nose nearly touching mine. His lips so close to mine I felt invisible ripples of energy like a phantom kiss. 'Worship?'

His eyes were serious. Dark blue like new denim. He wasn't kidding. He nodded, his sober look never changing. 'Absolutely. Worship. You should be worshipped, Nicole. And if you let me take you to the bedroom, I'll do just that. I've waited six months for a chance and here it is.'

'That's news to me,' I blurted and felt my face burn with heat.

'Not something I thought I should announce in front of your live-in boyfriend.'

It was my turn to nod. 'True. This isn't an offer of a pity-fuck, is it?' I sighed.

He didn't answer me, he just took the throw from my lap, hooked one big hand under the crook of my knees, one under my back and stood. He didn't talk at all as he carried me back. I thought about protesting. Thought about demanding that he put me down. Instead, I leaned my head against his shoulder and closed my eyes. I was tired and to be honest, I could do with a little worship. Whether it be for an hour, the night, or a lifetime.

Todd lowered me to the bed and lifted my sweater. His apartment was drafty like mine and I felt my bare breasts tighten with goose-bumps and my nipples pucker to the point of pain. He dipped his head and ran his hot tongue over one and I jumped just a little at the temperature change. He moved to the other nipple and the muscles in my belly galloped from the stimulation.

'This is not a pity-fuck, Nicole,' he said against my belly as he kissed a trail to the top of my jeans. Todd popped the button and lowered the zipper. Brushed his warm lips against the flat of my stomach. I jumped under his mouth and I laughed just a little. 'Ticklish?'

'Just a touch,' I said. His kisses grew firmer and he pressed his mouth harder against my lower stomach. 'Better,'

I sighed and let my hands settle in his light brown hair.

'Lift,' he said and I obeyed. I lifted my hips of the mattress and he peeled my jeans down. Next went my plain cotton panties. At least they were pink. 'Now see, the man is insane,' he said and smoothed his big hands over the ridge of my hip bones and down the flare of my hips. His hands went everywhere. Slowly. He took his time stroking my thighs, my waist, the backs of my knees. Then he followed the path his hand had taken with his lips and tongue and teeth.

I lay back and just let him. I let him explore me with his fingers and hands and mouth. I realised the room wasn't so chilly and the sounds of him kissing me were as soothing as the sounds of the ocean. I felt beautiful and for the first time in days, peaceful.

'Turn over,' he commanded gently and then just as gently helped me flip. He started at the nape of my neck and my body jumped and fluttered as his soft warm lips hit the most sensitive places. He kissed and stroked my shoulder blades before moving like a warm breeze down my spine to the small of my back. All the while, his palms stroked my ass, the backs of my thighs, my hips. When I felt like I might never take another breath from his gentle worship, he slid his hands under my hips, lifted me up to his mouth and kissed first one cheek, then the other. He touched his tongue to the very top of my crack, stroking the small indentation, stimulating the bundle of nerves. I sighed loudly, relaxing into his mouth and his attentions. He slid a finger into me, then another. My cunt jumped around his fingers, adjusting and then beckoning. More. I wanted more. He slid a third finger into me and began to flex and nudge deep inside of me.

I wanted to ask him to fuck me but I didn't want his ministrations to end. Patrick had never taken any time with me. It was always a matter of practicality with him. Was I wet enough to fuck? If not, a quick squirt of lube would do. Or if I was really lucky, five or so minutes of bored oral attention. I soaked up the attention to detail. Reveled in the fascination Todd seemed to have with touching and licking and kissing every inch of me before he even entered my body. He acted as if we had all night. And we did.

'How could you think that a word of that was true?' he whispered, still swirling his fingers in the depths of me. The soft sucking sounds of his digits probing and pushing in my cunt were almost secretive. 'You're very much to look at. Your hair is the colour of sunshine. Not just any sunshine. Morning sunshine. The kind that slants across my kitchen table at about nine o'clock in the morning.' His fingers stayed busy and I felt the tightening begin. The indicator of orgasm that always made me think of pent up energy about to be unleashed.

I hummed lazily and listened to his words.

'Your eyes are the most perfect green,' he said against the side of my neck and then punctuated his words with a wet open-mouthed kiss. 'Clear and sharp like emeralds. Do you know there isn't a fleck of any other colour in your eyes. Only green. No striations of blue or brown. I've never seen eyes that were pure green before. And never that colour.' He bit me gently on the shoulder and pushed hard against my G-spot. The first tentative flutter of orgasm echoed deep inside of me.

This time I did not hum, I sighed and followed quickly with a moan of pleasure. 'Todd–'

'I'm not done,' he said softly. I was going to give in, ask him to fuck me. That's where this was going and I figured I'd tend to him a little. His voice said he was perfectly fine right where we were. 'You have the most perfect ass I have every seen. One time, when you came out to get your paper,' he laughed softly before continuing, 'you were wearing a white nightgown. Nothing under it. And the sunlight from the hall window backlit you as you walked back in, spectacular. A true hour glass. So feminine and lush and beautiful.' On that word, another bite, this one a little harder and a deliberate flick of his fingertips deep in my cunt.

I sang out as I came. I don't know what I was singing but I know it was spiritual. The most beautiful orgasm ever. Crushing in its intensity, profound in its depth, divine in its origins – time and appreciation. I was being worshipped.

Todd rested his head in the hollow of my shoulder, working his fingers deep in me, pressing his lips against my now hot skin. He lovingly worked every drop of pleasure out of my orgasm. Wave after wave, each one growing weaker but no less pleasurable than the one before. When the last one faded, he pulled me taught against him, my face still resting on the mattress.

'And let's not forget your laugh, how it's infectious. Or your talent. Your art breathes, it's alive. And your kindness ...'

The tears came again. Luckily, no embarrassment came with them. With deeps sobs I let each thing go. The hurt, the deception, the painful words, the empty space that felt like it would swallow me up. With each new wave of sorrow he smoothed big warm hands over me. Touching me gently as I fell apart. It felt good.

After a moment, I heard the whisper of his clothes. The quiet sound of fabric hitting the floor.

'Let's turn you over,' he said and when I looked into his face he was smiling. I smiled back and turned willingly, as if boneless when he positioned me on my back. He pushed my legs open reverently, touched me slowly to make sure I was still wet and ready.

I was.

With any other man, under any other circumstances, I would have called him a pig. Viewed this as the lowest way to get laid I could imagine. But in the moment, looking at his face, replaying his words in my head, it resonated. It was real. There was nothing malicious in his face. His face was intent, his expression solemn but his eyes never stopped soaking me in.

The head of his cock nudged at me and my body instinctively fluttered around it, trying to draw him deeper. He hissed slightly with pleasure and that made the urgent flutter all the more demanding. I opened my legs just a tad wider, telling him with my body that I was ready. I understood. Without question, he slid into me, those beautiful eyes never leaving mine. They roamed over my face as if he could see

141

something I could not. Maybe he could.

He didn't close his eyes or bury his face in my shoulder as most men would, he stared into my eyes as he moved. Each thrust a little harder as the contours of his face shifted and sharpened. He was getting close and as I stared back into the blue of his gaze, I felt a thrill unfurl from my cunt to the top of my head. One long, unwinding ribbon of ecstasy. And peace.

He tugged me up by my wrists, his body bowing back some to accommodate. Like a human see-saw. We balanced each other as he thrust faster and deeper into me. My arms flexed, my head lolled, and I floated up with his strength. He delivered my worship on the swells and dips of another orgasm, the dark behind my eyelids blossomed with white flowers. White stains. I am used to sparks of colours, undulating waves of red or blue or green when I come. These were simply white. Virginal and pure, sipping up the black with every pulse that worked through my body. I heard his own cries of pleasure, soft and somehow muted as if his own climax was an afterthought. When he lowered me gently, arranged my limbs, wrapped himself around me, I continued to witness the dance of white behind my lids. Keeping time with the slowly fading echoes of pleasure.

'How do you feel?' he whispered as if afraid he may break some magical spell.

I inhaled the scent of him, watched the white begin to fade. When he pulled me close, my body instinctively mimicked his. I melted and bent into the form of him. If I thought it possible, I might have tried to climb inside of him. 'Clean. I feel clean.'

For the first time in days, I fell asleep.

Rebound Guy

Perry is my rebound guy. He's basically around to help me get over Scott. Not a problem. I can hang in for a bit. It's good to have the company. The sex. A person to hang out with. I haven't told him outright that he's just a filler. I assume he knows. Six years of intense relationship does not disappear over night but a girl has needs. Perry is good in bed.

I put the finishing touches on the outfit and steel myself for the evening. I love spending time with Perry but most of his friends make me want to chew my own wrists open. Tonight we are going to a party throw by Don and Diana. I hate them for many reasons but the foremost are their names. The double D thing. Also, they talk too fucking much.

I am told the party is to celebrate some big event in their relationship. I couldn't give a hoot about their relationship. Or them. However, an appearance at the shindig guarantees two things: really good liquor as they go for only the best and, most importantly, I will get laid.

When I answer the doorbell, Perry does a quick scan of my ensemble and smiles.

"Nice. I like the skirt. You look gorgeous."

"Thank you," I laugh. Even in heels I have to stand on tiptoe to kiss him. I am not short. At nearly six feet tall, Perry towers over me a good five or six inches. He is tall and big all over and I like that. I like that he makes me feel small whereas with most men I can stare them straight in the eye even while barefoot. "Now, about this party," I say and light a cigarette.

Perry frowns at my smoke. He doesn't like it that I smoke. He really doesn't like that I smoke around him. But, like I said, he is the rebound guy. He'll just have to deal with it.

"We don't have to stay long, Erin," he sighs in response to my unasked question. "And must you smoke around me? Really?" His green eyes turn a little grey with what I can only assume is frustration. Maybe anger. Whatever.

"Sorry, I'm nervous," I say and wave the smoke away from him as best I can. "I can assume that as usual I will be stuffed with jumbo shrimp and premium vodka and regaled with tales of love in the world of marriage?" I grin to make sure he knows I am joking. Kind of.

"Probably. Now if you can crush that death stick out we can go on our way and get this over with." He puts his big arm around me and guides me out of the apartment. He locks my door and takes my arm. I let him do all this because I like it when a man is in charge and even though he isn't, I let him think he is for now.

On the way to the car, I light another cigarette and listen to him let out a low growl. I smile at him as I pass through a puddle of light that spills from the street lamp. "Don't you want to know what's under my skirt?" I ask both to tease him and to make sure he knows that I fully intend getting fucked by him tonight.

"Of course I do. But can I guess?" He unlocks the car, waits for me to crush out the smoke and sit. Then he shuts my door. Ever the gentleman. When he gets in the driver's side he raises his eyebrows and waits.

I notice how big his hands are on the steering wheel. I've never really noticed before. "Sure. Guess," I whisper as I study his broad palms, long, thick fingers and square shiny fingernails.

"Purple thong. The one with the little gold circle dead centre in the back. I love that triangle. I always try to see if I can fit the very tip of my tongue through the little hole."

I swallow hard and can hear a dry click in my throat. Will I even make it to the fucking party? I wonder. I shake my head like a dog shaking off water. "Nope. Try again."

He caresses the steering wheel and I think of his hands doing that to my skin. That and more. The soft sounds of his rough hands caressing my skin and then, in my mind, the sound of that huge hand delivering a first delicious blow on my ass cheek. I suck in a breath and he cocks his head and grins at me.

"The white one. Same panties, different colour."

"Nope." In my mind I can see his big fingers sliding into my pussy. Disappearing from view but doing secret magical things deep inside me where I can't see them. I shift in the leather seat and it gives a seductive sigh as I move.

"Hmm. Are they new? They must be. After a month, I am usually very good at this game."

I nod. He gets a point. "They are. They are new."

Perry moves his hand to my thigh and heat flows up my thigh into my chest straight to my throat. I can feel my chest blushing crimson the way it does when I get horny. A scarlet stain of desire that I refuse to be ashamed of. "Let's see them," he whispers and leans in to kiss the hot blush on my skin. Just so I know he sees it, I assume.

I sigh and it sounds loud in the quiet of the closed car. "Okay, but then we go. The sooner we go, the sooner we can leave," I say, exercising my control. I turn to the side and raise my ass. He lifts my skirt almost daintily. As if it is made of vintage lace instead of soft, faded denim.

When he laughs, I smile out the window. He thinks it's funny. I think it's funny that he most likely assumes it's a joke. Sex with Perry is good but vanilla. Hot but generic. I always come but none of my kinks show up to play. I don't know if it's that I don't trust him yet or that I don't trust myself. Perhaps I am not ready to bare all to someone else after a six-year relationship.

He reads it aloud and I let him. "*Spank Me*. Nice. So, you want people to spank you, Erin?"

"Only those who read my panties," I joke but a shiver runs through me as I say it. In some small way I have let him in on a secret. One I doubt he had figured out. One part of me wants him to know and another part of me fears him knowing.

"Ready?" Perry asks as he smoothes a big hand over my bottom. Then without waiting for my answer he starts the car.

We are off to Don and Diana's place. The excitement is overwhelming. OK, so I'm lying.

I relinquish my coat and accept a vodka with a twist when we enter. The place is full of beautiful people in expensive clothes sipping booze that costs more than my rent. I sip too. I play along. I sink into the false security of being around people who have way more money than I can even dream of. That is fine. Money isn't everything. When I feel overwhelmed, I imagine them going to bed every night in their satin pyjamas and having sex in the missionary position. Not everything can be slapped with a price tag. When was the last time Don had spanked Diana until her cheeks were the colour of ripe summer cherries? How many times had she relished the hot welted skin of her bottom that proved that he owned her? How many times had she braced herself on hands and knees while he fucked her up the ass until she screamed? How many times had he given her twenty lashes with a whip? I had to smile just trying to imagine it. I would take my priceless orgasms over their pricey booze any day.

I walk into the next room and hear Perry's deep, comfortable voice. "Erin works for a rehab company. She prepares resumés and assists on job searches for people who have been injured in their current occupations." It sounds like he's bragging but I realize how very boring it sounds. Yes, it sounds boring but it really isn't. I smile at him and he smiles back.

I finally get him alone and I sip my vodka and whisper, "So, this big thing in Don and Diana's relationship … what is it? Renewing the vows? Baby? They learned to do it doggy style?" I ask and laugh. "I'm sorry. That was rude."

He doesn't frown, though. He just brushes my long dark locks out of my face and kisses my nose. "No. They have switched over to an open marriage. This is a coming out party, so to speak."

I feel my mouth open and close. I feel my cheeks heat and my chest flush again. Don and Diana? An open marriage? It had to be a fucking joke. Those two? The straightest of straight, the plainest of vanilla. Perry is laughing and I feel like I can't breathe.

"Joking," I say, "you are joking." He must be. It is the only explanation.

But Perry shakes his head and his almost black hair sways with the movement. I notice that here and there is a touch of silver. Just enough to make my new panties moist at the crotch. For the second time, I notice how very big and compelling his hands are.

I glance into the corner and see Don kissing a blonde. She is not Diana. She is tall and willowy. The back of her red dress barely hides the swell of her ass. Barely contains her ass crack. I swallow and my heart beats an erratic drunken rhythm.

"How about those panties?" Perry asks and I blink at him. I stare at him and wonder if somehow I got drunk and didn't notice.

"What?"

"I think that would certainly liven things up, don't you?" he asks and his hand when it touches my wrist is cold from holding his drink.

"My panties?" I say dumbly, unable to process that this man that I have written off is now provoking my very own kinks.

"Yes. *Spank me*. It says so right on them. White cotton bikinis, size medium according to the tag. It's an invitation, or am I mistaken?"

"What?" I sound stupid. I feel stupid. But my body is not and it is reacting to the information it is processing. My pussy has grown slick, my nipples have peaked and are attentive. My face feels like it is on fire and my breathing has gone shallow like I might pass out.

"Everyone!" He is no longer addressing me. He is now addressing the room. My head goes light as my cunt goes tight. "I think we have a lovely way to celebrate Don and Diana's new outlook on marriage. I have a special treat for you all!"

Half sideshow barker, half Baptist minister, he addresses the small gathering. "Perry!" I hiss. "Perry!"

147

He ignores me.

Perry takes my hand and I follow. I follow blindly, mutely, dumbly. I follow because part of me craves this more than anything. He sits on a celery-coloured settee and pulls me down next to him. "I propose a sound thrashing for my lovely companion. Her name is Erin. We've been dating for about a month now. I am the rebound guy."

The crowd chuckles in unison. Some of them tsk with disapproval but Perry raises his palms to calm them. He nods and smiles as if to say, *It's okay, I understand*. I feel my face grow hotter. Any hotter and I might lose consciousness. I bow my head both embarrassed and excited all at once.

"No, no, don't be that way," he goes on. "Erin is wearing very special panties and I would like to share them … share her with all of you. For tonight. In honour of Don and Diana."

I could leave. I know it. I could get up, slap his face, walk out. I do not. I wait.

Perry pats his lap and I stare for a moment. I breathe for several beats and weigh my options. The itching, creeping yearning is bigger than my pride and I hit the floor with my knees, bow my torso over his lap. I wait.

"Very good, Erin," he say slowly. "I wondered if you would or wouldn't." With that he flips up the back of my denim skirt and bares my white cotton panties with the hot pink words to the room. A low murmur sweeps through the gathering and he waits.

Quiet descends and he hooks his fingers into my waistband and pulls my panties down. The air and the stares and the wonder are as palpable to my bare skin as his blows will be. "Lovely, isn't she?" Perry says, addressing the crowd. "Are you up for ten?" he asks, now addressing me.

My stomach flutters and my knees shake. I feel a slow slickness grow between my thighs, slipping down the insides of my legs like water. My cunt flickers and clutches and flits. I squirm a little on his knees and my nipples pinch under my silk bra. I nod, not trusting my voice.

"I invite you all to count with me!" Perry barks and another murmur ripples through the room.

The first blow lands and my head flies back. I want him to fuck me right then and there. If not him, someone. Any man in the room that comes with a cock attached will do. His big palm blazes a trail on my pale skin and I cry out in pain and in excitement.

The blows rain down and with each the crowd gets louder. By the time they say five in unison, the sound of them hurts my ears. I see Diana in the corner. Her brown eyes wide, pupils dilated, cheeks flushed. She is shifting in place. She is wet and horny and ready under her plain blue dress. I know because I have worn that look before. I, however, do not need to worry about decorum because I am writhing on Perry's lap like a dog in heat.

We are up to eight and when he smoothes his hands over my ass, his fingers brush the seam of my sex. Tease around my clit. Hint at slipping deep inside me and bringing me all the way up to the peak where I want to be. I bite my tongue and focus on breathing. Two more to go and then I can see where it is he wants to go.

"Nine!" the crowd sings out in an overwhelmingly loud voice. I buck and squirm and wonder how red my ass is. How many welts I have. How my pussy looks, swollen and wet and bare to the men who are behind me. I wonder how many of them will masturbate or fuck their wives tonight picturing my tortured ass and my dripping cunt.

"TEN!" The sound is like a summer storm that has been contained in a single room. A crack and roar made up of excited voices and sexual energy.

I go limp on Perry's lap. I let the tears fall even as I relish the searing heat on my skin and the echoes of that heat deep inside me where I am wet and ready.

Perry bends and pulls up my panties, smoothes my skirt. Then he whispers, "Let's go."

I nod. I rise. I stand tall and proud as if I have just delivered a speech. Not at all like a woman who has been spanked in front of a room full of near strangers. Both Don and Diana hug me and whisper, "thank you" in my ear.

I might have been wrong about them.

149

Out on the street, on the way to the car, Perry runs his hand over my ass. Even through the denim it stings. I wince but I grow wetter still under my panties. I want him. I want him to fuck me. With his fingers, with his cock, with his tongue. Whatever he wants, however he wants, I want it too.

"I took a chance," he laughs. He opens the car and kisses my nose. "I know I'm just the rebound guy."

His eyes are large and sincere. Only a hint of his authority shines through. It is a statement not a question. No self-pity, just a fact.

I stare back. Remember the sting and the power and the control he has just wielded over me. I smile, let my hand sit on the thumping heat of my skin. I imagine what we will do when we get home. "Yeah, I'm not so sure about that," I say and slide onto the leather seat and let him shut the door.

Stick Garden

'What in the world is this?' I couldn't keep the laughter out of my voice even as Maddy frowned.

'It will be a garden.'

'What kind? A stick garden?'

She stood, deep red hair – the colour of Japanese maple leaves in autumn – swaying with the movement. 'No. Right now is the fall planting. There'll be vines, vegetables, tomato bushes and corn come the summer ...'

'And on her farm she had some sticks ...' I teased, singing in my best Southern accent.

Maddy swatted my ass with her slender but fast hand and I yelped. 'Enough of that, Nina, or no reaping of the goods for you.'

'But I live to reap,' I said and winked.

I teased her all through dinner about the stakes she'd driven into that large bare patch out back. She'd driven them down and tilled the soil and the whole thing was lit by marvellous moonlight by the time we went to bed.

I fell asleep fast. We live out in the middle of nowhere. A mile to the nearest house. There's hardly any noise out there at all, especially in the fall when the tourists head back to the cities.

She had the silk scarf knotted in the centre so the knot rested in my mouth like a ball gag. She tied it on me before I was even really awake. 'What are you doing?' I asked, but of course it was muffled and she had no idea what I was saying.

'Come on then, Miss Smarty Pants,' Maddy said in her no-nonsense way. She rarely raised her voice or showed high emotion. It was all about how quiet Maddy got. The more upset she was, the softer her voice. 'We'll show you the power of a garden.'

I fought but only for a second. I'd had nothing to do with bondage or submission or any of it before Maddy. But she saw something in me and the first time she told me to lie across her lap my world had changed. She marched me downstairs and I barely kept up with her in my tired stumbling steps.

'You shouldn't poke fun of things that will nourish you,' she told me sternly. My neck flared with goosebumps as my brain kicked into gear and I realised she was leading me out back. And I was naked.

'You've got a quick tongue, but how about my hard work? How about the teasing? How about the food that will feed you when harvest time comes?'

I shook my head. I had no way to say I was sorry. I had no way to tell her I hadn't realised how important it all was. But I knew deep down that she was about to extract her apology from my body. She would make me pay. And then she would reward me for my courage.

Two things happened simultaneously. My stomach buzzed with nervous energy and a hint of fear, and my pussy went wet and soft.

'What you need is some perspective. Let's take you out to the *stick* garden,' she said, and I shook with the chill of the fall night.

I put the brakes on and dug my heels into the soft earth. I could smell the dirt that she'd just turned and the moist scent of dew on greens. I could smell the autumn leaves beginning their breakdown cycle so everything smelt musky and rich. I dug my heels in and stared up at the fat white moon and shook my head. No.

It was a mistake, I knew it. But her small hand – so fucking small you'd never guess it powerful or wicked – landed on my ass and the crack reached my ears before the pain truly registered. But it did register and a searing heat lit up my right ass cheek like a flame was licking at my skin.

'Did you just tell me no?'

I blinked, tears prickling the inner edges of my eyes. My nipples stood out hard, cold and yet excited by the whole scenario. Teased erect by air and intent and lust for this woman.

I shook my head no again.

'I didn't think so.' She prodded me with her knee to the back of mine and I let her guide me dead centre into a white stain of moonlight. Maddy turned me and whispered against my neck 'Put your arms out, brat.' She kissed me hard even as my arms flew out to my sides in my obedience.

'Good. That's better.'

With a leather thong she took from her pocket, she tied first one wrist and then the other. I stood spread-eagled in the garden, each arm bound to one of her stakes. Maddy stepped back to stare and I realised how unbelievably bright the moon was. It was like a small spotlight on our little scene.

'What a pretty scarecrow,' she whispered and stepped forward to run her hand up the inside of one thigh before moving to the other. I shook as if I had a fever. I prayed she'd touch me where I needed it most.

I moved my hips just a bit, hoping against hope she wouldn't notice.

Maddy laughed and my heart jumped. 'Now did you think I wouldn't pick up on that little twist of the hips, Nina-pie? Bad, bad girl.' The swat to my ass landed and my back bowed briefly with the force of the blow. She was small, but she was a badass.

I shook my head no again. Maddy had taken my power of speech. More than ever I was at her mercy, bound out here and gagged. No way to call for help, not that help was anywhere near our house on any given day. The thought of being under her small talented thumb made my cunt flex with anticipation. I shut my eyes and said a prayer for relief. A touch, a kiss, a stroke.

Instead I got the sharp feel of a stick running the back of my leg as Maddy paced around me. 'You need to realise out here in the garden, that under the sun the plant will find warmth and light, and it will flourish.'

Maddy ran her hand over my hair, stroking me like a cat. Petting me. I shut my eyes to soak in the sensation of her gentle touch. Her hand slid down my neck, brushing my shoulders with a lulling attention. I sighed against the knotted scarf, letting her touch me however she wanted. The point is that she was doing it at all.

She traced the curve of my spine, ticking off each knob of bone until she hit my lower back and then palmed my bottom. I forced my body to be still. I forced my mind to stay unfocused and malleable. From behind, she slipped her finger into my pussy, even as her other hand guided the stick she held to scratch along my lower calf. The two sensations together confused my body – kept me off balance.

Her hand fell away and I sighed, moving like a leaf in the wind. I tossed and turned gently in my bonds, hoping against hope for more contact. Maddy clucked her tongue as she came into view; she shook her head and said, 'Try and behave, girl.'

I shivered seeing the glint in her eye. I knew that look. I nodded; my only recourse.

'When the rain comes,' she said, tracing the inside of my legs with that damn stick – a nod to my bratty comment about her stick garden, 'it will help the plant stay ... moist.'

The stick hit the fragile skin at the top of my thigh. She gave it a good whack and the flesh let loose a spark of pain. But my pussy went wet all the same, a magical process. The sharp bite of pain and then the pleasure bleeding in right behind it. The first time Maddy had spanked me, I'd laughed and cried simultaneously and then had simply gone boneless when she fucked me to orgasm with her fingers.

Whack, whack, whack went the stick and my heart lodged firmly in my throat as I tried so hard to breathe and not weep.

'The plant will get sun and get water. The plant will grow.' *Whack.*

'The plant will twine around these sticks, as you call them, and the plant will thrive.' *Whack.*

'The garden will not be a barren patch full of stakes and

furrows and naked dirt. It will be green and lush.' *Whack*.

'It will be sexy and abundant.' *Whack*.

I found myself nodding with her lecture. Nodding like a mindless, desperate bobblehead as she preached to me for putting down a garden she had clearly thought out, adored and worked to bring into reality. For *us*.

'It's for me and you, Nina, a gift to our home. A source of nourishment. Something we'll work together – as a couple. The woman I love and hard work out in the sunshine.' *Whack, whack, whack* ... She alternated, hitting the top of one thigh and then the other, but never ever hitting my clit. Never ever stroking it or even smacking it. She left welts that I could feel riding the tops of my legs like ridges of heat along my skin.

Maddy dropped the stick and my blood leapt. I tried to breathe but the adrenaline in my body was filling my veins, shutting down my logical thoughts. I trembled and the wind blew hard to lick at my naked illuminated skin.

She ripped the scarf from my lips and stepped in closer, toe to toe, face to face, barely an inch between us. 'Say you're sorry.'

'I'm sorry, baby. So sorry.'

'Were you bad?'

'I was bad.'

'Will you work hard in our garden? The one I've wished for us since we bought this land?'

I nodded, in my head demanding she kiss me, forgive me, touch me. 'I will. I will work hard with you. And then I'll cook our food and we'll eat and we'll can vegetables and we'll ...' I trailed off, losing track of my own babble.

'Tell me you love me,' Maddy said, her dark eyes darker in the moonlight. Her red hair nearly black in the silver air.

Oh that was easy. 'I love you, I love you, baby.'

She nodded. 'Good.' Then she pushed the knotted scarf back past my lips and smiled. 'To keep you quiet.'

When she dropped to her knees I did weep, tears streaking hot lines down my cold face. Her mouth found me, her lips pressed my pussy lips. Her scalding little tongue found my clit and she pressed hard with just the tip. Then with broad

155

flat licks she brought me close, right to the edge. Maddy stopped, laughing hard. 'Not so fast, smartass.' She held me still with her strong little hands.

Her fingers tickled over the welts she'd created. She pressed the fragile skin until I shimmered under her. I tried to pull away and she bit one welt just hard enough that a rush of fluid slid from my pussy. 'Does that hurt?' she asked, as if she didn't know.

I nodded, blips of pain firing off under my skin. She moved so that her hand slipped inside me. Fingers pressed deep into my cunt, curling in a come-hither gesture and my knees sagged. Cold and weak and tethered, I mumbled under the gag, *Pleasepleaseplease* ...

Maddy took pity on me. Pressed her lips back to me, licking me in silverfish darts as her fingers delved deeper, nudged my G-spot and I sighed.

'Come on now. Come for Mamma.'

She nipped my clit and the waterfall of pain did me in. I came with a muffled cry that had her chuckling in the sterling moonlight.

I gripped the stakes with a death grip until she pried me loose – finger by finger. She yanked the gag free. 'Come on now. Let go so we can get inside.'

'Inside?'

'You're going to get on your knees for me,' she said. 'Finish making this up to me.'

'Yes, ma'am.'

'Such a good girl,' she said and picked up her stick.

Pants on Fire

It's the first warm day of the year. Something about that first really warm day always makes me feel sexy. Ready to shed clothes and show some skin. Even if that skin is pale from months of sweaters and jeans. But I like to bask in the sun on the first warm day. Marc likes to grill.

The skirt is new. The panties are small. Flip-flops on my feet and painted toenails. A short-sleeved deep v-neck tee and I'm in heaven. I want to feel the wind on my face and my skin. Smell the fresh-cut grass. The neighbourhood is alive with the sounds of lawnmowers and week whackers. I listen to my thongs as I walk and I can't help but laugh.

Thwack, thwack…thwack twhack…

The sounds of spring.

"Chicken. I'm thinking chicken with barbeque sauce. Green beans. You can steam those inside and maybe some fresh bread." His handsome face is hopeful and alive and glowing from being kissed by the sun. It seems like we haven't seen the sun in months.

"Why is it that your head always turns to food when the weather turns?" I laugh.

"Michelle, need to know that man make fire. Man make fire then man make food," he grunts at me and when I pass him, he smacks my ass hard and I let out a little yelp.

"Hands to yourself," I snort and lower myself onto the chaise longue. I stretch my long legs out and sigh with happiness. I'll let them get just a touch of sun and then I'll coat myself in SPF 45 from head to toe.

"Why? You're gonna prance around in that … what is that? Is that scrap of denim supposed to be a skirt?"

I laugh again and close my eyes. In a moment he'll be back to food and fire.

"And a deep v. See how deep that v is. It makes me want to stick my face between your tits."

I'm smiling, eyes still closed, but his banter is making me wet. Between my legs a nice steady moist pulse has begun. "Hmmm," I say, noncommittally.

"You've painted your toenails. Let's see. What should we call that colour."

'Sweet Wine'

"Vixen red. That's it. That colour is most certainly meant to seduce men with spring fever. And then the flip-flops. Well, might I say, nothing like long toes and elegant feet."

I almost laugh again but it dies in my throat because now he is caressing my foot and the feeling of his hand on me shoots straight to my centre. Someone touching my feet has never been a big turn on but now, all of a sudden, it is staggering in its sensuality. His hand circles my ankle, gripping me, and just stays there. My skin feels like it's circled with fire where his skin is touching my skin. The sun that was just warm a few moments before is now a searing heat and I feel my skin flush but I shiver.

"And then we have your legs," he goes on.

"The same legs I've always had," I attempt to tease, but my voice is taut and my cunt is thumping and my nipples have pebbled against my blouse. What I really want to do is moan, not tease.

"The same legs I have been obsessed with all these years," he teases back but his voice is much more in control than mine. He releases my ankle and his hands are sliding up the insides of my thighs. I twitch under the pressure. He reaches the hem of my short skirt and stops, fingers splayed up under the fabric. So close to my panties. So close to the part of me that wants him the most. He stops. Right there. And lets his hands rest innocently on my skin. My mouth is dry and my pulse is pounding in my ears.

"You're stopping?" I whisper.

"All I'm interested in is food, remember?" His deep

throaty laugh fills my ears. I keep my eyes closed because if I see that evil smile I just might die of frustration.

"True. Mostly."

"Am I interested in food. Or am I interested in eating?"

That gets me. Right there. My breath freezes in my throat. "We'd have to go inside."

"Now why would we go inside on a lovely day like this."

A little pool of my own hot moisture escapes me and my panties are sticking to my clit. I would do anything to have them off me at that moment. To let the warm spring breeze blow over my naked sex.

He reads my mind, pushes his fingers up higher and strokes the drenched cotton crotch of my panties. I hear myself make a low sound. A sex sound. He lets me plead with my noises for a minute and then hooks the sides of my panties with his fingers and tugs them off. We're outside in the sun on a lounger and he's going to fuck me. Of that I am certain. The fact that we could be seen somehow makes it better. High fence or not, you just never know who's looking out of their upstairs window on a beautiful spring day.

I have my eyes clamped shut and I'm doing my best to breathe. He slides a finger into me, plays me softly at first. Even though I can't see him, I can somehow feel his head moving toward me. I can feel the air shift and change around me. And then his mouth is clamped onto me, wet and burning and I push up. Grind up. Force myself against his lips and tongue in demanding, steady bucks of my hips.

Warm and slick and quick his mouth moves over me. Never giving me time to adjust or sink into the pleasure. Constantly shifting his rhythm and pressure. Another finger joins the first and then a third. I feel myself stretch and pulse because the fullness is intoxicating. He withdraws the third finger and slides it slowly into my ass. Hand trapped inside of me, mouth smashed against me.

I sigh. When I come it's long and liquid and makes me feel boneless. Marc doesn't stop, though, that is his favourite thing. To just keep going, getting every drop of me he can. He knows me so well that his licks and kisses are feather-light now. I am sensitive and each drag of his tongue is an exquisite torment.

He flexes his fingers deep inside of me, coaxing every last flitter and spasm from my cunt and his voice is raspy when he says, "Turn over on your belly."

I turn without question. The sun that has been staining the inside of my eyelids red is now warming the back of my long, dark hair. I lie on my belly and he pulls his fingers free of me. I feel empty for a moment. The sound of his zipper tells me it won't be for long.

When he climbs on the chaise it groans with the added weight but holds. His cock nudges me, pushing insistently. He slides into me with a groan and I press my legs together hard to make my entrance even tighter.

"Fuck." That's all he says.

I nod. Yes, please. Fuck.

His body is pressed against mine, covering me and shielding me from the sun. I love the feel of him, slow and easy but with a barely restrained urgency. For just a second I remember that someone could be watching us right now. Watching as he fucks me from behind surrounded by bright green grass, glaring sun and butterflies. I tighten again and a shiver works along my spine.

"Will you come for me again?" he says and I can only nod.

For just a second his cock slips free of me. I take the time to slide my hands under my hip bones to angle myself higher. I let my fingers play over my swollen clit as he tries to enter me again. For just a second the head of his cock presses against my ass and he groans. That's what he would like. I know this and I smile.

Then he's back in me, sliding in and nearly out. Dragging out each second of friction and pressure. I stroke my clit harder until with a final forceful thrust I come again. A painted rainbow streaking behind my eyelids. I press my face into the mesh lawn chair to stifle my cries.

Marc continues to fuck me, slow and easy now. I can't help myself. I turn my head and with a voice weak from orgasm I say, "You really want to fuck me up the ass, don't you?"

"That's not why I'm doing this," he says, steadying himself on two strong arms. Staying still inside of me. The length of his cock steady and hard inside me.

"Liar."

"Not lying." I can hear the smile in his voice.

"Liar, liar pants on fire," I taunt.

"Pants on fire," he concedes with a chuckle.

"Go on then," I say and lift my hips, forcing him to move with me.

"Ah, Michelle…" he says and it sounds almost like he's praying.

When he slicks me with my own juices I relax into it. Gone is my fear of this act. It took me some time to like it. Now I crave it at times. Times like now. He slides one finger into my ass, slowly and carefully stretching me until my body gives in and relaxes. Then a second finger. He flexes inside of me and my heartbeat speeds up my pussy thump. Newly empty the alternate stimulation creates a sweet ache.

He presses against me, the big blunt head of his cock seeking entrance. I take a deep breath, relax, press back against him. There it is. That sweet, intense burst of pain that somehow only serves to excite me more. The head is in, then half the shaft, and in this part of me I can truly feel each millimetre of him as he pushes.

"Is it enough?"

"It is." My heart flutters because he's afraid of hurting me. My own moisture is serving its purpose, though, and all I feel is the pleasure of being unbelievably full. I want to come again. I want to come *with* him this time.

"You feel so fucking good," he says. He always says that when he fucks my ass and I always love to hear it.

I stroke my now tender clit, then give into what I really want. I shove two fingers into my cunt, grind against the heel of my hand. His body weight and frantic movements are bumping me hard against my own palm.

The chaise longue protests as Marc forgets timing and gives over to the feel of me. To the call of his body for release.

"Fuck, Michelle, I'm …"

And I come with him. Hard. I feel him spill into me, filling me with more heat as I come in a long, lazy wave. My body deliciously exhausted and filled.

He settles onto me, kissing the back of my neck, tangling his fingers into my hair.

"Remember how I said all you think about is food?" I ask, flexing my toes warmed from the sun.

"Yeah."

"I lied."

"Pants on fire," he laughs and lays his head down next to mine.

One More Night

She was rushing past the cottage two doors up from hers when she heard, 'Hey there Little Red Ryder Hood ...' and froze.

The deep baritone with accompanying backup slammed her back ten years. The hair on Ryder's neck rose up in a ghostly wave of fine blonde down and she spun, feeling off kilter already. Her eyes sought but could not find the singer, until she heard a deep chuckle that slammed her in the belly like a cotton-wrapped fist.

'Hubie! Joe?' she called. Feeling a little desperate, a lot crazy. 'Guys?'

There was no way. She had not seen them in nearly a year. No way at all, and yet she knew it now. Could feel it in her bones, that heavy knowing that mimicked the feeling she got after recovering from a long illness like flu or a drawn-out bout with a fever. A deep-seated awareness came over her.

The song that was being hummed somewhere in the trees sealed the deal. It was the boys out there. Ryder stomped her foot. 'Hubert Sullivan Usher! Joseph Michael Palmer! Come out this instant!'

And then she waited. Was she crazy?

No. They stepped into the clearing, one tall and dark and gruff like a bear in a man suit. The other long and lean and ethereal. Ice blue eyes and pale blond hair. The boys.

They had been friends all through college. Inseparable – the three of them. Friends, only, no funny business. But for that one night.

'So no man yet? No marriage, no kiddies, no picket fences?

It's been nearly a year, woman,' Hubie said. His deep voice was like a warm hand sliding up her neck and in the orange glow of the fire pit Ryder shivered.

'Nope. I have a thriving jewellery business. I have books, friends, good wine, nights out, invoices and paycheques.' She grinned. 'But none of that.'

Joe smiled, his eyes somehow surreal in the glowing flash of heated light. 'Hubie doesn't either, so don't listen to him. Nor do I.'

He said the last in that prissy, proper way that made him so endearing to her. She loved his almost stuck-up, uptight ways. But in Joe was a heart of gold and an old soul.

And a cock that could work miracles. Soft lips that know how to kiss. Really know how to kiss – and eat pussy. He rocked you to more than one orgasm while Hubie was ...

But she let that memory drift away on a curl of wood smoke. She couldn't go there. It had been one night a long, long time ago. Her 20th birthday. It had happened – just happened – after her drunken salute to herself and their youth. Her long monologue about their love for each other and how it would still fade, because nothing lasted for ever. It would fade and so would their youth. They were only going to be young once, only going to love each other this fiercely once. And how special were they that they had found each other. Three kindred spirits, friends, almost family but something more. She had let all the muzzy-headed words tumble out and then she had toasted herself and then them.

And then the boys had taken her. No one discussed it. It had just happened. A mix and turn and shift of three bodies. A mélange of forms and naked parts and soft words and cries. Orgasms and skin on skin and laughter and, at the end, a satiated peace and sleep.

The morning brought reality and no one had ever mentioned it again.

'... selling to?' Hubie said.

Ryder shook her head and tried to draw back the words that had come before the end of his sentence. She couldn't. 'I'm sorry. I spaced out on that. What?'

Hubie grinned, and cocked his head as if he had been tiptoeing through her mind. Reliving that night so long ago with her. 'I said, Ryder the daydreamer, your jewellery, who are you selling it to?'

'Oh! Tourists and some local new channels have been purchasing. Which is great, because then it ends up on TV and in the credits. And some local boutiques.'

'What were you thinking?' Joe said softly, grinning, poking the embers with a stick as he tapped his toe in the sand around the fire pit. His big foot was sheathed in his normal boat shoes, his khaki shorts knee length, his button-down shirt rolled and pushed to his elbows. Normal Joe – preppy chic.

'I was thinking about the jewellery show I'm doing tomorrow. How I should head off to my cabin and go to bed. I was thinking that this beer sucks ass,' she lied, taking the final swig.

'You were thinking about us,' Joe said, calling her bluff.

'Never,' she said, trying to tease with her tone.

'True story,' Hubie grunted, agreeing with Joe.

Ryder steadfastly refused to cave. It was that one time – a lifetime ago. No reason to even think about it.

At one point they were in you at the same time. You never thought that sweet full pressure could make you come, but it did. You straddled Hubie and drove yourself down on him over and over; he held your hands to his chest so you could feel his heart. All the while Joe rocked into your bottom, slipping into you on a cool river of lube. Working your ass, brushing your g-spot from a totally new angle. His hands on your hips, holding you so you didn't float away, or so it felt. Both of them. Holding you. You've never felt so safe.

'... fishing,' Joe said. His smile was ornery, knowing and smart-assed.

Ryder swallowed hard. Once they had been her very best friends. And for that one night they had been her lovers. Something she'd never been good at with Hubie and Joe was lying. She cleared her throat and steeled her nerves to admit it. 'What? I missed that.'

Joe laughed softly, drawing a heart in the sand with the

stick he held. The tip was charred from him poking it into the fire every few moments. He drank the last of his beer and said. 'We are here on a boys' weekend. Haven't gotten together for months. Figured we'd come down for some fishing.'

'Oh,' she said and set her empty bottle on the ground.

'Yes, oh,' Hubie said and his voice was a little gruff. A bit clogged sounding. His eyes seemed to stroke her like a hand in the firelight – over her breasts, her belly, her legs in her denim shorts and flip-flops. Ryder wanted to eye up his jeans to see if he had a hard-on but she refused. She kept her eyes above his belt. Joe's too.

'I'd better go to bed. I have to get up early. Vendors need to arrive at seven sharp. Doors open at nine.'

She kissed them each chastely, hugged them too. She pretended not to notice Joe's hard cock brushing her thigh when he pulled her into the embrace. She hurried through the woods to her dark cabin and resolved to put it out of her mind.

For two hours she lay there, not thinking. Deliberately not thinking. When every decadent sinful image drifted into her mind, she resolutely pushed it aside. At midnight, she got up and poured a glass of wine. At 12.15 a.m., she considered it and at 12.16 a.m. she banished the thought. At 12.30 a.m. she knocked on their cabin door.

It was Hubie who answered. His dark hair in a tangle and his chin sprouted with dark stubble that clouded his tanned skin with shadow. 'Well, look what the cat dragged in,' he said softly and swung the door wide for her to enter.

Ryder still wore her white nightgown. She had tossed a grey cardigan over it and her feet were bare, and now dirty, from the beaten path from her cabin to theirs. 'Were you sleeping? Did I wake you?

'Hell, no, woman. We're watching some dumb-ass movie on cable and drinking beer.'

'What movie?' she asked dumbly.

'Shit if I know.' He touched her lower lip and Ryder felt her pussy go liquid and soft. A fierce surge of lust swelled in her chest and she breathed out like he'd squeezed her too hard.

'Who's there?'

She turned to see Joe and, when she did, her heart raced at his pale good looks. A smile lit his face and she realised that she still loved them. After all these years. Loved who they were, what they had meant to her once and what they still meant to her now. 'Little Red Ryder Hood,' Joe whispered and crossed his arms over his chest.

'I ...' Ryder lost her words then. It hadn't taken long to feel that old familiar belonging with them. Something she had rarely experienced thus far in her adult life. She loved her life and her business, but she was missing the rush of real life. The visceral reaction to love and lust and fucking. She didn't have time.

'You what?' Joe asked, cocking an eyebrow.

'You ...?' Hubie echoed.

'I want it back,' she sighed. She blew all the words out on a rush of air. She was so eager for them to hear her that she rushed it out of her mouth in a tumble of soft speech. 'I want it back. I want that night back. That feeling – you two. I want one more night.'

Then she waited. Her heart pounding like some tribal drum, her throat shaking with the force of it, her stomach dipping almost sickly from nerves. Joe turned on his heels and Hubie took her hand.

What did it mean?

'Come on, Ry,' Hubie said and tugged her gently.

'We thought you'd never come to your senses,' Joe said over his shoulder and her whole body seemed to relax.

It would be OK.

In the living room it was Joe who pulled her in for a hug. Engulfing her in his strong but lean arms while Hubie – his best friend in the world – closed in behind her. His broad chest pressed to her back, his cock pressing the small of her back. Joe kissed her, hands in her hair, his hard-on pressed to the cleft of her sex through the thin nightgown.

'I just want it back for one more night,' she said again.

'We can do that,' Hubie said, pressing his lips to her

shoulder, her neck, the crown of her head. His kisses rained down along her back and his hands pushed up her nightie as she shivered like she was cold.

'No problem,' Joe said, pushing at the nightie too. Together they got off her cardigan, her nightgown, her panties. She worried briefly, stupidly, about her dirty feet but the thought drifted away as Joe's tongue touched hers and Hubie's fingers came from behind and started slow, lazy circles on her clit.

She gasped, tasting beer on Joe's tongue as his finger found her nipples and he pinched just a touch too hard. 'I remember you like a bit of pain,' he laughed softly and pinched her again.

The pain sizzled from her breasts to her cunt and it flexed, tight and eager around nothing at all. Hubie felt the swell of her hips as she tilted toward Joe and said, 'Let's see if it's still true.' He dipped his fingers, each as thick around as a cigar, deep into her pussy and he pressed against her g-spot with a precise kind of determination. 'Still true,' he said in her ear, and flexed again. He dropped to his knees, kissing a trail along the curve of her back, the wings of her shoulder blades, the swell of her hips. His fingers stayed buried deep in her wet pussy, his mouth never leaving her flesh. He trailed a wet line down until his tongue found the swell of her bottom and he started to lick and kiss her from one side to the other.

'Not to be outdone,' said Joe, with a chuckle. He kissed down the front. His tongue sliding in a slow, sinister dance between her breasts, over her belly button. He kissed one hip bone and then the other, all the while Hubie gave great attention to her ass.

Ryder clutched at Joe, Her hands buried in the pale floss of his short hair. Her one hand waved wildly behind her, finding purchase on Hubie's bare shoulder. He wore nothing but cut-offs and Joe nothing but gym shorts. They'd been drinking beer, watching movies, she thought wildly. Minding their own business until she had barged in and–

Joe sucked her clit in and nipped it. Hard enough that in her head a dark violet sizzle took up like a faulty neon sign.

Ryder sucked air into lungs that felt too small to hold it and her pussy cinched tight around Hubie's thick fingers.

God how they made her feel. Singly. Together. She never felt more free to be herself than with her boys. It had always been that way, still seemed to be.

The first orgasm slammed her and it was a blindside. One moment she felt so good, the next her cunt was rippling with harsh waves of euphoria. Tight, tight, tight around Hubie's probing fingers, her juices flowing out to meet Joe's ministering tongue. She held onto each one of them with a hand, swaying between them like a sapling in a storm.

Joe was the first to ditch his shorts. His cock standing out straight and true, ginger hair at the root and a birthmark on his right hipbone. Hubie laughed in that locker room way and Joe flipped him the bird. Joe's hands cupped her breasts, thumbing her pink nipples into small spikes of flesh. He drew her to the sofa as Hubie dropped his cut-offs. Hubie's cock was huge. He was a big man overall and not to be outdone in the cock department. A thrill worked through Ryder, she had forgotten. She stared at his thick hard-on and the nearly black hair at the base. His thighs, three times the size of hers, seemed like tree trunks.

'Don't' worry, Ryder, I'll go slow,' he said, meaning he would take his time. Let her adjust.

She nodded. She trusted Hubie with her life. Joe too. She could certainly give them one more day of trusting them with her body. Hubie dropped like a boulder to the sofa and she sat, her back to Joe's front, and watched him stroke his cock and watch her. Then Hubie leant in and kissed her while Joe tugged her hair enough to make her scalp sing.

The pain blended it all together. The soft kiss, the echoes of her orgasm. The feel of mouths and fingers and now cocks. She wanted them both now and later and in a million different ways. 'I feel greedy,' she blurted.

'Good,' Hubie said and patted his lap. She climbed on. Straddling his lap as he stroked her wet slit with the head of his cock. Ryder hummed low in her throat at the sensation of soft flesh on soft flesh. Of his hard cock pressed to her eager entrance. He held her hips almost reverently and she started to lower herself one inch at a time. Watching as her body swallowed his length and his mouth came down hot and insistent on her nipple. Hubie bit her and she jumped, but it was Joe who laughed.

'Come around here, smart ass,' she said, but there was no real heat in her name calling. She lowered onto Hubie, her eyes drifting shut at the pressure and the fullness of being stuffed with him. He lifted her and dropped her, lifted her and dropped her, as if she weighed nothing more than a sack of flour. And when he dropped her, the head of his cock nudged her g-spot and it winked to life. Some small secret thing waking for another go at pleasure.

Joe came to where she pointed. Standing behind the sofa that sat in the middle of the main room, dividing the dining space form the TV space. He stood facing her as she rode Hubie, his cock poking impudently over the back cushion.

Ryder took him in hand, meaning to make him suffer for laughing, but when she felt the silken slide of his hard-on in her hand, she caved, wanting nothing more than to make him feel good – to make him come. Ryder stroked Joe and Hubie fucked her, biting her again so that she hissed but her cunt went taut around his thrusting member. She lowered her lips to Joe and kissed the tip of him so that he groaned.

'A kiss?' he sighed.

'How about a French kiss?' she teased and pressed him into her mouth with her hand, before sucking down the length of him so that he had to clutch at the back of the sofa.

Hubie stopped for a moment, watching them and then he said, 'Jesus. Gonna make me come if I watch you.'

'Don't watch,' Joe laughed. But the laugh was breathy and high, as if he couldn't quite get it out.

Hubie held her hips tight, thrusting up and whispering words that she couldn't quite hear. When he pushed his broad finger into her bottom, she cried out, coming. Lips working around Joe who was shoving into her mouth, losing his manners a bit. He held twin hunks of her dark red hair in his hands like reins.

'Stop,' she said and they all froze. Both of them had been moving with a greater sense of purpose, almost frenzied. She knew it was close. It was close to ending and she said, very calmly so they knew she was serious, 'I want you both in me. Again. Like last time.'

Neither of them argued. There were no jokes or jibes or teasing. It was a nearly solemn but rushed rearrangement of bodies. An almost holy (to them, anyhow) tableau. Hubie lay on the ugly brown rug and pulled her down. She lay flush to him for a moment while Joe waited, breathing shallowly, touching his cock to stay hard. Hubie kissed her, his big green eyes on hers. 'Hey, you say the word and it's–'

'Over. I know. But I won't. *I* came to *you guys*.'

'So you did, Little Red Ryder Hood, but still.'

Ryder kissed him. Loving him for protecting her, even if it meant from himself and then she sank down onto him again. Taking him in the second time was as good, if not better, than the first. The break had set her body on high alert. All the nerve endings in her pussy danced and clamoured for the feel of him. She whispered to Joe and he lubed himself well, his cock shiny with the stuff.

'I don't want to hurt you,' he said, pressing the head of himself to the tight eye of her anus.

'It always hurts at first,' she told him, and it was pretty much true. 'Plus, I like a bit of pain.' And that was pretty much true too.

She stilled and Hubie held her hands to his chest again. For some reason it reminded her of praying, the way he held her hands in his bigger ones. The temple of Ryder, she thought and smiled. And then Joe was in. That pinching bite of pain having passed as simply as a breath.

He started to move, her pushing back, relishing the feel of having both of them in her body at once. Loving both of them. The three of them joined physically the way they had always seemed joined emotionally and mentally. It was natural for her and that was good enough for Ryder.

And the boys.

Somehow it was not an awkward dance of three. They

found a rhythm of give and take and up and down. She crested to orgasm only to crash down, her forehead to Hubie's hairy chest as he started to come, shaking under her as if he were fragile. Her fingers in his mouth and Joe's snaking around to press past her lips into the wet recesses of her mouth.

'I missed you, Ryder,' Hubie said as he came. His big awkward hips slamming up so that he could bury root deep into her. His heart beating so hard that his coarse rug of a chest jumped under her fingertips.

And then Joe was with him, holding her hips and slamming into her. He came with his lips on her shoulder and a simple, 'We love you, you know.'

And she did know. Which is why she wanted one more night. And that night wasn't over. Which made Ryder smile.

When We Were Two

"This is the story of how we begin to remember," Steve said and locked the front door.

"What are you talking about?"

My mother drove off. She beeped three times and I saw a flock of hands waving from the car windows. Her exhaust pipe plumed in the cold air as she took my children for four long days.

"How we begin to remember what it is to be Steve and Laurie."

I folded the throws scattered around the living room. I fluffed pillows, glanced back out the window, looked for something to keep me busy. With a house full of kids: fourteen, twelve, nine, and seven, it's never hard to be busy. Now it was quiet. Silent. Eerie. I wanted to whip out my cell phone and call my mother. I wanted to demand my busy, chaotic house back.

Stephen read my face. He took my hands and kissed me. It took the edge off the anxiety but not entirely. "What do we do?" I asked. And sadly, it was a sincere question.

"Relax and enjoy it. I know it's odd. It seems entirely new. Like we have never, ever been alone before," he laughed. "But close your eyes and think way back. Way back when. Once upon a time, we were two. Not mom and dad. Steve and Laurie."

I closed my eyes and found it hard to breathe. My ears kept straining for the sounds of siblings fighting or something being broken. The sounds of a shower running or a too loud stereo or someone on the phone demanding that the caller, *"Shut up ... Noooo ... oh, shut up!"*

"That was a really long time ago. I don't think my memory goes back that far," I laughed. But it was a nervous, high laugh. A dead giveaway that I was telling the truth. Spitting out a fact disguised as humour. "I can't remember what it was like before they filled the house up with noise and kids and chaos."

And it was true.

"I seem to recall that you liked this," my husband said and dropped to his knees. His jeans made a whispery sound on the hardwood floor and he peeled my leggings down like he was unwrapping a present. My black Danskin leggings that were so much easier to put on than a fancy outfit. Even faster than jeans when it came to a hectic schedule.

Instinct took over. Anyone could walk in. I pressed my thighs together and twisted away from his face. Contorted in the opposite direction despite the fact that his face being near me, his breath on my plain cotton panties, made me wet between the legs. Made my heart speed up from something besides anxiety.

Steve put his hands on my hips. Hips that has supported four pregnancies and were definitely wider than when we started our marital adventure. "Shh now, Laurie. No one here but us. Now just let me. Come on, let me."

I did. I let him peel down my panties in the bright sunny living room. Let him touch his tongue to my clit. I let him slide his fingers into me and probe against those sweet wet spots that made me clutch at his big shoulders. I let out a little cry as he slid his fingers free of me. When he latched his lips over my clit and started to lick more of those lazy circles, I felt tears leak from the corners of my eyes. It felt so good to let go. He felt good. I let my thighs fall open in invitation. He could finish that or he could slide into me. I was happy either way.

How quickly I had changed my mind. It was starting to come back to me in bits and pieces. Like a dream that you only recall hours later when you sit quietly with a cup of coffee.

"Not yet," he said and continued his languid tour of my

174

cunt. "We used to take our time. Remember?"

"Not always." More of it came flooding back to me. The time when we were two. Sometimes we were hurried. In a frenzy of clothes and hormones and I could barely breathe until he slipped his cock inside of me and fucked me. "Sometimes we were like crazed animals," I laughed. This laugh was lower. More sultry. Not nervous at all.

Stephen kissed the jut of my hip bones and the swell of my belly. Little silver stretch marks tattooed that skin. I hated them for the most part, but when he kissed them they seemed important. Meaningful. He drew his tongue over the surge of flesh that were my hips, the little landslide of freckles that I loathed and he loved. He kissed my ribcage below my breasts. He did all of this slowly. As if we had all the time in the world. And we did, or so it seemed.

His tongue wrapped the very tip of my nipple and an invisible cord of pleasure inside of me was tugged. I felt the warm sensation of want shoot from my nipple to my pussy. I spread my legs wide and wormed my hand between us to find his erection. He skittered away from me, "Not yet, not yet," he scolded.

"You are stubborn."

"I am remembering. I am recapturing the time long ago. Now we constantly wait for the knock on the door or the sick kid or the fight that interrupts. Or we have to wait until the middle of the night and then we're both tired. This is nice right now. This is what it used to be for us. This is what we are going to make it again. Starting now. A new leaf."

His mouth came down on me again. Hot and wet and very welcome. I arched back, into his embrace. Calming myself. There was time to be frenzied later. Four days. Four days of … whatever we wanted.

A little breathless at the thought, I pushed him away. He argued but then his eyes found mine and he let me go. His curiosity won over his desire to keep his mouth on me. "I seem to remember," I said, climbing slowly to my feet. I stifled a small groan. The wooden floor was unforgiving and I was no longer twenty, "that you liked when I danced for you."

175

A ribbon of unease unrolled in my belly. Could I pull this off at forty-something? Could I be the sexy dancing siren? He smiled up at me. His face a mess of dark stubble peppered with grey. More lines around his big blue eyes. His jaw line a bit softer than it was back in the day. Gorgeous. He smiled wider and I had my answer. I could.

I touched my toe to the stereo button and our station came on. Something classic, something slow. I moved to the music as best I could. Focused on his eyes on me. Of how his mouth had felt on my skin. I closed my eyes and let that feeling take over my motions. I let my hands peel off my plain mom bra that Stephen had bunched down under my breasts. I tossed it over my shoulder with attitude, as if it were the most expensive black lace lingerie.

My husband growled low in his throat and I forgot my self-doubt.

"There she is," he said and reached up between my legs to touch me.

I let my head fall back. Let his touch and the music move me. Push me and pull me. "Who?"

"The Laurie I fell in love with. She's always been here but I haven't seen her so clearly for a long time."

Me either, I wanted to say. I didn't. I swallowed the words and focused on how I felt.

"You are more beautiful now than ever."

"After four babies?" I laughed, swaying my more generous hips. I squeezed my breasts and swayed to the music.

"Absolutely. More beautiful after every one. Most beautiful now," he said. Then he was on his knees again, his head pressed against my lower belly as I moved. I slid down to join him, pushing him back.

"If memory serves, this is something else you like," I said and kissed my way over his chest. I trailed my tongue down his belly and the muscles fluttered just under his skin. His breath caught, a sound that never fails to make me wet, to turn me on. The sound of stealing a man's breath is amazing. The fact that I still could, even more so. I smiled and captured his cock in my mouth, sliding the length into my throat. I had memorized his taste and texture long ago but this time seemed new. New flesh. New meaning.

His hands went into my hair. Immediately and forcefully. I sucked him harder. I worked my tongue over every ridge and dip and swell until I felt light-headed.

"Come on. Now, Laurie. We've been patient enough," he laughed and I laughed with him.

"And we have the rest of today and then three whole days after," I agreed.

"Yes, yes, we can have dinner and go for an encore," he said and tugged my hand. Pulling me up to him.

I straddled his hips and ever so slowly lowered myself onto him. I stared him right in the eye. My husband. My friend. My gaze never left his and that itself brought a huge power with it. A renewed connection.

"Baby," he said. Nothing more. Just the one word.

I came. My body squeezing around him as he lost his patient rhythm and thrust up under me, his hips beating an erratic tattoo against the scuffed but polished hardwood floor.

"Baby," I said back and watched his face when he came. I had seen it more times than I could count but it seemed like the first.

When I kissed him and he pinched my nipple, I laughed. I felt grateful. Grateful for our family and what we had built, but grateful that for just a few days, we could be two again. To be adventurous again. To have sex on the floor in the sunshine.

"Do you remember?" he asked.

"I do."

Yes, Tim

"Fu-uh-uck," I hissed. I dragged the word out while trying to back my SUV up without crashing into anything. Or killing anyone. "Please do not let me kill a worker," I sighed, inching backwards. I was completely blind. I did not want to end my day with manslaughter.

"Ho!" I slammed the break so hard I shot forward. The cans rattled and shifted in the back of my vehicle. The smell of old soda and beer made my stomach roll over. It was a cloying scent that would linger for days.

A face appeared at the door and I started. I pushed the button and the window whined. "Sorry. I can't see sh–crap. I didn't flatten anyone, did I?"

He gave me a small but friendly grin. "Nope. And you didn't dent your truck. That's the main thing. Pop the back for me?"

His face was long and lean. Weathered without being aged. Prematurely silvery hair that had once been blond it seemed. His eyes were the colour of steel and his lips were thin without being pinchy. Overall, a handsome face that made me feel calmer. I read his name tag. Tim.

"Sure. No problem."

I hit the button and heard the back door disengage. I opened the door and it thunked the concrete wall. I was a tad close. "Shit." Now I had dented it. I sucked in my breath and squeezed between the wall and the SUV. Once around back, I started to unload the huge bags of crushed cans into a pile.

My small company collected cans from the employees. We kept all the cans from our modest business meetings. Held weekly, they were small but generated a surprising amount of

178

recycling. One of my design clients went through a six pack of diet soda per meeting. I figured by the time I had finished her Zen-meets-punk-rock bathroom, she'd make up roughly a third of our can collection.

Every month I cashed in the cans and the proceeds went to a local charity. It was my small way of giving back to the community and doing something positive with the people who worked for me.

"– gonna get ruined." Tim was staring at me. What had he said?

"I … uh … what!?" I shouted. The place was possibly the noisiest place I had ever been and that included the circus and the rock quarry during blasting.

"I said, your shoes are gonna get ruined!" he yelled as a huge machine spilled a waterfall of aluminium into a giant bin below. Imagine if it rained rocks. And wrenches. With a few hammers for effect. I shoved my fingers in my ears and cringed. How could he hear at all? I'm surprised they weren't all deaf.

"It's fine! They're old!" I said and jumped when a huge boom filled the warehouse.

He laughed and guided me to the open bay. His hand on me made me feel warm. I looked again at his face. Nice face. Warm, friendly face. His hand was clean but busted up from working with metal all day. It looked out of place and completely right on my brown suede coat. "Your coat will get ruined in there, too. You've never been here, I take it?"

I shook my head. Somehow my gaze had become pinned to his lips. Pale pink. So pink they almost looked like he had lipstick on. Completely incongruous with his masculine appearance. I found myself shifting a little bit at the thought of those lips coming down on mine. On my lips. On my belly. On my hipbones. My thong rubbed over my now swollen clit at just the right moment and I sucked in a breath.

"It's OK. It's old," I breathed. And tried to tear my gaze from his mouth. I managed to do it. My eyes fell upon his grey Dickies jacket and the wide chest underneath. Lean and tall, Tim was what I looked for in a man. No excess. Every muscle, every ounce put to good use.

"Still. Don't want to ruin something perfectly nice and useable. No waste. Remember?" he said and winked. His big hand slid up my forearm and rested at my elbow. He held my arm that way. Somehow completely proper and completely irreverent at the same time. Heat shot through my arm, up into my chest and flushed my cheeks what I could only assume was a cherry red.

"Right. I'm sorry. I didn't realize that they shouldn't be in so many bags. My assistant Tammy usually brings them." As I was explaining, a worker was ripping open all the little grocery sacks that held the cans.

"It's fine. Really. That's what we get paid to do. Right?" Another wink and a squeeze of my elbow.

I felt more than my cheeks flush and my breath caught in my throat.

"Listen to boss man," said a laughing voice. I turned to see a smiling Mexican man. He had a lilting accent and an easy grin. "That's what we get paid to do. You da man. You talk like one of us."

"I am one of you," Tim said. He smiled at his worker and then at me. It was clear this was good natured ribbing.

"Yeah, yeah. You wield the whip."

"Yes. I am a whip-wielder. I am brutal," Tim said. But when he said it, his face was a bit more serious and he squeezed my arm a little. I didn't take it as a threat. But I wasn't stupid. He held a strength and a serious nature that was thinly veiled behind that easy smile.

"I'm sure you are," I laughed. OK. I tittered because I was suddenly nervous. And I wanted him. I could kid myself and waste the time or I could admit it. I chose the latter. I very much wanted to have Tim fuck me senseless. Whip or no whip.

"Fucking rich bitches thinking we got nothing better to do," said the other man. It was clear by the look on Tim's face that this was not good-natured ribbing and not OK.

"Peter, you can go to my office. I'll finish up."

Rich bitch? I nearly laughed. I had scrimped and saved to

become independent. Eaten more peanut butter sandwiches and Ramen noodles than I cared to remember. The smell of Shrimp noodles still made me gag. I flustered and clenched my fists. Then I covered my ears and yelped as Tim pulled a lever and another river of cans rained down from the sky.

When it was done, I did the only thing I could think to do. I was pissed and hurt and oddly attracted to him. So I worked. I opened bag after bag and handed them to Tim who dumped them in the sorter. On my final squat I felt a nice icy breeze and realized my white lace thong was not peeking, but popping up over my waistband. Probably half my ass was visible. I patted it with my hand as my throat seemed to close. Dear Christ. I had mooned him more times than I could count.

"I'm sorry. I was enjoying the view too much to speak up." And there was that grin again. Ready. Slow. Sensuous.

I wanted to smack him. I wanted to kiss him. Shove my hands in his grey-silver hair and see what those lips really felt like. I wanted to scream. Instead I said, "How much did it come to?"

His grey eyes probed and I hid my embarrassment. I had spent years polishing myself and here I was, smelly, sticky, with my ass hanging out. I had been called a fucking rich bitch, which was a riot. I was abnormally attracted to the owner and all I wanted was to go home and take a shower. And drink a bottle of vodka. Alright, a few drinks. Not a whole bottle. Hopefully.

"Let's see." He tapped the computer. Somewhere in the building a huge bash sounded. I read the sections. Copper, Iron, Lead, Aluminium. Anything to keep my eyes off of Tim. "Fifty two pounds. Name?" His eyes slipped over me, showing his interest.

"Jessie. Jessie McCarthy," I stammered.

He hit the print icon and the printer spat out an invoice. "Sign this and ..." he stopped and smiled. The corners of his eyes crinkled in the most appealing way and I wished for the warmth and solidity of his hand on my arm again. "... and follow me, I guess because Lana is gone."

I looked at my watch. It was five already. After five,

181

actually. "I'm sorry. You're closed."

"Spoiled," said Peter as he sauntered out. He looked pretty proud of himself. "I waited in your office but you never came. And now it's quitting time. So, I'm leaving. Unless you want to pay me overtime to rip me a new asshole."

Tim scowled. "I want you in on time and back in my office in the morning."

"Yep." Peter started to stomp off but Tim put a hand on his arm.

"You owe the lady an apology," he said.

I wanted to say he didn't. To tell him to never mind. The look on Tim's face told me not to. Hush, it said. Be quiet and let me do this.

"I'm sorry," Peter ground out.

I nodded.

But he kept talking. "I'm sorry that you're spoiled and rich and that you had to come in here and smell us and hear us and be around us working folk."

My father was a janitor. My mother picked crabs for a buck an hour to earn extra money. I had baby sat and delivered newspapers to add to the family income all through school. Spoiled was so far removed from me that it wasn't funny.

"You can clear out your locker, Peter," Tim growled.

Peter nodded, laughed and spat at my feet. "Gladly. Plenty of jobs out there for a low life like me." And then he was gone.

"I have to go."

He nodded and didn't argue. "Come on and get your money first. Don't forget that."

"Right. Sorry."

"No. I'm sorry. He's an asshole and I'm damn ashamed that someone like that could work for me. And you're not spoiled. Anyone who's worked an honest day can tell that. He's just too hung up on what he doesn't have to see what's around him."

"How did you know?" I asked. "That I'm not rich. Never have been."

182

"Cause the rich women do not squat down and help slit open disgusting smelly bags of cans. Here you go. Twenty-five dollars and twenty cents." He handed me the money and his fingers brushed my palm. Lingered. Traced the lines of my hand. "Enjoy it."

"Not me,"

"Who then?" His eyebrow went up with the question and my stomach seemed to bottom out.

"Someone who might need it more," I said but then said no more.

I stopped for a latte. At the counter, I noticed the boy who was grinding the beans. His eyes, the colour of storm clouds. Not dead-on but close. His eyes made me think of Tim. I remembered how hot my skin felt when he looked me over the way he had. How they didn't seem to miss a thing. The feel of his gaze had been almost like being touched physically. I shuddered.

"You OK, Jessie?" Amy asked. She handed me my usual and I chugged a sip. It scalded like hell but I needed the fix.

"Nope. I am a spaz. I am sure of it. Now, will you do me a huge favour and make another one of these and toss some biscotti in a bag?" I handed her a twenty. "And keep the change."

"Oh, big spender," Amy said, working a liquid miracle with her petite hands. Within a minute I was holding another warm concoction.

"Yeah. Just call me Rockefeller, toots," I said and nearly ran to the car.

I expected to have to hunt for him, but he was the only one still at the recycling centre. My heart stuttered when I looked at him. Serious face, big hands. I went wet between the legs when he gave me that slow grin.

"You're back."

"I am. Here." I handed him the coffee and shook my head. Very smooth.

"Thanks." Tim sniffed it and then laughed. "Vanilla?"

"Yeah. I shoulda realized it's kind of girly," I said.

"Maybe just regular coffee. Or espresso." I shrugged.

"No. I like vanilla. I like coffee period."

Then he set the cup on the work station and touched me. With one finger. He slid his finger up my arm to my shoulder. He paused while I tried to breathe. Then he traced the line from my shoulder to my clavicle. My skin felt like it was on fire.

"I … uh …"

"Listen. You should have stuck around. About Peter," Tim leaned in and smelled me. Inhaled me like I was an elusive scent.

"Mmm?" I could feel his breath on my neck and my nipples went tight. Sensitive.

"He hates everybody. Even old Joe. A regular. Joe who has about five dollars in his bank account and one tooth. And it's not even a good tooth," he whispered and pressed his lips to the slope of my throat.

A bubble of laughter escaped me. My pussy was thumping now. A pulse that kept time with my briskly beating heart. God I wanted him in me. Some part of him. Tongue, finger, cock. All of the above. I couldn't remember wanting that bad. Needing. Seeing a man and thinking, *I have to have him.* I looked at Tim again and fisted my hands to keep from stroking him through this work pants.

"That's terrible."

"That he hates everyone?"

"No. That Joe's one tooth isn't even a good tooth."

"Ah," Tim said and slid his finger below the waistband of my jeans. His skin seemed to brand me. Heat and want flickered through me wickedly. My knees felt ready to sag. "Come on, girl," he said and took my coffee from me. I let him. Then he snagged my two wrists in his one hand and led me. I went willingly. I would have gone anywhere he tugged me. We walked through the door marked OFFICE and he shut the door. The click sounded loud in the tangible silence.

"I don't normally do this," I blurted. I don't know why. I wanted to explain.

"I'm not in the habit, either," he said. Then he started

popping the buttons of my white blouse without a word. "I want you out of all this."

His work scarred hands worked against the crisp white cotton. The buttons like little pearls in his big fingers. "Yes, Tim" I agreed.

I shucked the shirt like it was smothering me. His fingers worked over my plain white bra, gently pulled down a cup and released a nipple to the cool air. Then his tongue captured it and the warmth was shocking. "Fuck. You are gorgeous."

I grabbed his head with my hands but he snagged my wrists again and pinned my arms above my head. Against the shelf that held folders and boxes and ledgers. I liked the feel of being at his mercy. It made my cunt frantic. All I wanted was for him to fuck me. However he wanted. It didn't matter to me. Just the sensation of it was all I asked for. Just that. Nothing else.

His other hand tugged at my jeans. Wrangled my zipper. Pushed at them until they obeyed and slid down over my hips as I wriggled to help them along. His lips never left me. They nipped at my mouth, slid over my throat and my shoulders. Rolled hot circles around my exposed breast. I pushed into him. Seeking and finding heat and his hardness. I wanted to tug at his pants. Find what was waiting beneath the stiff utilitarian fabric, but he held me fast with his big hand.

"Turn around, Jessie," he said and I did. I spun in his loosened grasp like a ballerina in a music box.

His belt jingled merrily and I held my breath. Anticipating his freed flesh coming in contact with mine. He bent me over a clean cart. The sharp scent of new plastic filled my head along with the sharper underlying smell of the plant itself. He kept my wrists pinned but now they were held behind my back. I teetered on the edge of the cart, my belly pressing so hard against it that I saw stars. Then his cock found my soaked slit and I forgot about the spots and lack of air and everything else. He slid into me with a satisfied grunt. The sound alone had me teetering on the edge of coming.

"Stay still, girl," he said and I went limp.

"Yes, Tim." Not docile by nature, it felt right anyway. I

absorbed his motions, accepted the hard length of him. I didn't move back against him. I took him in.

Tighter and then tighter still. I felt my body gearing up for release. I wanted it and yet I wanted to keep it in the distance. In the future. So I could have him here this way longer. Or better yet, he could have me as he wanted me for just a bit more time.

"Fuck, you are so tight. So tight. And your ass ..." he trailed off as the first ripples of orgasm shot through me. Halfway through, he pulled his cock from me and I cried out. "Just wait. Shh."

And he shoved into my ass. The pain was intense. It ate up my pleasure and then somehow enhanced it. I came long and hard. The pain flowing through me, dancing with the pleasure that threatened to overtake me. I let my head hang limp as he clutched at me. His fingers bit into my imprisoned wrists. His free hand yanked at my hips. When he smacked my ass hard enough to make me bite my tongue, a single tear slipped free of me. But he was fucking me so hard and the pain was so good. I came again on a sob.

Tim lost his rhythm. His body beat against mine in a frantic tattoo and he came. His teeth found my shoulder and nearly broke skin.

We stayed that way for a moment. Me teetering on the edge of the receptacle. Him buried deep in my ass. Softening but still hard enough to fill me.

"Did I hurt you?"

"Just enough," I laughed.

"Coffee's cold, I bet."

"Have a microwave?" I asked. His hands smoothed over my bottom. The spot where he'd struck me was hot and sensitive. He patted it hard enough to make me jump a bit.

"I do. Will you stay?"

"Of course."

"Better yet, come home with me?"

My body grew hotter. I didn't answer. I pulled free of him. My wrists sore and chafed. My ass sore and wet. My pussy ready for more of him. All of me ready for more of him. The way he was. The way he took from me. The way that made me feel. He studied my face. Steel grey eyes. Serious face. Easy smile. Then his lips compressed and he reached out. He grabbed my arms and gave me a squeeze. Hard enough to hurt.

"You're coming home with me."

"Yes, Tim," I said and smiled.

Nothing but the Boots

Cat rummaged through the boxes. She'd bought her monthly allotment of clothing for *Lush* and *Ripe*, two plus-sized stores with one-word names that always seemed to make her smile. Her eyes found those fabulous purple boots again.

"I really need them." She said it sincerely to her own reflection. Her pink lips lingering on the word *need*. She'd been considering trying to seduce Sam the delivery man and wearing these boots and nothing else might do it.

She flipped open the box, ignoring the rest of the clothing and shoes that littered her studio apartment. The boots were the bomb. Her fingers tickled up the synthetic material that made up the shaft. It reminded her of a mix of well-worn leather and patent leather. "Superhero boots," she muttered.

Her eyes found the clock even as her fingers fondled the footwear. She had time. Her brand new assistant was supposed to arrive today, but not for another hour. Cat knew it was crazy, impulsive and just plain stupid, but she did it anyway. She shucked her tight-leg jeans, her tee and her knickers. She stood there, in her abundant fullness and nothing else. Wide hips that curved up into a smaller waist, large breasts, ample belly, and kick-ass legs. Her legs were a deadly weapon, she thought. The boots would make them look fierce.

"I have to test what I'll look like when I put the moves on Sam in nothing but these boots." She sat on her bed, which was smack dab in the middle of her studio apartment. It sat in a patch of sunlight, its weathered white antique frame squatting squarely in the middle of her wide-planked hardwood floor.

She took all the packing out of the boot and felt a nearly sensual arousal course through her. It was very easy to imagine greeting Sam in just these decadent purple boots and then having him attack her like a wild wildebeest. That made her snicker and her breasts swayed slightly, ticking her thigh as she started to pull the boot up over her foot and ankle. Mid-calf they were stuck, arrested in their upward momentum.

"Uh-oh." The material was not nearly as giving as she had expected and, due to the nature of synthetics, the heat of her body had caused the shaft to stick on her leg. Tight.

Cat tried to yank it up to no avail. "Fuck no," she groaned.

Then she tried to push it down. The boot would not budge. "These are so going back," she growled. Panic swelled in her chest and she tried to suck in a great big breath to still her nerves. It was a boot. She wasn't caught underground in a cave or anything, she was stuck in a boot. She rolled onto her back, splayed on the bed in all her naked glory – too bad she was alone! She hooked her fingers under the top of the boot and started to push.

"Move, you bastard! Move."

Nothing. She couldn't get it up, she couldn't get it down. The foot bed of the boot dangled off her foot, mocking her, the heel pointing the wrong way toward the window.

"Baby powder?" she said, thinking aloud. But she didn't have any.

Her mind raced. Lotion would make it worse, and the more panicky she got the more she sweated and the more she sweated the more she was sticking. "Cornstarch!" she crowed but then she remembered she didn't have any of that either.

She sprawled there on her bed, one purple boot half on, defeated. And then –

The doorbell rang.

"No," she whispered.

Cat grabbed her foot and yanked. She yanked and yanked and yanked and the doorbell rang again. Her eyes scanned the room. She was never going to get those jeans on over this Frankenstein boot. All her other clothes were still in the dryer down in the laundry room. And she didn't have time to raid

189

her closet because the doorbell was ringing yet again and someone was knocking on top of it all.

"Hello? Mrs Barbieri? Catherine Barbieri?" he yelled.

She groaned and rolled to her belly. Her eyes found the kimono and she felt hope. At least it was something.

"Yes! Hold please," she sang out as if she hadn't a care in the world.

"I'm Greg. Greg Irwin, I'm your new –"

"I know! I'm coming!" she yelled and pulled the kimono on. She held it tight to her waist, clenched in a death grip, but the peach and pale blue-patterned cover-up still hoisted and accentuated her generous cleavage.

Oh well, George would have to deal with it.

She stagger-stepped in her half-on boot to the front door and yanked it open , her mood already sour. There was no point in attempting dignity. "Come in, George," she growled.

"It's ... um ... Greg," he said and took a tentative step inside.

He looked scared to death and Cat did not blame him one bit. Worst part was, she recognized this man. This was not her first meeting with Greg. She had met Greg at a singles event her friend Mary had dragged her to. She and Greg had shared some pretty steamy glances but had never had a chance to talk in the crowd.

"Of course it is. Sorry, *Greg,*" she sighed.

She saw him make the mental connection and he said "Hey, aren't you – "

"Yes, yes I am," she sighed and turned her back to him and hobbled across the floor, trying very hard to appear unflappable in her silk kimono and her fucked-up footwear.

"I didn't know my big boss would be –"

"Naked under a kimono and stuck in a stolen boot?" she asked.

"Naked?"

"Buck. Or is it butt?" Cat asked.

When she turned, clutching valiantly at the front of her robe, his face had gone red but his eyes took a very lingering tour of her anyway. He was very tall and lean and dark-

190

haired, wolf-blue eyes peered at her from under a fall of too-long fringe that needed a trim.

"I don't know," he admitted.

"I personally like buck naked. As in skin, I guess," she babbled, as if this were a perfectly ordinary conversation. Cat noticed – but tried not to – the slick warmth of arousal between her legs. The way young Greg was eyeing her up was turning her on. Almost making her forget her sweaty foot stuck in the pilfered boot.

"That sounds good," he said.

"Coffee?" she asked, waving the carafe at him and trying to pour herself a cup one-handed.

"Sure."

She poured two and he started to doctor his with sugar and cream. "Yours?" he asked.

"Two sugars, cream it until it's pale," she said. Then her cheeks went hot from her own words. "I like it light," she amended.

They stood and sipped their coffee for a moment while he tried not to study her figure and failed. "So did you ever meet anyone at the … thing?"

"No. Never did. I mostly went to make Mary happy."

"You?" she asked, feeling her nipples spike at his gaze and willing them to behave and return to their normal state of being. She failed.

"Never," he said.

He moved a step closer and said softly. "I wanted to come talk to you all night but that dreadful woman who ran the party kept interrupting me."

"She wanted you," Cat said. She looked at his body in those jeans and a white button-down and a dark grey sweater vest. He wore brown work boots and his hair was windblown. Of course that woman had wanted him!

"She did?" His confusion seemed genuine.

Cat laughed and his eyes followed her face. He smiled and her pussy went wetter.

"Yes, she did. The *duh* is implied."

He shrugged. "News to me. I mean, I know you're my new

191

boss – if I work out, but I have to admit…" he trailed off.

Cat realized she was holding her breath. Her kimono had gaped open a bit and she watched his gaze travel over her outline. His eyes on her was as tangible as a touch and a stroke. She shifted and her kimono gaped. "Admit what?" she said, a bit too fast.

"I only had eyes for you that night."

"And now your eyes are on me again," she laughed, feeling her heart bang crazily.

"Because you're standing in the sun and I can see right through that robe," he admitted.

"Oh … God. I'm sorry!" she blurted.

"I don't mind,' he said and blushed.

Cat cleared her throat. "Ready for your first assignment?"

"I am."

"Help me get out of this damn boot."

Greg chuckled lowly and her stomach sizzled with the sound. She went to the bed and sat down. She put her leg up, her calf muscle standing out and her skin flushed with her arousal. "Ready?" he asked.

Cat nodded and was surprised – to the point of jumping a bit – when he first took his hand and ran it down her leg from her knee, over her calf, to the place where that damnable boot remained stuck. His fingers curled slowly into the lip and he caught the purple fake-fabric-from-hell (as she now thought of it) and he tugged gently, inching the boot down, a bit here, a bit there.

She tried to hold the robe closed and not seem turned on. She was failing. Her body was tensing with the effort of acting as if this was just no big deal.

"You have to relax," he whispered, giving her the smile that had so captivated her at that singles event. He'd been so handsome and mysterious she'd even considered attending other parties to try and catch another glimpse of him. She hadn't though, figuring someone as cute as him would have snagged a girl by now.

"Relax," he said again.

"I'm trying!" she blurted.

When he bent his head and kissed the inside of her knee her whole body seemed to sigh with pleasure. Her mouth popped open in surprise and she shivered.

"It will make this all easier."

"OK."

He inched and wiggled and pulled and she-finally, finally! – felt the boot sliding grudgingly down her leg.

"You have very nice legs," he said, touching her muscle.

It jumped and fluttered and so did she. "Thank you. God, don't touch me," she sighed.

He laughed. "I'm sorry. Am I fired?"

"Nope."

"Am I hurting you?"

"Far from it."

Greg went still and his cool appraising eyes met hers. "Then what?"

She shook her head. He tugged.

"What if I said please? Would you tell me then?"

He was almost to her ankle and suddenly she was afraid of when the boot did come off. "Nope."

"Please?" he said anyway.

"You're turning me on," she sighed. "But then you knew that, didn't you?"

His fingers, bold now, traced from knee to ankle and the boot popped free. He touched her instep and then kneaded the ball of her foot and she thought she might actually come.

"I was hoping. I probably should resign," he said, pushing his lips to her knee again, then her calf. He kissed her ankle and said, "Let the robe fall open ... *please.*"

All the many ways this was inappropriate flew through her mind like a tickertape but she did. She let it fall open and when he stood, studying her, she shifted with nerves and excitement. "Gorgeous. And what are the odds we meet up like this again? With you all damsel in distress and me all willing to help."

He climbed onto the bed and leaned over her – not touching her yet, she noticed with frustration – and kissed her. His mouth soft and full on hers, tasting like sweet coffee and young man.

"The odds are staggering," she whispered.

"I agree. And yet here I am. And here you are … naked."

His hand covered her breast, stroking softly. Cat tried so hard to stay still but failed. She danced under his hand and he pinched her nipple just a bit and she gasped. "I am. I am naked," she babbled.

His mouth followed his hand and he sucked so that she felt the tug and pull of her arousal go from nipple to cunt. "I like you naked. I liked you clothed, too. I really liked you in a see-through cover-up and one purple boot."

"I looked stupid," she said as he traced down the sides of her body with his warm hands. Her pussy flickered happily at the attention and her stomach quivered. She was caught between begging him to hurry and begging him to go slower.

"You looked captivating. Crazy blonde hair, flushed cheeks, those breasts … oh, sweet Cat, those breasts."

She smiled but then he put his hand to her pussy and started to touch her. Greg stroked her outer lips and then parted them to touch her clit. He watched her face which turned her on even more. "May I?"

"Youmayyoumayyoumay …" she said in one long word like a chant.

He bent his dark head and pushed his face to her pussy. His tongue found the distended nub of her clit and he licked her. The flat of his tongue dragged over her and his thick fingers pushed into her. His other hand pinned the curve of her thigh to the bed and she felt both empowered and helpless and immensely aroused. When she came, he kept licking past the release point so that she jittered under him laughing.

"Condoms in the bedside table," she murmured.

He found one, then lost his pants. His proper shirt and nice grey vest followed suit. His body was long and hard and the jut of his cock was just what she needed to see. He rolled the rubber on and when he was sheathed, climbed between her legs, kneeing them a bit further apart. He took the time to run his hands up her thighs, pet the flare of her hips and then follow the dip of her waist. Greg bent, pushing his tongue into her belly button the way he'd touched it to her sex.

"You can officially start work *tomorrow*," she said. "For now, please … you're killing me."

His crooked grin only served to amp up the moisture between her legs and when he ran the head of his cock to the soaked split of her she grabbed his arms to steady herself. The world seemed to be moving in time with her pulse. "Stay still, boss," he chuckled and then slid home.

Cat thought she would weep with joy. His cock nudged her perfectly so the very first tickling of orgasm rubbed up against her. Greg held her hips flush to the bed, bent his head and licked her breasts. Baby kisses along the left one before sucking the nipple and repeating the whole process on the right one. His thrusts were slow and measured, not in a hurry. The man was not in a rush.

Cat wrapped her legs around his waist and her body allowed him deeper. He groaned, moving his hands from her hips to trap her wrists high above her head.

"I wasn't expecting such a spectacular first day," he whispered. When he kissed her, his lips tasted like her own juices.

"Me neither, me neither," she said.

"Boss lady?" he said in a teasing voice though his tone had grown thick.

"Yes, subordinate Irwin?"

He shut his eyes, his fingers going tighter around her wrists, his hips moving faster. "I'm going to come, ma'am." He was still smiling but his eyes were closed.

He thrust harder and Cat rose up to meet him, mashing his pelvic bone to her now tender clit. "Me too, I think. Me too. I keep repeating myself," she said quickly.

And then she did come. She came and her orgasm made her tight around his cock. He lost his battle to hold it off.

She lay there, looking up at the sun-speckled ceiling, still in her kimono which was filleted down the middle, spread out on either side of her like great butterfly wings. Greg lay atop her, up on his elbows just enough so as not to crush all the air from her lungs.

195

"I feel like the universe smiled on me today," he said. The look on his face said he was serious.

"For real?" she couldn't help asking.

"Yes, for real. I kept ... wondering about you."

She had thought of him too, she realised – often, in fact. More than once he'd been the fantasy in her head as she masturbated at night. Heat rose in her face and she laughed. "Yeah, me too."

"So, am I still hired?"

"I think we can totally see how it goes," she said. "Probably improper but so is answering the door butt and or buck naked."

"Be right back," he said and he was gone. Perfect little toned man-tush disappearing toward the kitchenette. He returned with powdered sugar from her pantry.

"What's that for?"

"Can you take off that kimono?" he asked, ignoring her question.

Cat shrugged it off and then he was sprinkling her legs with powdered sugar. He smoothed it over her skin and her eyelids fluttered at the soft pleasure he was bringing just touching her.

"What is this for?" Cat tried again.

"It's to help me do this." He slid the one purple boot on her leg and it went up effortlessly with the aid of the silken powder. Now why hadn't she thought of that? He found the purple boot's partner and slid it on too.

"Now what?" Cat asked. But his cock was already growing hard and twitching and his eyes strayed to the still open bedside table drawer where the condoms were.

"Now we repeat that, to see if we liked it. But this time, in nothing but the boots."

"I'm pretty sure I liked it," she said. His fingers found her, stroked.

"I know. Me too. But best to be certain," he said and pulled her to him.

"True story. If you're going to be my assistant, I do want you to be thorough."

"I aim to please," Greg said, his hands exploring her again.
"My God," she said. "I've noticed."

Girl Crush

'There isn't much I wouldn't do for you,' I said and then laughed. The laughter was nerves.

'Then just think about it. I know it's cliché but it's something I can't get out of my head,' Scott said. He pulled me close and smoothed my hair. 'We're on vacation and we're here to be wild and free. And maybe a teeny tiny bit dirty,' he snickered and then delivered a hot wet kiss to my collarbone.

'I'll think about it,' I sighed on a shiver. That one hot kiss had awakened every nerve in my body.

'Dinner?'

'Dinner,' I agreed and followed him out.

The dining room was gorgeous. The hotel had gone all out to make it magical and elegant and sexy all at the same time. Long, white tablecloths on the small, intimate tables. Candlelight. Low lighting from the crystal chandeliers. We had been at the Palms for two nights and every night I looked forward to dinner. The setting alone was erotic.

'My name is Callie and I'll be your server tonight,' the waitress said.

'Hi, we had you the night before last,' I said, accepting the menu.

Callie nodded, her long, dark hair hiding her face for just a moment, and she smiled. 'I remember. How are you? Enjoying your stay?'

When I glanced up, her eyes were fixed on the low-cut V of my red dress. She caught me looking and her pale cheeks were instantly stained with rosy pink. Scott's big warm hand crept up my thigh, hidden from view by the tablecloth. Had he planned this?

'Lovely,' I said, my voice a little high. *She* was really lovely. Callie. Tall and slender with all that long, dark hair. 'Thank you.'

Still blushing, she nodded and shared a glance with my husband. 'Sir, what can I get you to drink?' she asked in a small voice.

'Whatever's on draft,' Scott said. 'What about you, Paige?'

'A glass of Merlot,' I said, looking not at him but directly at Callie.

She dipped her head and hid behind that hair again. 'Yes, ma'am. I'll be right back with your drinks.' She scampered off like a puppy.

'What have you done?' I hissed, swatting Scott's big arm. 'Did you set me up?'

He laughed. It wasn't a malicious laugh but the kind of laugh that comes from being married for a very long time. 'All I did was request to be seated in her section. She has a girl crush on you.' He put his arm around my shoulder and stroked by bare skin. I sighed and allowed myself to be pulled close.

'What the hell is a girl crush?'

My husband leaned in and whispered right in my ear. His hot breath ignited all the little nerve endings in my face. My pulse throbbed and my nipples grew tight under the bodice of my dress.

'When a younger girl has a crush on an older woman. Well, in this case. Can be any time. High school, work place, whatever. Usually she looks up to the other woman. Wants to be like her or look like her or learn from her. Remember the article I read? I tried to read some to you.'

'You're always trying to read things to me. Sometimes I just …'

'Tune me out?' he whispered and subtly let his hand drop from my shoulder to my breast. One quick pinch of my nipple, so fast it was like a magic trick, and my cunt flooded in my expensive silk panties.

199

'Mmm-hmmm,' I moaned.

'Bad girl. You should know better. I only read you things that are pertinent.'

Callie returned with our drinks. Her cheeks were still flushed and she continued to hide behind the sleek curtain of dark, chocolate hair. Her eyes flashed to me, skittered over me and then darted away. She nearly toppled Scott's beer on the table. 'Sorry, sorry,' she murmured, her voice sweet and low, 'I'm all thumbs tonight.'

'It's OK,' I said, touching her hand gently. I suddenly felt very powerful. Powerful and sexy. The fact that Scott's hand had started snaking up my inner thigh under the table didn't help matters. I fought the urge to squirm in my seat. She sucked in a breath and stared at my hand. My eyes sought and found the hard nubs of her nipples behind her plain white blouse. I took my hand away and handed her the menus. 'We'll both have the steak special.'

She nodded and then practically bolted from our table. Scott's blunt finger wormed under my panties and slid straight into my wet, moist heat. 'Wetter than wet,' he snickered in my ear. 'Are you still considering it?'

I slouched just a touch in the booth so that his finger slid deep into my cunt. He quickly added a second finger and I had to control my breathing. 'No.'

Scott hooked his fingers inside of me. Nearly inaudible wet sounds emanated from under the elegant table. He probed my G-spot expertly until I gave into the quick but intense orgasm he provoked.

'No?' he smiled and then subtly stuck his fingers in his mouth and licked them clean.

Little white-hot echoes sounded inside of me at the sight. My pussy flickered and twitched, wanting more of what it had just been given. 'No. I've decided. Find out what time her shift ends.'

'Will do,' he said with a small, victorious smile.

I wasn't nervous. Why wasn't I nervous? I should be, shouldn't I?

Scott wasn't nervous either. He sat on the hotel bed and watched me. Watched me touch up my make-up. Watched me smooth my short blonde hair. Watched me straighten my dress and wash my hands and spritz a little perfume on my pulse points. He watched it all with a small, secret smile. And when my gaze met his in the mirror, I smiled too.

'She knows, right?' I asked again. I wasn't nervous but I was concerned. 'She knows why I invited her up.'

Scott gave me another patient nod. 'Judging by the way she flushed that lovely raspberry colour and how hard her little nipples got … *again* … I'd say, yes, she knows. And if she doesn't and she wants to leave, then she can.'

'Right.' I heard the hesitant tapping on the door and my stomach bottomed out.

'She's here,' Scott said, and I could hear the excitement in his voice. This had been his fantasy for years. A tried-and-true fantasy of many men. His wife with another woman.

I found that suddenly it was my fantasy, too. Him watching me. Me and the lovely Callie.

She looked almost startled when I opened the door. As if she hadn't expected us to actually be here. 'Come on in,' I said, taking pains to keep my voice low. I didn't want to scare her.

She stood in the centre of our luxurious hotel room looking terrified but aroused. Her brown eyes were wide, the pupils dilated, her breathing rapid. For all intents and purposes, she looked as if she might run or have an orgasm at any moment.

'Can I get you a drink?' I offered. 'You seem really scared. Are you scared?'

She shook her head no and then let her eyes take me in. Her gaze levelled me from the tip of my head to the toe cleavage peaking out of my pumps. She surprised me by speaking. Loudly. 'Can we do this? I know why you asked me here. I knew the moment you touched my arm. And I am nervous but I really want this and I'd like to start.'

I heard Scott's soft laughter from the corner.

'Of course we can,' I said and began unbuttoning her

blouse. She reached through my arms and untied the knot at the base of my neck. The halter of my red dress fell away, leaving my breasts bare, nipples eager.

'Oh my,' she said and then she dipped her head just as I freed the last button and she sucked my nipple into her mouth. Her tiny pink mouth.

A rush of heat shot through me. From breast to cunt. Belly to scalp. How different the feel of her delicate feminine mouth was from Scott's. More gentle. Wetter if possible. Reverent.

Her small hands roamed over the skirt of my dress, caressed my waist, and I tackled the button of her black slacks. Now I wanted her bare. I wanted to see her small breasts, the hollow of her belly button, what was nestled between her thighs. Trimmed? Bare? Shaved? Wild? I couldn't wait to find out.

My voice was more authoritative than normal. 'Step out,' I commanded as I shoved her jeans down along with her panties. I had only caught a flash of red, and beyond the colour, I had no idea what they looked like. I didn't care.

She stepped out but her hands never left me for more than a second. It was as if she were memorising me with her hands. She was smooth and bare and creamy. I glanced quickly at Scott. The fly of his trousers was tented, the small smile still on his lips. He stroked the bulge under his fly with those big hands. I felt another hot rush of fluid slide down my inner thighs.

I ditched her clothes and her bra and then shimmied out of the rest of my dress. Before I could take off my silk panties, Callie had dropped to her knees and buried her face in the sodden material that shielded my cunt. The intensity of seeing another woman face first in my crotch was overwhelming. I plunged my hands into her soft hair and felt her hot breath heat the silk.

I heard Scott's zipper in the near silence.

She licked her way around the border of my panties and my knees felt unstable. I waited patiently as she explored. Her tiny nose nuzzled my belly as she traced the covered seam of

202

my sex with her kitten pink tongue. I felt like I would come already.

I shoved the thong down and widened my stance. 'Would you like to do it for real?' I asked softly.

She didn't even answer but rubbed the tip of her tongue over my already swollen clit as if she were taking a tiny sample taste. Very delicate and tentative but eager. My pulse slammed in my throat and chest and clit. My body thumping with each beat of my heart. I brushed her hair back so I could watch her. Her slender throat working, her eyes closed, her tongue probing and pushing and licking at me. I was fiercely wet and very hungry to see what she tasted like. Curiosity had turned to full-fledged desire.

'Back up,' I sighed, and she did but her large brown eyes looked confused. 'It's OK,' I smiled. 'Let's go over there.'

The blush returned, turning her normally creamy complexion ruddy. She dropped her eyes but nodded. I took her hand, wanting her to be comfortable, and led her to the bed.

I lay on my back and motioned her over me. I had deliberately lain sideways across the bed for Scott. This way he could see us both. See her mouth and tongue on me and mine on her. I heard the secretive wet sounds of his spit-dampened fist pumping his cock. My pussy twitched at the sound. Ready. I was ready.

When her cunt was over my face I could see how wet she was. Swollen and rosy and dilated. I did it all at once. Plunged my tongue in between her wet lips to find the tiny pink nub of her clit. Thrust two fingers into her blossoming pussy. She sighed against my own pussy and the vibration rocketed through me.

She tasted sweet and slightly musky. She tasted exotic and new. I worked my fingers into her moist heat, licked at her, drank her. Each time I licked her pussy clean a fresh wave of her moisture coated my face and my chin. My lips tingled with the feel of her.

Scott groaned in the corner. I groaned on the bed as her

slender fingers pushed into me. Explored me. Her tongue never stopped. Hot and fast, reminding me of the way tiny silverfish move in the ocean. Graceful and darting. Fast and intentional.

I suckled her clit and nibbled and her pussy clenched around my fingers, giving little warning signs of orgasm. I glanced at my husband as his fist pumped faster over his purplish cock. His face was divine. Intent and aroused and happy. And he was very close. Fifteen years of marriage earns you the knowledge. From the way his lips were parted and his eyes half closed, he was about to shoot and I wanted to go with him.

I played ring around the rosie with her beautiful pussy. Licking everywhere but where she wanted me until my fingers were trapped in her tight wet heat. Then I focused on her clit until she squirmed over me. Scott shifted, his fist a blur. I bucked myself against Callie's mouth and she started to finger-fuck me in earnest. I hooked my fingers inside of her and felt the swollen, suede-soft G-spot. I pushed it, stroked it and sucked her clit into my mouth.

She let loose over me. Her juices coating my face, her eager little tongue lapping at me even as she cried out. And over I went. I let her soft tongue and long fingers tip me over just as I saw my husband come. A freshet of semen shot from his fist and I rode wave after wave of pleasure.

Callie collapsed against me, twitching and cooing from time to time. I felt my breathing slow, my orgasm fade.

No one moved. Scott stared at me. His eyes barely took in our beautiful guest. It was me he was watching.

'I have to go,' Callie said softly. Her gaze lingered on my body for just a moment, and when she smiled she looked more certain of herself. 'I have to pick up my son from the sitter.'

I rose and kissed her softly on the lips. Her tongue was a searing heat in my mouth for a moment and then she turned to get dressed.

'We're here for two more nights,' I said. I handed her the blouse. 'Do you work tomorrow?'

'Yes, I do. Would you like me to come back?'

I didn't even glance at Scott.

'I would. If you want to.'

She buttoned her blouse and grinned. 'I'll be back. I'm sure I'll see you in the dining room first.' Then she touched my arm and kissed me again. 'You're so pretty.'

I couldn't help but laugh. 'And so are you.'

I didn't get dressed even after she left. I sat in Scott's lap and noticed he was hard again. I kissed him deeply and sighed, 'See what she tastes like?'

'Delicious.'

'Mmmm-hmmm.'

'So how do you feel about my fantasy now?'

'I think it's *my* fantasy at this point. And next time you read me something, I will definitely pay attention.'

Tech Support

"I've done it again," I whisper into the phone. Extension eleven is lit up; Tech Support. The hot little red button that matches my wildly beating heart and the moisture in the crotch of my panties. "Can you come quickly?"

Well, not too quickly, I think and grin.

"I'll be right there, Doris," he says and I can hear the smile in his voice. For some reason, his voice reminds me of sinful dark chocolate melting on my tongue.

I wait and cross my legs. That's not good. I uncross them and swivel my seat. I bounce my knee and I wonder how long it can take him to walk down the hall. It has been an eternity since I hung up the phone. Hasn't it?

I hear the heavier walk of a man. Women swish and sway down the centre aisle all day, but when a man walks past it's different. A different vibration and different rhythm. The cubicle walls shake just a bit more when a man walks by. I hold my breath and only release it when I start to feel light-headed.

There he is, dark hair and glasses. Brown eyes and a tired smile. He has been working overtime and the sleep deprivation is showing in the lines around his eyes. A little too heavy, a little too pale, a little too average for my normal likes. My heart kicks up into overtime and I feel my pussy clench just a bit. I am way too worked up.

I take a deep breath. "Sorry," I say softly. I am lying through my teeth. I am not sorry at all. Not one little bit. But he thinks I am and his cheeks flush with red and he smiles. He shakes his head.

"Believe it or not, I'm grateful for you, Doris. As long as

206

you work here, I have job security." He moves into the tiny confines of my cubicle and the air grows charged around me. At least my nipples think so, because they stand at attention and rub against the warm white silk of my blouse.

"Glad I can help," I joke. I brace myself for what will come next. The top three buttons on my blouse undone, I am prepared today.

"Doris, Doris, Doris, what am I going to do with you?" Mike asks.

Fuck me? But I don't say it. I hold my breath instead and his arms go around me. He stands behind my office chair and reaches his arms around on either side of mine. There they are. His hands. On my keyboard. All the while his breath is on my neck because his head is next to mine. I can see the fluorescence reflected in his glasses as he fixes my mangled program. I was never really good with tables. They stump me. So it is not hard for me to fuck them up to earn a visit from Mike and his hands.

"You can click and drag this over here, you know?" he says and I watch him work that mouse. To me, it's like watching porn. The dark hair on his knuckles makes me weak in the knees. The way the tendons flex just below the skin. And the scar on his right index finger that looks like a crescent moon has starred in many of my fantasies. The way it would disappear as he fucked me with his fingers. The flash of white flesh dipping into my pink recesses. I shiver.

"I didn't know that," I say to prolong exposure.

"Yes, you did. I told you last time." His hot breath slides down into the vee of my blouse, caresses my cleavage.

"Oh. Oops."

"I need an admin assistant to work this project tomorrow. Can you help? Faye is busy and she's a pain in the ass anyway. I know it's Saturday but please. Can you do it?"

"Me?" I say to his middle finger. Then I tear my gaze up to his open, friendly, clueless face and say, "Sure. What time do you want me? Should I be here! What time should I be here?"

"Seven."

207

"I'll bring donuts for everyone," I say. He punches a few keys and I watch his big fingers dance over the tiny keys. I squeeze my inner thighs together and a warm ribbon of pleasure fills my pussy.

"What everyone? You and me, kid. Skeleton crew."

My mouth goes dry and I feel like I might faint. Go all girly and pass out and slide right out of the chair. "Oh," I manage.

"You're all fixed up." He squeezes my shoulder and the pressure from his strong hands stops my breath. "See you in the morning?"

I nod. The moment he is gone, I scamper off. Run to the small private bathroom as fast as my two-inch heels will let me. I slump against the mauve-coloured door, prop one heel on the sink and get myself off. One orgasm, two orgasms, three orgasms, like brightly coloured poppies blooming just for me.

I walk back to my desk. Cheeks flushed, heart erratic, body warm. I cannot believe I have just done that. There's no telling what I'll do tomorrow when it's just me and Mike. Nothing. Nothing at all. I will control myself and act like a pro. Mike has no interest in me. Sadly.

"I did it again," I say and stare at the red indicator on my phone. Only, this time, I really have done it and not on purpose. "I don't know what I hit. The whole thing is gone. It's gone!" My voice is going up and my eyes are tearing up. Damn.

"I'll be right there," he says and laughs. His easy laughter makes me feel worse. Here we are on a Saturday working overtime and I screwed up. I lost the document because I wasn't focused on the inventory list. I was focused on my vivid dirty movie of me and Mike. And his fingers. The way he would pinch my nipples before running his finger slowly down my chest, between my breasts, and over the flat of my belly. How my stomach would do that fluttering thing it does when something almost tickles but doesn't quite and...

"What's gone?" Mike says and stands in the doorway of

my cubicle with his hands on his hips. His watch band is thick black leather, like a biker. I've never seen him in jeans. He looks completely normal and totally different.

"The spreadsheet for inventory."

He walks forward, grinning. "I doubt it's gone."

"It is. I was typing and poof! Gone! Blank document."

Mike reaches around me. A move that should be very familiar but somehow never grows old and says right in my ear, "Just minimize it. You must have hit Control N by accident. New document. Remember?"

Now I feel stupid. But the wave of goosebumps that has gone up my neck lets me forget how stupid I feel. My nipples peak in my pink and black skull T-shirt and I am fighting the urge to squirm. We are alone. In the office. Completely. I can't seem to swallow. "Sorry." I say it so much, I should get it tattooed on me.

"I like this," he says and I notice that his voice sounds different. More assured. Deeper.

"What?"

"This T-shirt. The snaps right here –" He takes his hand off my mouse and slides one finger down into my cleavage. His finger is hot and hard and I watch it dip between my breasts and I am mesmerized.

"Thank you."

"You're welcome. But I'd like it better open," he says and tugs.

The final two silver snaps let go with a *pop! pop!*

I shift in my seat and it doesn't help. It does nothing to dampen the pulse that has started to beat steadily between my thighs. I close my eyes and focus on the inhale.

"And I like the way you look when you get all flustered. And the way your breasts move up, up, up when you are trying to get a deep breath. Like right now," he says right against my earlobe. Then he dips his head and kisses me right above my heart. His lips are warm and soft and I can smell his shampoo.

"Oh," I say, brilliantly.

His hands come back in and gather me up. Wrap around

me and then tug me to my feet. I go very willingly. Like some pretty boneless thing. "I like these jeans. They are well loved," he says, hooking his hand in the front. Then he tugs and my little silver buttons give up the ghost. I am bare inside my denim and his hand slides down into my pants and covers me. He presses just his middle finger to the cleft of my sex and puts a hard pressure on my clit. I sink back against him.

Mike pushes my jeans down, but only to my knees. I go to kick them off and he steadies me with his hands. "No, leave them there."

So I do. I am bound by my own pants when he tilts me forward slightly and from behind pushes a finger into me. He adds another and my cunt flexes around him, welcoming. Damn. And I can't see it.

"You can watch my fingers next time," he laughs and I feel my eyes roll back. So he does know. I smile.

I close my eyes and picture the crescent moon scar being swallowed by my red-flushed pussy. I hang my head down and the computer fan kicks on with a whir. Mike strokes me slowly until I feel that tightness start. His other index finger rests with still but firm pressure on my clit. I'm making little sounds in my throat now.

"Almost there, Doris," he says and I feel the velvet head of his cock nudge me. I push back and try to widen my stance. "No, no, nice and tight together," says Mike, pushing against my hips with his palms. Holding my legs together so tight that my knees and ankles touch. He pushes again, tilts me forward more and slides home. One finger back to my clit and he starts a slow steady stroke that accents the intense friction. The chair rolls a little and he steadies us.

He puts his finger in my mouth and I lick at it. His fingers have the heady perfume of sex and attraction. He continues to stroke and rock and I come. Easy and sharp like a firecracker going off in the summertime.

He lets me hold on to the chair now and it rolls forward until it bangs the desk. I am now stretched out like a trapeze artist, my legs still snug in my denim cocoon. "Say it for me, Doris," he says.

I don't get it. Say what? But that is mostly because my brain has gone shiny and white with endorphins and I am slow on the uptake.

He's thrusting high and hard now, panting with his eagerness. His breath fans out over my back and my nipples grow even harder as the fine hairs on my neck stand. He gives me a clue. "Tech Support," he says in his professional voice.

I'm right there again. His finger is pushing me closer to the edge. His pressure is hard. Almost too hard. Just as I like it. I get it, now.

He lets out a groan as I whisper, "I've done it again."

I come around him and Mike's loud orgasm follows close behind. He thrusts all the way until the last flicker works through me. Then he laughs and smacks my ass lightly.

"Why yes, Doris. Yes, you have. And I hope you'll do it again."

Oh, no worries there. Mike can count on me.

The Known

I am the known in our neighbourhood. The men all know about me. There is talk. An underground railroad of information, tips and words of advice. I don't mind.

I am the talk of the women, too. A sad marriage. A woman to be pitied. A man who doesn't want me any more and more time to myself then I can shake a stick at. If they only knew. But they don't and I like it that way. I am someone to be pitied, or so the word on the street goes that way. A husband disabled by disinterest. We don't fuck any more, they all gossip. And it's true. We don't.

I'd rather fuck their men anyway.

I am the great secret who is not so secret. I follow the fires; the chimneys, the pits. The smell of wood smoke and ash, like some mythical creature of campfire lore. Under the moon, bright and savage, I find my mark. Sometimes the fire calls out by a cool summer pool, luminous turquoise water that makes you think of slaked thirst. Of chilled heaven and cleansed souls. But always there is fire.

The husbands who don't invite me with orange flaring night calls do not tell their wives. That would be wrong, they'd be outing their buddies who do call out to me. And besides, if they tell, if the day ever comes that they want me for themselves, they're screwed.

Tonight I wind my way through Joshua's back yard, past his lilac bush and past his wife's white cat who's name is Pepper. She glares at me with moss-coloured eyes and blinks like I will disappear. 'Good kitty,' I say.

Their fence squeaks on its hinges, I know this from meeting Joshua out here, so I hold it tight and try to move it slow. It helps. He taught me that and I still remember. I also remember that his skin tasted like oranges and he babbled when he came. Words like love and glory and mother and home. I remember the feel of his fingers tugging at my braids while I sucked him dry.

I move past the red car in their driveway and if I close my eyes I can remember him fucking me in the back seat in the dead of night while snow fell on the windshield, licking at the glass, whispering as he thrust into me. He had been outside though, by his trusty chimney, pretty much sending me smoke signals to come and give him something that his wife couldn't. So I answered.

My feet sink into the lush lawn next door as I cross. Inside, Mr Hampson's dog barks three quick chuffs. Mr Hampson, Todd to his friends, cries when he climaxes. He likes you to play with his balls and he lives to eat pussy. And he's good at it too. Todd liked to kiss the insides of my thighs and along my legs until I pleaded and promised him anything if he would just put his mouth to me. And then he would and the world would stop and all it would be was the hot sopping length of his tongue on my clit. He also liked to bite.

His dog woofs once more but he sounds bored. I hurry through the yard and across the street. The black top still warm under my feet from hours ago when it lay assaulted and warmed by the mid-day sun. The fireflies flicker around me like shorted out Christmas bulbs and the cicadas are shrieking like monkeys in the concrete jungle. This is suburbia, but don't be fooled, the city is a bullet's path away.

I really cannot pinpoint the fire yet. It's just a glow ball of light in the semi-darkness. It's never really dark here with the street lights and garage lights and motion sensors and whatnot. But it is darker than day time and the orange glow of a fire in summer shimmers in the purple night, a big enough beacon to follow.

I walk past Mark Abrahams yellow sports car. His phallic symbol. Trust me, he needs it. His wife eats his self esteem for breakfast and then spits it at him all day long. He is so armoured from emotion that when he comes he clenches his jaw like he's angry. If you tell him he's hung his face softens like he's taking his final breath before he dies. If you tell him he's good, he damn near kisses your feet. My heart breaks for him when I see him out, but he smiles at me, remembering how I let him pull my hair when he fucked me from behind. He called me special. I called it therapy.

It is Edward's property glowing for me. I see it now as I round the side of his small white cottage. The black shutters suck up the light like some kind of supernatural sponge. The tongues of yellow fire are reflected in the old glazed windows and I worry that his wife will see. But then part of me wants her to, right? It is the women of our cosy little neighbourhood who squawk and crow about me. And then when they go to sleep and dream their righteous, perfect dreams, I fuck their husbands in their own back yards. A wolf in sheep's clothing. A predator in the guise of a victim. Or, a woman who knows what she wants. I prefer the latter.

'I didn't think you'd come, Heather,' he says and he's feeding the squat fat clay pot another handful of sticks. 'I though they made it all up.'

I smiled, suddenly feeling a little shy, worried. I always feel this for a few moments. But usually they end up on their knees, begging me silently (or not too silently) to understand them, if only for a night. So I do. Because I do understand them. They simply want communion, company, acceptance.

'Here I am.'

'What do I do?' He turns to me and there is a haunted hollow of dark shadows under his eyes. Too much stress, too little sleep, no one who listens. I've seen it all before. The marriages that go from love affairs to business meetings. You go here and I'll go there and it's your turn to do the dishes, change the baby, do we have time for three point seven minutes of sex? No. Not tonight.

'What do you want?' It is the most basic of questions and yet it seems to stagger him.

'Sex.'

'I figured.' I smile at him and he smiles back. He has a nice smile, if not tired. Wary. 'What kind?'

He's a shy one, so I am bolder now by measure. I go to him, wrap my arms around his neck and stand there, waiting. Offering my lips up for a kiss and he takes my offer. Holding my head in his hands and pushing his hot, eager mouth to mine. I open my lips and he makes a soft sound like he's surprised. I push my body to his, feeling the long ridge of his hard cock along the front of me. I move so that I rub him and that sound is back, filling my head and starting a pulse of excitement in my belly, in my cunt.

'Any kind. Any kind, really. Just something,' he whispers.

Ah. A man deprived of softness, curves, touch and kisses. 'That's fine. You tell me.' He stiffens. 'Show me,' I amend. He goes with that.

He pushes me back into the shadows where no one can see. Back in between two trees where the lawn furniture, freshly spray painted dark green this year, resides. He pushes me onto the chair and tugs at my gym shorts. My old, soft tee is over my head before I can even shiver. He's fast and he's eager and he's intent now, his breath blowing hot over my faces. His kisses settling on my skin even hotter. Only half of his face is speckled with the orange glow from his fat clay pot. I find his cock with my hand, his lips with my tongue. We are a tangle of sunburned limbs and secret dreams. Mine to find a man who wants me as fiercely as fire wants oxygen. His to find a woman who what? Fucks, listens, cares, loves? Pick one.

'I thought you were a fairytale,' he says, his finger thrusting and bending deep inside of me so that my ass leaves the crosshatched wrought iron chair to chase his touch.

'Like Santa Claus? Make me a fire and I will come?' I laugh softly because I'm about to.

'Yes, do. You're so tight. You couldn't, couldn't you? Is it the fire or the men?' he asks but dips his head to suck my clit before I can answer.

The answer is yes. Yes to all of the above and no to all of it too. It is whatever it is. It is an urge, a need, a thirst I have and only they can fix me when it settles in for a visit. It lives in my chest and my belly. It pulses in my pussy until I am half mad with want like some stray cat in heat. And the fires crop up more in the summer when the heat of the city drifts into our part of the hood. That hasn't escaped my notice.

'It doesn't matter,' I whisper. And it doesn't because he's pulling at his shorts and I feel the smooth, stiff head of his cock between my legs. I hook my legs and tug him into me, wanting him to forget whatever it is that made him come out here and build the fire for me.

'No. I guess not. I'm glad you're here, Heather.' He kisses me like we are true lovers and my throat grows a little tight.

'Me, too.'

He fucks me softly at first, the antique lawn chair bouncing under us. It's older than I am and it gives and springs back with each thrust. I open my legs for him, and meet each pounding surge into my body. I bite at his throat and feel the blood jump under his skin. I close my eyes memorizing the feel of his fingers digging into my skin and his new beard scratching my face. 'Bite me,' I whisper, tightening my pussy around his cock so that he wavers. He stops and his eyes are wide and his breath is rushed.

'Won't he see? Your husband?'

I shrug, sliding up and down the length of him in little waves of movement and he closes his eyes to steady his body. To not come. To keep control. 'He won't care.'

The knowledge that that is true nearly makes me start to fuck him harder so that he will break. But it is not his fault that Jack won't care so I bare my throat and I clench my cunt and I move up just enough that he had to capitulate and he does. He dips his head and bites me, his fingers moving over me. Face, lips, mouth, I suck his finger and he fucks me faster. Throat, shoulders, collar bone. He steadies on the undulating chair for a moment and then nipples, belly, hips thighs. As if he's proving that I am real.

I am truly real. And really coming and I say so, his teeth still locked above my pulse like some great night-time beast. 'I'm coming. Will you come with me? Please?'

He comes with me in a rush of breath and body and words I cannot decipher. It is the please that breaks him. It always is.

It is not an order, a to-do list, a demand. It is a plea. A request. A need I have. They get to be my knight in shining armour, my big strong man, my provider. They get to give me what I'm pleading for. They like it. And so do I. It helps that hunger that overtakes me.

He sits back on his knees, his cock still buried deep inside of me. He paints his fingers over my belly like he's laying down a design. His breathing normalizes and he's smiling, I can see that by the one side of his orange and yellow face. 'Will you come back?'

'Will you invite me?'

He nods. Kissing below my breasts, fingers tangled in my small patch of pubic hair. 'I will. I'll build you a fire.'

An offering

'Then I'll come.'

And so will you.

'I need you,' he says. 'I want you. Is that OK?'

I nod. Because I need him too, right now. And I want him. But I won't say it out loud. I'll just watch for the flames and the smoke.

Vigil

It was easy enough to lose myself in the inner workings of The Joint. Completely doable to build small, token relationships with the regulars as my long-term token relationship dissolved. I bussed tables, chatted up artists and writers and stay-at-home mums while Richard ran around and got lipstick on his collar. And his boxers. I made foam and espresso that would curl your toes and doled out croissants with a smile and a small flirty laugh for garnish.

All the while I was doing the death-watch for my marriage. The mental equivalent of sitting in the corner waiting for our union to take its last garish dying breath. And I wasn't just waiting. I was an avid audience, eagerly awaiting the death rattle. Richard, for all intents and purposes, was clueless.

I wiped the counter and waited. Any moment now the door would open and three people would walk into the café. Brie, the recently divorced soccer mum. She'd be here for her morning jump shot of caffeine to get her through more legal papers and her volunteer hours at the kids' school. It was not easy to have your heart breaking while trying to look *that good*. Then would come Jason, a brick mason. Jason would get a froofy caramel latte, make a joke about it, flirt and then be on his way. Low-slung faded jeans fitting his hips in a way that made me think sinful thoughts. And then would come Jose. Jose the teacher who taught rehabilitated addicts to work in the community. Jose who likes his espresso strong enough to peel paint.

The tiny bell dinged and I looked up, ready to greet whoever was first through the door. The greeting died on my

218

lips.

He nodded to me, inclining a beautiful face with high cheekbones. Flawless burnt caramel skin stretched over his bone structure and my heart did a small flutter. I nodded back, my voice gone. He found a table, set a sketchbook and messenger bag on the seat to mark his spot. He loped toward me with a lazy, sure walk. My throat felt too small but I couldn't not watch him.

'Morning.' He grinned and my mind took in the slightly crooked front tooth and the soft pink colour of his tongue.

'Good morning, what will you have?' For some reason that sounded dirty and heat rushed to my cheeks. He caught the look. My embarrassment.

The flash of a grin, his long hair swaying over his shoulders. Long, long dreadlocks caught up in a bit of leather. He was a god. An idol. Something magical. His voice deep and dark and secretive. I had clearly lost my mind. 'What's good?' He leant in. 'I like strong but sweet.'

That sounded dirty too and I cleared my throat to stall, tried to smile. 'We have a half and half. Half espresso, half hot chocolate.' My eyes skittered nervously but avidly over his broad chest, his black tee with the Green Lantern insignia on it. I knew that thanks to my nephew Max.

'Sounds good, Nicci,' he said.

I blinked. 'How did ...' I didn't even get it out before he leant in a little more, stalling the breath in my lungs. He touched one long ink-smudged finger to my red nametag. *Nicci, Owner*. I laughed. Too high, too long, too loud. He grinned again.

'I can read. And I'm Frankie. Frankie Winner.' He stared. I stared.

'Hi.' My face grew hotter and my cunt was doing that thing that it did when getting laid was imminent. Only it wasn't imminent. But my body sure as hell wanted it to be.

'About that coffee ...'

'Oh right! Shit! Sorry.' I turned, a flurry of nervous hands and anxious energy. Were the curls in my hair standing out from my messy top knot in 20 different directions? Did I wear my good ass jeans? How many coffee stains were on my polo already and had I remembered to put on make-up? His laughter washed over me, calming me but revving me up too.

The door jingled. 'Nicci!' Jose yelled and I waved a hand at him, trying to find the chocolate syrup.

Ding! 'Good morning, girl!' Brie.

Ding! 'Honey, I'm home!' That was Jason's daily joke.

All the while I could feel Frankie Winner's eyes on me. Making me crazy and off centre. And my brain wouldn't stop worrying at his name. Why did I know his name but not his face? I turned too fast and hot liquid splashed onto my hand. One more scar in a sea of tiny burns. But I hissed anyway.

'Easy. Hey, you are one busy lady.' Big strong hands, a shade darker than mine, pushed a small white napkin to the spill and I hummed low in my throat before I could stop myself.

'Thank you.'

'My pleasure.' My hand continued to shake so I set the cup down. 'What do I owe you?' he asked.

A kiss? 'Nothing. First cup is on the house.' Before he could balk I pointed to a small sign on the wall that said: *New to us? First cup is on the house!* I managed to smile at him when he grinned even though all I could hear was my heart and my ears ringing. I watched him saunter off and managed a nice big breath.

'Oh, girlfriend. You are practically panting like a dog and your eyes are glazed. Did he diddle you or something?'

'Brie!' I squeaked, turning to get her drink automatically. I loved the safe, easy routine of getting regulars their orders. 'My God. Hush.'

'Sweetheart, if he didn't, he should. When you look that satisfied before a man touches you, you need to get together.'

I laughed, but again —too high, too long, too loud. Frankie Winner looked up from his table and winked.

'My goodness. I didn't think it was possible but you just got more flustered.' Brie leant in and whispered to me, 'That man has the ass of a Greek god.'

'Oh, holy shit.' I hung my head, shaking it. I was a mess.

A hot, hot mess. 'Brie, behave yourself.'

Brie pushed her long blonde hair out of her face, dropped a dollar in the tip jar and grinned, 'Mark my words. You are getting some of that. Mark them!' she called and rushed out into the cold wind, headed to her lawyers or the kindergarten. Who knew which. I had forgotten to ask.

I waited on Jose and Jason. My eyes kept popping up to peek at Frankie only to find Frankie watching me. His big hand moved pencil over paper without any apparent concentration. My insides would light up and heat would course along my skin and I would look away, busy myself with the usual morning rush. For the first morning in a long while I was not angry that Richard wasn't here to help. I was not obsessing over what – or who – he might be doing instead. It was a lovely respite from my normal melancholy.

'You have any of those almond biscotti?' Mrs Rush, another regular, asked. I looked at the photos of her grandkids, boxed up some goodies for her, refilled her decaf. But even as I did so, my eyes kept straying. And every time, every damn blessed time, his big brown eyes were on me. Like fingers. Like a touch. Probing.

The rush ended in a flurry of clacking silverware, dirty cups, crumpled paper napkins. In a heartbeat and a clock tick it was only me and Frankie in The Joint. I busied myself bussing tables, wiping off dark red Formica tops, throwing out scraps and debris. I could hear the rustling swoosh of his pencil over sketchpad and the sound stirred something in my chest, it sounded so reverent and hasty. I didn't talk. I was too afraid.

'So, you own this place alone?' he asked softly, without looking at me. His dark eyes stayed down on the paper now, as if he knew they made me so nervous I couldn't think. Him looking at me. The *way* he looked at me.

'I am co-owner but seemingly sole worker,' I laughed. The shop only stayed open from seven to seven. I worked most shifts; I had a college student who did relief shifts and a few friends I could call in if an emergency should happen. Beyond that, my shop was small and tidy and pretty much a one-woman deal.

'Ah, is the other owner a man?'

'A husband.'

'Hmmm.' *Scratch, scratch, scratch* went his magical pencil.

'Not a real husband. More of a cardboard cutout,' I laughed. There it was again – too high, too long, too loud. I ducked my head, grabbed a stray fork.

'Not a good man?'

'I thought so once.'

'But you were wrong?'

I nodded.

'That's OK. Everyone's wrong sometimes.' His fingers flew, his mouth turned down a bit as he drew.

I inched closer, drawn to him. Curious. Terrified. 'I'm done,' he said to his sketch. 'You can take the plate if you don't mind. I'll want another coffee though.' His hand flew faster and the scratching symphony seemed to fill my head.

'Right. No problem.' I went to him like I was perfectly calm. Took the napkins and empty sugar packs. God, he had put sugar in the already sweet concoction? I smiled. And then there was my own face staring back at me. His fingers moved over my jawline, smudging it, softening the sharp angle he had drawn. 'That's me,' I breathed.

'Yes, sister, it is.'

'Wow. I ...' I put the dish tub on an empty table and snapped. 'You're Frankie Winner! You draw *Vigil*!'

The smile nearly swallowed his handsome face it was so big. 'You know *Vigil*? Come on, you don't look like a comic-book nerd. How do *you* know *Vigil*?'

'I have a nephew named Max. That nephew thinks you hung the sun. And the moon. All the stars and possibly are a god.' I was smiling, my heart was going. And then I caught myself, caught his gaze on me and my knees felt weak.

'Ah, then I have to give you something for Max.' He pulled a copy of his comic book from the messenger bag, extracted a Sharpie, and wrote on it. *To Max, You have a smoking hot aunt and good taste! Frankie Winner*

222

I laughed. 'I can't give him that!'

'Oh, OK, then. Be that way. Picky, picky,' he teased, signing another with a quick slash of black ink. Just a signature. Max would levitate. My eyes went back to my eyes. My nose. My face on his paper. A fiercer me. A warrior me. I bit my lip.

'Why are you drawing me?'

His eyes found mine and I held my breath. Everything was so loud and bright. The clock ticking, the humming overhead fluorescents. 'I draw things I like. When I see something striking, I draw it. Especially for the books.' He nodded toward the messenger bag where more comics peeked out.

'You're putting me in there!'

'I think I am.'

'Am I a superhero?' I blurted and then wished for all the world I could rewind and not say it. I had sounded way too excited. Way too silly. I toed the cracked black-and-white tile floor and tried not to fidget.

'I don't know. I guess we'll have to see. She's not even sure if she is yet. It depends on how strong she is.'

I watched him touch my hand and a zinging tingly sensation filled my fingertips before I realised it was him. His fingers were warm, his eyes searching. 'I'm keeping a vigil of my own,' I sighed. 'And I'm afraid I'm not very brave. Maybe you could just make me a throwaway character. Kill me off in a page or two?' I tried to chuckle but my vigil statement had lodged in my throat. The truth sucks. I was keeping vigil over a dying marriage.

Frankie's fingers crept around my wrist, his fingers a darker circlet of skin against my own. I liked the look of his hand on me. He had a small scar on his hand, a teak-coloured slash against the beautiful smooth flesh. 'I bet you're stronger than you think.'

His phone rang and the door jangled. I looked up. Mr Foster, my regular eleven-thirty. 'Hi, Mr F,' I called, not wanting him to release me. But Frankie's hand dropped and he closed his phone after a soft goodbye.

'I have to run. I'll be back.'

'You liked the coffee then?' I was fishing. Hoping. Wishing. And we both damn well knew it.

'I liked the coffee fine. I like the ambience better.' He gathered his stuff and turned fast, his mouth coming down on mine warm and chocolate flavoured. His tongue found the tip of my tongue and the kiss went from soft to hard and then back to soft. A gentle break and he touched my lower lip with his finger. 'I'll be back for that refill. Think about how strong you are, yeah?'

'Yeah,' I said. Totally lying. But so was he, and that was fine. He wouldn't be back and I would not think about my strength. Or lack thereof.

It was all wiped down. The dishes washed. The lights out. I sighed, tossed the trash sack into the dumpster. I wanted a glass of wine, a frozen dinner and my pyjamas. Maybe the latest in reality TV so that all the nut-jobs on TV living their lives for cameras could make me feel better than I felt about my own life.

Unless Richard was home. If he was home it would be round 1,239 over where he'd been, who with and why we were married to begin with. Or maybe not. I wasn't in the mood. Whoever he was fucking deserved him. With any luck he'd stay with her tonight.

'You should be careful, anyone could sneak up on you out here.' My ears picked up the sibilant sway of his dreads on his corduroy jacket before I actually registered his face. I should have been startled; instead I was suddenly too warm in the cool fall air.

My pussy thumped along with my heartbeat. My pelvis growing warm and soft and wet all of a sudden. A purely visceral reaction to the close proximity of Frankie Winner. 'I know.' It was barely a whisper and a sudden gust whisked most of it away. His hair looked blue in the half light from the streetlamps.

'A guy with bad intention. A guy who's had a head full of you all day.' He took a step toward me and I took a step back. My jeans snagging on the rough brick wall of the small alley.

The light over the back door to The Joint had blown ages ago. I wished it was glowing, throwing off lemon yellow light as his mouth came closer so I could see him better. He smelt like cinnamon and cloves and leather.

'A head full of me?' My brain fuzzy, body humming. His lips touched mine and his hands found my hips and pushed me harder against the chilled brickwork.

'You.' Lips on my neck, my collarbone, hands on my ass, hauling me forward so that his hard cock ran the split seam of my cunt. Even through my jeans my clit thumped; I grew wetter between my legs. Desperate.

I touched his hair, the warm weight of it in my hands. I pulled from each side like I was pulling reins and stood on tiptoe to put my tongue in his mouth. Feel more of him, taste more of him on my lips. 'I don't know why,' I said against his chin.

'It didn't help that I had a picture of you staring back at me while I tried to work. Staring at me when I did a short singing up the street at the Comic Block. Making my dick hard and my heart hurt. You might turn out to be a bad girl. A femme fatale,' he said, hauling me to him again, rubbing me against his length even while his lips never stopped.

'I don't think that's me.' But even as I said it, I hooked a leg around his slim waist, opening my body to him despite the barrier of fabric.

'Trust me, baby, it's you.' He palmed my ass, lifted me again, thrust against me.

'Should we go–'

'No.' He bit me gently but enough to make me jerk, my hair catching on the coarse wall, my breath catching in my throat. 'Here. Now. Pants.' He was laughing and I was helping. Too many fingers on my button fly, we warred each other even as we each tried to help the other. 'I couldn't stop staring at my sketch,' he said, head still down.

'I couldn't stop thinking about your kiss,' I admitted. I pushed at my pale yellow panties, watched the sunshiny silk slide down my dark legs, pushed by his hands. My pussy so wet and so ready and ruling my entire brain at this point in time. His fingers slid up my leg, tickling, blazing an invisible trail of fire. 'Touch me,' I said. There for a moment I was brave. I was strong.

His eyes found mine, inky dark in the city lights. 'Like this?' He dipped a finger inside me, withdrew it, ran the pad of his finger over my clit. I pushed my hands flat to the wall to keep from floating off. To keep from falling down.

'More, please,' I closed my eyes, letting my head tip back.

'Look at me.' It wasn't a request but there was respect in his tone.

I opened my eyes. Watched his eyes as he slid his thick warm finger deep inside me again. He curled that finger deep in my cunt, touching a spot that made my hands grasp at nothing. 'Why?'

'I want to see your eyes. I want to see you come. You're beautiful.'

I shut my eyes. His fingers stopped. I opened my eyes.

I tugged at his belt, wrestled it until the buckle sang out and then my fingers found his zipper. Pulling free of his hand, I dropped to my knees, pulling the jeans down with me as I went. Long and hard and perfect, his cock nestled in his boxers until I tugged at those too. He was dark silk on my lips. Cashmere on my tongue. He thrust a few times, his hands steadying my head as he pushed into my mouth. 'Sorry, God, sorry,' he said. 'Your mouth is just too good.'

I smiled in the dark. Liking that. Seeing this in my head like a comic book. Blocks of black and white. Words streaked in the dark air. *Bang! Thrust! Pop!* I licked up the length of him, the dirt and the grit biting my kneecaps. His fingers pushing at my temples, my forehead, my eyelids. I swallowed him and breathed him and wanted him that much more. I was brave.

'Come on up here, come on up here.' Frankie's voice was rough and scratchy like his pencil on his paper. His fingers, stained with ink and calloused from drawing ran up my neck, over my face, pulling at my tee until my breasts popped free. His tongue was on me, rolling my nipple over his tongue, sucking until I felt a tug in my pussy. 'Spread your legs,

Nicci. Spread your legs for me.'

I opened, pushing my back to the wall, letting him at me with his perfect cock and pretty words and talent. When he broke free of my breast to kiss me, I sucked his tongue like his cock. Kissed his full lips hard, bit his lower lip until he jerked at my hips roughly and thrust into me. Filling me. Pinning me to the wall with his body, a pretty ochre butterfly with a broken heart and one remaining flicker of hope. He pushed into me, touching me softly, rough, fast, hard. Just touching me. Feeling me. I was real to him. Real and beautiful.

My throat clogged a little and I let it. Something in my chest felt like it was cracking and I let it. A melancholy wave of sorrow crashed over me and I turned my face up to it, letting it come. Brave. Free. Distanced. The ending of my vigil. The ending of my last tiny threadbare shred of caring for my marriage. My fingers clutched at his shoulders like I was drowning. My eyes leaked like I was dying. My mouth worked, soft, soft words I could barely hear, like someone praying in church. 'Please, Frankie, Please. Please, please, please.' Over and over. Please what? Please don't let me go? Or please set me free? I didn't know.

'Come for me, Nicci. You're right there.' His lips whispered against my earlobe; he bit me softly, his teeth sharp and hard against my skin. 'You are right there. Your cunt's like a slick fist. Perfect. So fucking perfect.'

I came. And when he pushed harder, higher, faster, his mouth crushing mine and my back scraped raw from the mortar, I came again. Screaming out like some bad-ass bird of prey. Screaming out and letting go of all of it. Letting go of the me who had spent so much time letting it go. Letting it slide. I was done waiting. And I was done hoping about things past. When he came, I listened. To his breath, to the expletives, to the rustle of his clothes and the sway of his hair.

Frankie grinned at me in the dark. His eyes watching every flicker of emotion. Every bad feeling dropping away like dirty feathers. 'Wow. You *are* a femme fatale.'

'No. I was just ... ready. And you were ...'

'I was?'

'You were you.'

He laughed, his laugh as dark and rich as the coffee I served. 'What's that mean?'

'I wanted you.' I lowered my head, smiling. Frankie handed me my panties and I got myself together.

'Enough to go for it?' He turned me, took my arm. We headed past the back door of the shop.

'Enough to speak up. Enough to be strong.'

'So where do you want to go now, bad-ass woman?'

I thought about it. I could be shy or I could be coy. I could go home and look back fondly on tonight. One of those memories to treasure and polish and put in a memory box and take out as the years flew by. Or I could move forward. Be brave. 'I was thinking maybe you'd like to take me home and make me dinner,' I said. False bravado rushed over my lips and I held my breath waiting. Waiting for my fate.

Frankie's hand snaked around my waist. 'Hmm, I thought you'd never ask. I have some drawings I want to show you. And then maybe I'll draw you.'

'In a superhero costume? For *Vigil*?' I asked, my body still pulsing from my orgasm. My heart still lifted from my new-found freedom.

'I was thinking more like naked.' He smacked my ass and I yelped. We headed down Main Street. 'But I'm sure you'll see yourself in *Vigil*.' His face went serious for a moment. He was even more beautiful under the full moon.

'Oh, yeah? Who will I be?'

'You'll be the brave one. The badass.'

When he kissed me, I tugged his hair. To get him closer.

Not All Love Stories are Great

It would have been much more interesting if she had been running from something, Molly realised. A much better story to tell if she were a widow, or running from some horrible ex. Even if she were walking out on a philandering husband. All of that would have made her moving down to Deep Water Lake that much more exciting for the locals to talk about.

That wasn't the case.

The real story, in fact, was rather boring and stupid. She had grown tired of all parts of her life, most of all the total lack of a love life. A fresh start was something she looked at as a last-ditch effort. Maybe this would be the whirlwind-spurring moment in her life.

'Or just another place to live a boring life,' she murmured to herself, standing in the entryway of her new home. What had once been a small in-laws house was now a single cottage for rent. The owner had given her six months to rent and then the promise of the right to buy if she desired. It was a win-win as far as Molly could tell.

'Pretty place, don't you think?'

She turned so fast she dropped her bag, her mouth hanging open, eyes flying so wide that the light was suddenly too bright. 'Oh, my holy God, you scared me!'

'Sorry,' the woman said. She was laughing though. Even hiding her face behind her big red mittens, Molly could tell by the slant and sparkle in her eyes that she was laughing.

'Yes, pretty,' Molly sighed, smiling despite feeling like a moron.

'I'm Ella Simon and I live next door. Well, in front of you. In the big house. I keep the property for my brother Samuel.'

'Samuel Simon, Samuel Simon ... That always sounded like a nursery rhyme to me. Even when I was talking to him about renting, I wanted to say it aloud,' Molly giggled because now her nerves were shot which always put her in a nervous laughter kind of mood.

'Good thing Mother didn't call him Simple, then.' Ella bent and grabbed two light boxes. 'Let me help you. Leave the heavy stuff, Sean can get it soon enough. He'll be home in an hour or so.'

'Sean?' This is the point in the past where Molly would have felt a quickening of the heart. No more. She simply felt a minor blip of curiosity.

'My surly and ferociously glum son. He runs our sporting goods shop since he's back at the homestead. Lives in the keeper's cottage by the boathouse. Close-knit family, we are,' Ella grunted, setting down her burden. 'These days I think they call it dysfunctional.'

Molly didn't quite manage capping her laughter and she smacked her palm over her mouth to try and contain the tail end. But it didn't matter because her new neighbour, aka her caretaker, was laughing with her. 'Sorry. Seems you got me in a laughing mood.'

'It's perfectly fine. You know my father used to say, better to laugh than to cry.' Ella pushed the boxes flush to the wall and threw her hands high. It made Molly look up and she saw the cottage's perfect high ceilings again. The outcropping of the wooden loft that would be where she slept. The perfect blue October sky through the ceiling light that painted a round circle of sunshine on the floor of the main room.

'Wow.'

'Had you forgotten?' Ella beamed.

'I had. I had forgotten how gorgeous it was. I'm fairly certain I'll want to buy. But how do you feel about that?'

Ella waved a hand. 'Ah, Samuel and I have decided it will do wonders for our bank accounts. Plus the main property will still be ours. It's Sean who has an issue but he won't buy it himself. Just wants to gripe.'

'Why is he so ferociously glum?' Molly asked, feeling

silly and nosy all at once. She shook her head. 'Never mind. It really isn't any of my busin–'

'Girl problems. He ain't got one.' Ella snorted and shook her head. 'That was mean. I am his mother, after all. He had one and now he doesn't. It can put a crimp in a man's good humour.'

Molly, who had never had a man – not for real, anyway – nodded sympathetically. 'I'm sure he'll get over it.'

'He's not hard to look at, so maybe he'll at least get lucky and that will brighten his mood.' Ella winked and Molly couldn't help it, she was giggling again. No wallflower, her new caretaker, no sir. But maybe a good friend, eventually. She could hope.

'Wow. I hope that works out for him.'

Ella grinned. 'Yep. Me too. I'll bring you a snack later. And some tea. No one should have to move *and* forage all at the same time. You like Earl Grey?'

'I do.'

'How about pumpkin cookies?'

'I do, I do!' Molly said.

'Good deal then. I'll be back in a bit. When Sean rolls home, I'll send him over.'

'Thanks, you really don't have t–'

Ella waved a hand and frowned. 'Don't even. He won't mind helping you out. And even if he is grumpy, ignore him. That's an order.'

Molly felt the overwhelming urge to hug this woman. All she had been missing lately was someone in her life who cared. Someone to boss her around and maybe coddle her a bit. Already Ella Simon was doing just that. Even the prospect of a surly son didn't scare her.

While putting away linens, insanity struck. One moment she was folding sheets, biding her time until help arrived to get the big furniture into the house, the next she was dancing. And not only dancing – dancing and singing top volume to one of her favourite Motown songs that happened to play on the radio.

'Bernadette! People are searching for the kind of–'

'You don't get out much, do you?' he said.

Molly threw an armful of sheets in the air like New Year's streamers and let out a horrible shriek. Which was pretty mortifying, to say the least.

She stared, heart pounding, hands shaking. She wanted to punch him right in the neck. That was her first instinct. Then she wanted to slap his face, that was her second. Mostly because of the smirk on his handsome face. Then her eyes took in the deep coffee brown of his eyes and the small streaks of green that swirled around the pupil, the big broad shoulders and the leanly muscled upper body and the anger turned to a sharp, hot zing of lust. She shook her head, frowning. 'No, I do not get out much. Not much at all. You *must* be Sean.'

'Oh? And why must I be?' He set a tray of cookies and tea on a moving box and bent to retrieve her red-and-white sheets printed with flamboyant poppies. He held them to his face and sniffed. 'Nice.'

Molly felt herself blush all the way to the roots of her hair. She grabbed the sheet, her fingers brushing his for just an instant. Less than a heartbeat. But enough for her to feel an unwelcome stab of attraction. 'Because your mother described you to a "T". And yes, it is nice, it's English lavender.'

He grinned again and it made her belly flutter with anxiety. Molly turned, stuffed the sheets in a messy square among the otherwise neat hive of bedding.

'Would that "T" happen to be a grumpy jerk with a bad attitude?' he laughed, took a cookie from the tray and snapped it in half. Those dark brown eyes were on her and Molly felt his gaze as tactile as a physical touch on her skin. She found herself wet between the legs with nowhere to run. He was in her home, after all.

'A little,' she stammered. Then she poured a cup of tea, wishing she hadn't because her hands shook so bad the small china top rattled in the pot.

Sean laughed softly and her body responded with a shiver that she tried to ignore. It was simply chilly in here.

Sean bent to get another cookie, his breath – warm and spiced – ran over her shoulder like a shower of invisible water. Electrically charged water at that. A mild current seemed to skitter under her skin, her nipples spiked, her scalp tingled. She had wanted excitement. She had wanted attraction. She had not wanted her body to go haywire over a man she wanted so desperately to dislike. 'My mother's wrong about me. I can be very charming,' he said, his lips almost touching her hair.

Molly bit her tongue and froze; maybe if she didn't move, he wouldn't provoke her any more. She would pretend he was an angry bear and play dead. 'I'm sure you can,' she said, the words issuing from a throat that felt two sizes too small.

'I'll go grab your desk. I'll need your help with the futon and the sofa though.'

'Fine, fine,' she stammered. 'Thanks so much.' Molly waited until he was out the door before she looked his way. The red screen door was swinging shut, offering her a limited view of his broad back, his faded jeans and the way his dark wheat-coloured hair curled along the collar of his green tee. It was too long and she imagined that wet, it was much darker and the curl more pronounced. For just a breath she wondered what his skin would taste like, but she pushed the thought away. 'Moving to a new life doesn't mean jumping the first man that looks at you, Molly,' she muttered and sipped her tea. It was too hot and she swallowed fast.

Bernadette gave way to Jimmy Buffett and Molly put a few bath items away in the small hallway linen closet. She kept her eyes on the front door and, when she saw Sean struggling to walk the desk up the slate path, she hurried to push the screen wide. 'I can help you!'

'Don't need help,' he grunted. 'If I needed fucking help, I'd ask for it.' He frowned at her, his jaw set from the strain and struggle of manhandling the small but heavy wooden desk up the walkway. She reached out to help him get it up the one step to the small porch and he glared at her so hard that she pulled her hands back as if she'd been burned. 'Just let me do it,' he growled.

'You're really rude!' she blurted and then put her head down, mortified that she'd let her emotions run away with her. Clearly he wasn't angry at her. He was just angry.

'I try. Now are you going to stand there passing judgement on me, or are you going to tell me where you want this deceitfully small desk?'

She had to stifle a smile at that. It was small but weighed a tonne since it was made out of walnut and not fibreboard. 'In the nook just off the kitchen.'

He nodded approvingly and muttered, 'Good choice.'

Molly found herself mysteriously pleased that he agreed with her.

Sean Simon came back through, brushing his hands on his pant legs. 'What do you do anyhow? Not much work up here, but for local shops that have low-paying jobs.'

'I teach yoga,' she said. When he stared at her harder she said, 'And I write about it. Health magazines, yoga sites and the like.'

'What in the world are you going to do at Deep Lake?'

'Teach,' she said, feeling her cheeks colour all over again. She'd never been much of a blusher and now this angry, harsh stranger was turning her various shades of red.

'Where? Out in the woods?' He laughed at his own joke, snagged another cookie from the tray he'd brought and popped it in his mouth.

'Actually, yes. The new retreat out there has hired me to–'

'Great. That's what we need. A bunch of hippie-dippie women running through the woods, hugging trees and stretching.'

'Hey!' Anger rushed through her but from somewhere calm inside herself she was watching him. Simply observing. The more reserved, non-offended part of Molly paid close attention. Even as he spit out his nasty little words his eyes were roaming her. He studied her from top to toe. And was that a blush of his own on his rugged face, colouring him red below his new crop of stubble? 'Look, Sean, I know you don't want to be here. And I can see why you're having–'

Molly bit her tongue, her heart pounding. She'd been

about to say something mean of her own. Too mean. Meaner than poking fun of yoga, which lots of people did.

Sean squinted, frowned, watched her. 'What?'

'Nothing. Can we just get the sofa and–'

'Sure. When you finish that sentence.' He rested his back against the knotty-pine wall. The sun had shifted and she saw that his dark blond hair was shot with red streaks and some of the emerging whiskers matched.

'I don't know what I was going to say,' she lied, studying her brown flip-flops. She pulled a loose thread on her leggings and waited – prayed – for him to get bored and move on.

Instead, he pulled a pocket knife out and started to clean under his nails. How many times had she watched her grandfather do that when she was small? And it was always followed by a lecture that any man worth her while would care for his appearance. Nails, hair, shaving. 'Darned socks and clean clothes,' she muttered.

Sean looked up and the late afternoon sun turned his brown eyes to whisky. 'Pardon?'

'Nothing,' she said. 'Something my grandfather used to say to me.' Molly realised his clothes were clean, his nails short, his hairstyle a bit too long but current and fashionable. She shook her head; she was confusing herself. But Molly didn't miss that her heart was a runaway drum beat in her chest or that her panties were sodden at the crotch or that she wanted to know if his lips were as soft as they looked.

'Well, you can't change the subject, Miss Molly,' he sighed. 'Are you going to finish your snippy comment or are we going to stand here and grow old?'

Molly felt ultimately defeated so she murmured softly, 'I was going to say that I can see why you have women troubles.'

Sean barked laughter so fierce it startled her and she jumped. 'Oh really?'

'I'm sorry. It was mean and you upset me and I get my feelings hurt easily and ...' She trailed off. And when Molly raised her head he had bridged the gap between them. His handsome but annoyed face filled her vision.

'I'm not having women troubles. I'm done with them.' He leant in even as he said it. His nose an inch from hers, his mouth blowing little puffs of warm words over her lips. Molly tried to stare at the bridge of his nose to appear confident. Instead, she stared at his lips and it was increasingly hard to stand still.

'That seems a shame,' she breathed. 'What happened? Why would you be done with ... women?'

It was a shame, because Sean Simon was oddly captivating. And handsome. And he was so close it was easy to smell the dark, wood and spice and cold air smell of him. A rugged man who worked with his hands. Rough hands, nicked-up hands, hands that could haul wood and tie knots and grab a woman in just the right manner to excite and provoke just the smallest shard of fear.

'She left.' He leant in even further and Molly tingled. Where his imaginary line of energy crossed hers, little sparks and flashes of nerve endings, fired.

'Why would she do that? Another man? Another woman? There had to be a reason.' Her mind was at war, trying to logistically figure what he was saying and trying to stifle the urge to lean in and kiss him. Which was so unlike her but it was an urge that had managed to sink its teeth and claws into her, spurring her on.

'She just left. She wasn't happy. Not all love stories are great ones.'

Molly lost the battle. 'Then it wasn't really a love story,' she said and stood on tiptoe, pushing her lips to his and her body to his. Fear ripped through her fast and furious; would he push her away? Would he storm off? Toss her aside and leave, talking of the crazy woman who'd accosted him in the cottage?

Instead he yanked her in and kissed her back. Sean took three big steps forward, forcing her backward as he moved. Molly felt the apprehension in her throat war with the excitement in her belly. She pushed her body flush to his even as he hustled her back like he was the law and she had been wrongful. Her back hit the opposite wall, rattling a small shelf that held kitchen implements and cookbooks. '*I* thought it was a love story,' he said, pulling back.

Molly felt her lips tingle like she was being shocked. They were still pelvis to pelvis, though he was now watching her face instead of kissing her. Molly's heartbeat filled her ears and it was all she could experience for a moment, until she felt his cock, hard against her front. She swallowed hard to try and find her words. 'I'm sorry.' She went to kiss him again and he pulled back. Even as he retreated, his body rocked against her and she felt the friction where they were pressed together.

Visions of this man, naked and moving over her – moving into her – flashed through her mind like a fast-forward movie. From kiss to penetration to him thrusting into her, filling her pussy with the full length of himself. Her legs locked behind him, greedy, yanking him down. Her lips on his shoulder as he moved, his mouth on her throat, her cheeks, her eyelids dropping kisses until he finally pinned her flush, kissed her hard, driving them both hard and fast to climax.

Little sparkles clouded her vision and she realised she felt light-headed. And he was still watching her.

'Don't be sorry for me,' he sneered, sounding more brave than he appeared. His eyes looked weary and wounded. She rose up, too fast for him to back off, and kissed him again. Running her tongue the length of his lower lip until he made a broken kind of noise in his chest.

His hands slammed hers against the wall even as he pinned her with his pelvis, crushing the evidence of his lust to the line of her sex. She shivered though the room seemed way too hot. He pushed her wrists harder and pain shot up her forearms, just enough to accent the pleasure growing in her pussy. He held her there and then ... pulled back from her.

'I'm not looking to get fixed, Miss Molly yoga. I'm not broken. How about we go get that sofa?' he said. His voice was harsh but he wouldn't meet her eyes.

'Right. Sure. I'm sorry. I don't know what came over me,' she said. Her heart twisted sideways, her stomach bottomed out. She had never felt more shunned or wounded before. And that was saying something.

They got the futon in and then the sofa. And he was gone. Muttering about work to do and a shower and good luck and all that jazz.

Stuffed cabbage. The one thing she actually made well. She made stuffed cabbage to christen the cottage. To make it her own. Plus, she rarely indulged in cooking because it was only her. Molly made simple dinners – grapes and cheese, a homemade pizza bagel, quick pasta. Rarely did she make anything that required real time. But cooking helped her be peaceful and she needed good feelings after Sean had both sparked her interest and lust and then pushed her away so fast and so far she nearly developed vertigo.

'It's fine. I'm not even settled. Romance can wait,' she sighed. But she didn't even believe herself and her forced good humour. Molly lifted the lid to peek and the front door crashed open and Molly jumped. She dropped the lid from one hand, as the spoon fell from her other. Scorching tomato sauce splashed her hand and she yelped.

Sean rushed forward looking both annoyed and startled. 'Jesus Christ, I came to apologise.'

'Knocking works!' she yelled, clutching her burnt hand. Already she could feel her heartbeat in the wounded skin.

'So does cold water,' he said, gruffly. He tugged her hand free from under her arm where she was guarding it. 'Come on. It's a burn – don't stick it in your armpit for God's sake.'

'Why are you yelling at me?' she sighed but let him tug her to the sink and shove her hand under freezing tap water.

Autumn rain tapped the skylight. A noisy voyeur to her clumsiness and his asinine version of an apology. She studied Sean's profile as he held her hand and refused to look at her. He looked handsome and tired and irritated. 'Why did you come here tonight? To yell at me?'

He turned his big brown eyes to her, frowned. 'No. To say I was sorry for being a jerk. I think it's hard for me to talk about Dawn. There is no reason for our split. She got tired of me. She left.' He turned the water off, bent to open a cabinet. 'There's burn cream in here somewhere. I'll just find it and–'

'Would you kiss me again?' Molly asked. Her voice rushed out of her before her mind made the connection. Why had she said that? Because she wanted it. Where had she found the nerve? She didn't know, she didn't care.

He froze, hand halfway from the cabinet. The small first-aid kit fell from his fingers and he grabbed her hard, her face trapped between his hands. Sean kissed her. His tongue pushing past her lips, stroking over hers, his cock already hard against her as he pulled her forward into an aggressive embrace.

'Are you angry with me?' she managed. This was not like her; she was shy around men. She was the wallflower, the one who did not entice. All of that swirled through her head as his tongue danced against hers and the heat of him made her feel like she was blushing all over. He nipped at her lower lip with his teeth and a spark of pain flared, making her cry out but making her pussy that much wetter. She was so ready. So willing. She wanted him that bad.

'Yes,' he said.

His hands slipped under her arms and he hoisted her, none too gently, to the counter. His fingers dipped below the waistband of her leggings and he tugged like his life depended on getting them off.

'Why? Why are you angry? What did I do?' she gasped, raising her hips to help him. Was she really going to do this?

Yes. She was. Because something about him spoke to her. And what it said was in a secret language that even she didn't understand. Yet. But right now, that didn't matter. Instinct said yes. Desire, need, want, lust, urge – all said *go*. So, Molly went.

'You did nothing.' Sean kissed the side of her throat. Molly jumped; she was unbelievably ticklish there. He laughed softly in her ear, sounding almost malicious. 'Sit still, will you? I'm trying to make things up to you.' He held her legs flat to the granite counter with his big hands. Quickly pushing them apart so he could slip his body between her legs.

Then her leggings hit the floor, the stuffed cabbage bubbled and he kissed her until her toes curled in her rag-wool socks. 'Why are you mad?' Molly pushed her hands in his hair, tugging enough so that he made a sharp sound. Good. Let him hurt just a bit. Just a *bit*.

But he countered by running his thumb across the crotch of her panties, red-and-white candy cane panties to be exact, and her clit zinged with delicious pressure and sensation. 'Oh, that is cheating,' she said.

'True. But I have to clear my head somehow. Look, I really didn't want to notice a single living woman. Or explain Dawn. Or feel the urge to ...' He had started wrestling with the thin elastic bands at her hips to pull the panties free and her pussy thumped with anticipation. The roar of blood and steamed cabbage and his harsh breathing filled Molly's head. He kissed her again, to shut himself up she suspected.

Molly pulled back, using his hair as reins. Sean winced and glared at her, only the glare softened and his gaze settled on her mouth as if a thousand dirty things were going through his mind. She couldn't help it – she scooted forward on the counter just a hair so that his cock seated perfectly in the seam of her pussy lips. 'The urge to what, Sean?' she breathed, releasing twin clumps of wheat-coloured hair.

'To be with someone. Not just the urge. The ...'

'The?' He came at her to kiss her and she dodged it. Her pulse bounced around her body, echoing in her neck and wrists and cunt. She swore she could feel his pulse answering hers.

'The *need. The need* to be with someone. With you. OK, I said it. I need to be with you. And I don't know why. You sing horrible Motown and your furniture weighs a tonne. And I don't like this need. And really, I don't want to but–'

'But?' she demanded, feeling angry all over again.

'But I have to,' he said and yanked her panties so they gave way.

She was in mid-kiss when he dropped to his knees. She

sucked in a breath at the absence of his mouth on hers and then again when he pressed his lips followed by his hot, hot tongue to her clit. Sean slipped two fingers deep inside her, curling and pushing until she wiggled on the cool stone counter, her socks tripping along the lines of his back. She caught a toe in his blue polo collar and then, when he sucked her in, lapping at her with his tongue, she damn near choked him. 'Easy, Molly,' he snickered, but he kept licking, murmuring against her pussy, the vibration of his words scrolling up into her pelvis, her womb, her belly. Molly shut her eyes and let her head fall back. It hit the wood cabinet with a bang and she laughed, but then she sighed as his fingers continued to push and work and stroke deep inside her and she came. A white hot ball of release rushing at her and dragging her under in a series of small spasming echoes.

'Oh, God, that was good,' she said, feeling no embarrassment. It was good and she wanted more. 'Can you come up here now?' Her voice was weak and she laughed at herself.

Sean was frowning again. 'I should run from you,' he said, tugging at his belt.

She smiled. 'Is that how you run?'

'No, this is how I ignore my instincts.' He pulled the buckle free and started on the button. Molly, again having an out-of-body, or possibly just out-of-character, experience leant forward and tugged the button until the whole row submitted and opened for her.

'Maybe your instincts are wrong. Maybe you should be here.'

Sean pushed his jeans low and stepped out of them. His boxer briefs hit the red tile floor next and he came to her, his cock erect and, in her opinion, quite fine indeed.

'I'm on the pill and I'm clean and I'm ...' she petered off as she took him in hand, running her fingers along the smooth silken heat of his erection. She brushed the small weeping slit at the tip with her thumb, spreading a crystalline bead of precome across his pink flesh.

'Me too,' he said, pushing to her. Thrusting past her still

groping hand to press the tip of himself to her wet entrance. 'I mean, I'm not on the pill, obviously.' He grinned, looking a bit drunken and stunned.

Exactly how she felt.

This is where she should laugh because it really was funny, but the laugh didn't want to come. What came instead was her body's call for him, so big and so swift it took her laugh and her breath. 'Dear God, *now*, don't make me wait any longer,' she said and then let her head fall to his shoulder, waiting to see what he would do.

'Jesus, woman. You are more than a mind-fuck,' he said, sounding utterly defeated. Sean thrust into her and Molly bit her lip to keep the sounds in. Otherwise her noise might be so big she'd never bottle it back up. He moved in her perfectly. His motion tripping sympathetic nerve endings in her so that each move he made was nirvana. Each thrust was heaven. Each beat of his heart pounded against her breast in time with hers.

'I mean even if you hate me, don't stop,' she said. The rush of words spilled over her lips as he moved into her deeper, a bit faster, scooting her millimetre by millimetre toward the yellow tiled backsplash.

'Fuck. I don't hate you. I'm rather ...' He sighed, but his fingers bit in to her hips, securing her so he could tip her just a bit, holding her perfectly so he could move deeper still.

Her orgasm rushed at her like a fork of lightning. She wondered briefly how they had gone from him sneering at her to fucking her on the counter. But then his lips came down on her. First, on her nipple, then migrating to her mouth in a crushing kiss and she forgot to care. 'Rather what? Rather horny? Hungry? Angry?' she demanded. Even as she said it, her fingers dug into his broad shoulders, plucking at the shirt he still wore, anchoring him to her so he wouldn't poof and disappear.

'Taken with you. You got into my head from the word go. You are ... different. Now shut up and kiss me.'

Her burn still thumped with her pulse but so did her pussy. When Sean stiffened against her and simply said, 'Molly?'

She let her orgasm come up inside her, turning her insides to a silken fist around him as he came. When he came he simply said 'Damn' in her ear. But she smiled. It was the biggest compliment he could give her.

The smoke detector sounded and they both jumped, her legs still hooked around his hips, her lips still on his chin, his fingers in her long mussed hair. 'Oh, yeah. Hey, would you like to stay for dinner?' she said, with the straightest face she could manage.

Sean said, 'Yes.' And he stayed.

Molly signed the final paper and the realtor beamed. 'Aren't you glad I talked you into signing that six-month plan?'

Molly grinned. 'I am, Katie, thanks. You'll come to the housewarming?'

'Wouldn't miss it for the world.'

'I'll show you out,' Ella said and ushered the realtor down the hallway.

Sean wrapped his arms around her from behind. 'Jeez, that's my ma. Nothing like the bum's rush.'

'I think she's just eager to start celebrating,' Molly snorted. His lips pressed to her nape and she shivered. Mentally she calculated just how long she could hold out before demanding he make love to her.

'Soon,' he whispered in her ear. Reading her mind as Ella reappeared.

'Well, I want to give the dogs walkies and then you come over and we'll feast! We will celebrate Molly being here for good. This is so karma ... kismet ... destiny! The moment I saw you, I knew you were right for–' Ella's eyes flew wide and she turned on her heels.

'*Ma!*' Sean barked.

Ella kept her back to them. 'The house, Sean! I knew she was perfect for the house. But it would be a great love story if I had set it up, yeah?' She turned and winked.

Molly had to bite her tongue to keep from laughing. They'd never know for sure.

The front door slammed and Molly turned in Sean's arms.

He was already walking her backwards toward the sofa. 'Your mother!' she said, but she opened her mouth for him, accepting the warm thrusts of his tongue.

Her belly tingled, her pussy grew ready. She was never anything but ready for him. Head over heels in love in the blink of an eye. A rather ordinary life to love that was so grand it hurt her heart sometimes.

'Would not come back in here if she were on fire,' he chuckled. 'Walkies are 20 minutes. I have 20 minutes to ravish you and put you – and myself – back together again.'

'Like a dirty version of Humpty Dumpty,' she joked. He pushed up her denim skirt and stole her blue silk panties. Molly gasped, feeling him rubbing the hard bulge of his cock, still swathed in denim, to her pussy.

'Yeah, something like that.'

Molly reached for his button and he blocked her hand, dipping down out of reach to suck at her clit for a moment. His tongue darting in wet hot circles that made her drop her hand and close her eyes. Then the merry jingle of his buckle and the rasp of his jeans coming down. He grabbed her ankles, his palms hot and rough on her skin, and pulled her closer to the edge of the sofa.

'Hurry,' she said. Now that she was ready, she was beyond urgent. Her body hummed with a deep aching need to have him inside her. And she really didn't care that it was daylight or the door wasn't locked or any of it at all. She owned a house, she had Sean, and this was the cherry on the sundae.

'I'm getting there,' Sean said, slipping the crown of his cock along her wet slit. He painted her with her own juices, laughing softly when she would thrust up to try and capture him inside her. 'Impatient, aren't you?' he said.

'With you, yes.'

He tortured her further by slipping just the head of himself into her pussy. Her body clutched up around it, uselessly greedy, trying to draw him in so they could start to move together. Creating heat, creating friction.

'Oh my God! Put it in!' Then she clamped a hand over her mouth in shock.

'Such a mouth you have,' he laughed, slipping into her languidly. One inch at a time, pausing to let her body adjust and crave more.

'Sorry, sorry,' she chanted.

He kissed her again. A sweet kiss. A love kiss. 'It's OK.'

He moved gently, rocking into her like they were atop waves. Sean's hips swinging like a metronome, touching off each nerve ending that built to a wave of euphoria. Molly started to come and she gripped at him, trying to stave it off. 'Ella's right. It would make a great love story.'

He stilled, his hips barely moving, his cock barely moving and her body froze up in mid-orgasm. On the razor's edge of bliss and torture. 'But not all love stories are great,' he reminded her.

They stared eye to eye for longer than two heartbeats but less than three and then he began moving in her faster, losing his control. She lost hers, coming with a soft cry. 'But this one is,' she said, kissing him, holding him tight as he came.

His mouth settled on hers. 'Yes. It is.'

Also by Sommer Marsden

A collection of three novellas: Life is full of hard lessons. From finding out who you really are under an endless Montana sky to meeting the fascinating stranger when your life has taken an unexpected turn in the responsibility department. Then there's the workman you'd do just about anything to see again and the boss you can't help falling for, even though he's taken more wrong turns than you can count. Want, need, craving, playboys and personal assistants--the men of Hard Lessons know what it's like to find a guy that makes your heart beat faster.

Life is full of hard lessons--Forgiveness, redemption, love, lust, pain, sex and discovery. The key is finding someone to learn with.

ISBN 9781907761522   £7.99

Also from Xcite Books

Power Play

Control is everything. No matter whether you like to wear the trousers or be ordered out of them, these stories will have you hot in no time.

Every nuance of sexual domination and submission is explored, from tongue-in-cheek role play to intense BDSM.

These stories reveal the lives of the 'slaves' and their 'masters' and even one or two who like to swap their roles.

ISBN 9781907761720   £7.99

Xcite Books help make loving better
with a wide range of erotic books,
eBooks and dating sites.

www.xcitebooks.com
www.xcitebooks.co.uk

Sign-up to our Facebook page
for special offers and free gifts!